THE PRINCESS
AND THE ODIUM

What Reviewers Say About Sam Ledel's Work

Rocks and Stars

"I think Sam Ledel told a great story. I adored Kyle even though a few times I wanted to shake her and say enough girlfriend. I wish the ending was a bit longer, but that's the romance addict in me. I look forward to Ledel's next book."—*Romantic Reader Blog*

Daughter of No One

"There's a lot of really smart fantasy going on here. …Great start to a (hopefully) long running series."—Colleen Corgel, Librarian, Queens Public Library

"It's full of exciting adventure and the promise of romance. It's sweet, fresh and hopeful. It takes me back to my teenage years, the good parts of those years at least. I read this in a few hours, only stopped long enough to have lunch. I hope I won't have to wait too long for the sequel—I have high hopes for Jastyn, Aurelia, their friend Coran, Eegit the hedgewitch and Rigo the elf."—*Jude in the Stars*

"A fantasy book with MCs in their very early twenties, this book presents a well thought out world of Kingdom of Venostes (shades of The Lord of the Rings here)."—*Best Lesfic Reviews*

"Sam Ledel has definitely set up an epic adventure of star-crossed lovers. This book one of a trilogy doesn't leave you with a cliffhanger but you are definitely going to be left ready for the next book. …As a non-fantasy lover, I adored this book and am ready to read where Ledel takes us next. This book is quality writing, great pacing, and top-notch characters. You cannot go wrong with this one!"—*Romantic Reader Blog*

"If you're a huge fan of fantasy novels, especially if you love stories like this one that contains a host of supernatural beings, quirky characters coupled with action and excitement around every tree, winding path or humble abode, then this is definitely the story for you! This compelling story also deals with poverty, isolation and the huge chasm between the royal family and the low-class villagers. Well, fellow book lovers, it really looks like you've just received a winning ticket to a literary lottery."—*Lesbian Review*

Broken Reign

"Sam Ledel has created a fascinating and at times terrifying world, filled with elves, sirens, selkies, wood nymphs and many more. …Going on this journey with both young women and their fellow travellers still has this fresh and exciting quality, all the more so as new characters joined the story, some just as intriguing."—*Jude in the Stars*

By the Author

Rocks and Stars

The Odium Trilogy

Daughter of No One

Broken Reign

The Princess and the Odium

THE PRINCESS AND THE ODIUM

by

Sam Ledel

2021

THE PRINCESS AND THE ODIUM

ISBN 13: 978-1-63555-894-4

THIS TRADE PAPERBACK ORIGINAL IS PUBLISHED BY
BOLD STROKES BOOKS, INC.
P.O. BOX 249
VALLEY FALLS, NY 12185

FIRST EDITION: APRIL 2021

CREDITS
EDITOR: BARBARA ANN WRIGHT
PRODUCTION DESIGN: SUSAN RAMUNDO
COVER DESIGN BY TAMMY SEIDICK

Acknowledgments

Thank you to Bold Strokes Books and to my incredible editor, Barbra Ann Wright.

A zillion hugs to Alyssa for reading the early drafts.

To the readers who came along on Jastyn and Aurelia's epic adventure, thank you.

Dedication

For those going on journeys of their own
and discovering what it means to stand up
for who and what they believe in.

CHAPTER ONE

Jastyn stared out at the calm waters of the Southern Sea. The blue-green waves carried her modest wooden ship steadily onward. Behind her lay the selkies cove, or what was left of it after the invasion. The elves had come and gone quickly, like a raging storm that hadn't found its true target and moved on, content with the devastation it had wrought. Ahead of her was the land she hadn't seen in six months. Venostes, the kingdom she had reluctantly called home for nearly twenty-three years, a kingdom taught to despise her. Yet, here she was, the Odium child returning home.

Adjusting her woven navy and gold belt, she squinted at the wave crests shimmering like jewels in the sunlight. A memory flashed like the light in her mind. *Ten thousand rubies to whosoever can bring the princess back to Venostes.*

Shaking her head, Jastyn laughed at the first time she'd thought about the reward since its pronouncement from King Grannus Diarmaid. It seemed like ages ago when Jastyn had stood on that market road with Coran, concocting a plan to rescue Princess Aurelia Diarmaid while simultaneously securing a key to the cure for her sister Alanna. At least, Jastyn had thought Aurelia was the key. She'd been convinced of it, unable to fathom another meaning to the Red One's words. The mercurial leprechaun had told her a noble sacrifice would be required to obtain her sister's cure, and Jastyn had been sure Aurelia was the noble in question. She had been so convinced, in fact, she'd dragged Aurelia across the realm, knowing she might have had to face grave dangers, maybe even death.

Jastyn wouldn't have let anything happen to her. Their frightening excursion through the mountains had been awful, but they'd survived. Jastyn had been prepared to handle the obstacles she'd imagined lurking, waiting inside the caves. However, another complication entirely had surprised her on their journey. Love had found its way into her heart. She had fallen in love with Aurelia, and that love complicated everything. When Jastyn had realized she'd been wrong about the meaning of the noble sacrifice, she had been relieved, confused, and grateful. Still, keeping Aurelia ignorant of her fears had betrayed Aurelia's trust. Jastyn had been prepared to fight against whatever had wanted Aurelia's noble blood in exchange for the cure. She had not been prepared for the heartbreak involved in revealing her plans and watching Aurelia walk away, maybe for good.

When she'd told Aurelia the truth on the beach one week ago, Jastyn's world had crumbled. She could handle many things: hunger, cold, even the dirty looks the villagers in Venostes threw at her for being marked an Odium, a bastard child. Aurelia's dismay upon learning what Jastyn had kept from her, however, had been too much.

Closing her eyes, Jastyn let the salty breeze cool her warming face. She leaned against the ship's railing, listening to the water and the sail beating steadily against the wind.

"Tove says we should have Venostes in sight in two days' time." Jastyn opened her eyes. Her best friend Coran stood beside her on the deck in a worn navy tunic that fell to his knees above old boots, the only difference in their outfits being the color of his black pants to her brown ones. His red-orange hair whipped wildly in the wind. Jastyn's own braid flopped like a fish's tail, the plaited end patting an irreverent beat against her chest. "Fastest travelin' I've ever done," he added. "These selkies are some sailors."

Her father, Tove, manned the helm, despite most of the sailing being done by his magic, which he'd cast three days before when they'd set out. He said something to Fortan, the only other soul aboard their ship heading east. The two of them conversed quietly, their sealskins perched atop their heads seeming to listen along. Jastyn imagined they were discussing recovery plans for their cove, which was left in disrepair after the elf attack.

Seeming to read her mind, Coran said, "Revna says they'll be fine. They'll rebuild, Jas."

Gripping the rail, she cut her eyes to his freckled face. "It was in pieces, Coran. Their home was obliterated." More memories surfaced: young selkies emerging from the water on the heels of their parents the day after the attack. Tears running from their dark eyes as they transformed, sprinting to what used to be their safest place. Barks of anguish ringing out, echoing across the cove.

"It's all my fault," she murmured. "All of this is my fault."

"Come on, Jas. You know that's not true."

"Tell that to my family."

Coran grimaced. "We'll get them out."

She gripped the rail tighter, forcing her dark thoughts away. She tried to think about the one good thing that had happened during all of this.

Inside the satchel draped over her chest, she found the three vials holding Alanna's cure. Her head swimming, she pinched the bridge of her nose. There was so much at stake: she needed to get the cure to her sister but only after she figured out how to prepare it. Additionally, her family had been thrown into the dungeon in Venostes, and Aurelia had been kidnapped...again. The Dark Fae seemed to be everywhere at once. All Jastyn had wanted was the cure for her sister. She stared into the bright sunlight as the ship pushed through the waves. Now, the entire realm seemed to be crashing down around her.

Coran placed an arm around her shoulders. She jumped, pulling back.

"Just me, Jas." His hazel eyes met hers. She and Coran had been through so much together. She didn't know what she'd do without his unwavering support, even if she felt like she didn't deserve it sometimes. "We'll get through this. We always do."

"I just hope we're not too late."

Later that night in the ship's cabin, Jastyn pushed around her half-eaten fish, listening as Tove and Fortan discussed the state of their colony.

Fortan wiped his mouth clean with a torn cloth, then sipped his wine before placing the cup atop their makeshift table, a collection of barrels formerly used to hold mead. His youthful features seemed bright after days at sea, despite the glint of pain Jastyn caught from time to time when he looked west, back toward their cove. "Njal and Yrse say there's a boat of pirates incoming within another week," he said, "so we'll have a new ship to help us rebuild."

Across from him, Coran said between bites, "I s'pose they *are* pirates. I'm not one to knock takin' what you need. Is it true what they say about what happens to those on board?"

Fortan smirked. "Like you said, they *are* pirates."

At Jastyn's silence, her father leaned forward, resting his elbows on the table. His lean frame looked small in the brown tunic, especially compared to the broad-shouldered Fortan. Thick black hair fell to his shoulders. He said gently, "You can't keep blaming yourself."

"The Dark Fae was after me. I drew him there, brought him into your home."

Fortan watched her carefully. "It's not he who did the damage."

"The elves are doing his bidding," Coran added.

At this, the selkies frowned. "They were there to capture Her Highness?" Tove asked.

Putting down her fork, Jastyn sighed. "They were. The elves took out the prince. If they can eliminate Aurelia, the elf queen or the Dark Fae will have a much easier path to the Diarmaid throne."

Coran's face scrunched. "I thought the Dark Fae was after you, not the throne."

Feeling exhausted with the weight of the last six months, Jastyn shrugged. "So did I. But I think the two are tied together, the Dark Fae and the elves. Something or someone is manipulating them. I don't know." She rubbed her temples, a headache forming.

Everyone let Jastyn's words hang over them like a heavy cloud. She was almost grateful for the gloom. Maybe then they would understand how dreadful she felt.

An awful sense of dismay had settled into her chest since her fight with Aurelia. Obtaining her sister's cure had been a moment of daylight. Alas, darkness had followed. When she'd thought things looked ready to change, like the days might grow longer or the bright sky might last, the world always had a way of reinstating its dark will upon her once again.

"Let's focus on what we do know, eh?" Coran nudged the conversation along. "We know Aurelia was alive at the beach. She was with the queen. That's gotta be good news." At Jastyn's unconvinced look, he added, "The queen is more than capable of holding her own. Trust me, I've seen her use magic more than once at solstice festivals. They'll be okay."

"If she's anything like her daughter, I imagine you're right," Fortan said, smiling and brushing aside the long black hair that fell down his back.

Jastyn met Coran's gaze resolutely. "Tell me again about the beach."

His look told her he wasn't enthusiastic about repeating this story for the fifth time. Still, he took a drink, then said, "Rigo hadn't returned from the ships. I'd been hopin' he'd be back to help talk to Aurelia."

"I like that elf," Fortan interjected, nodding to no one in particular.

Tove asked, "Have you received word from him yet?"

Jastyn and Coran shook their heads, and Jastyn could only hope Rigo was all right. Coran continued. "Sif found us on the beach, but as soon as she did, an elf snuck up and attacked. Once he'd shot Sif, Aurelia went after him." His freckled fingers tapped the tabletop. "I tried to stop her."

Jastyn snorted, letting herself smile as she conjured an image of Aurelia, a look of stubborn determination on her face. "I'm sure that went well."

"Yeah. Fortunately, Queen Dechtire showed up. She had her riding cloak on, like she'd just come from the stables." His gaze flickered around their group. "I think she'd ridden across the realm. But as soon as the queen had taken care of the elf, the sky grew dark." Coran gulped down his wine. "I remember I was cold all of a sudden."

"The Dark Fae." Jastyn rubbed a finger into the wooden surface next to her plate.

He nodded. "That was when Her Majesty did somethin' to me." He narrowed his eyes, seemingly trying to recall. "Put me to sleep." Then his eyes widened. "I just remembered somethin' else." He glanced around, and Jastyn made a prompting gesture with her hand. "There was a woman walking up behind the queen."

"A woman?" Tove asked.

"I didn't recognize her, but it all happened so fast." He frowned. "She's gotta be that someone or something workin' with the Dark Fae." His sentence held an intonation of hope as he looked to Jastyn.

Fortan asked, "You think this woman might have the princess and the queen?"

Shrugging, Coran looked at Jastyn. "Maybe. She seemed human. I think."

Tove said, "Perhaps they were taken back to Venostes."

"We can only hope," Jastyn said, throwing a glance out a small, circular window.

"Did Aurelia ever speak of the unrest in Venostes?" Tove's question drifted over to Jastyn carefully, as if he was treading lightly on the subject. Jastyn glanced up after another bite of fish. Her father's dark eyes were kind and helped coax her into speaking.

"Aurelia was shaken by her brother's death and the idea that somebody could have wanted him dead. She seemed unable to understand the dark workings within her kingdom. But we didn't talk about it much." Jastyn pictured the night Aurelia had received a message from her maiden while they'd been traveling. Aurelia had seemed dazed, empty even. Jastyn had brought Aurelia a gift to make up after a spat but had returned to their campsite to find her dizzy with disbelief about her brother's funeral.

"Something nefarious is definitely happening," Fortan said, playing with the coin at the end of his necklace, his brow furrowed. "Something more than just the Dark Fae."

They all sat quietly. Jastyn tried to put the pieces together. Her gaze fell to the lone candle flickering in the center of the table in a puddle of wax within a metal tray. Her mind was too foggy, like the halo of light surrounding the flame. It buzzed with worry for Aurelia but also rang with concern for her family. If what Eegit showed her was true, they were locked away in the Diarmaid dungeon. But why? Who had ordered that? Could the queen have wanted them captured before she left in search of her daughter? She recalled the way Dechtire had fallen back against her husband after learning who Jastyn was that night in the Wood. She'd seen the fear, the disbelief in her eyes. Jastyn's jaw clenched at the idea of the Diarmaids' relentless tirade against her family.

Prior to meeting Aurelia, Jastyn's perception of the royal family had been like stone. She'd despised them and had every reason to. Their unjust laws had imprisoned her mother when it was discovered she was pregnant without a husband. They had helped shape Jastyn's low lot in life. However, Aurelia had slowly chipped away at the jagged points of her hatred, revealing shining fragments of hope and possibility. But as long as it had taken for Jastyn's view of the Diarmaids to change, it had all disappeared as she had watched Eegit's vision, staring helplessly as her mother, stepfather, and thirteen-year-old sister had been dragged from their home at the hands of the royal guard.

"So," Coran said, and Jastyn knew what he was going to ask. It was the question she'd been trying to find an answer to since Tove got this ship at Revna's approval, and they'd set sail. "What's the plan?"

When Jastyn didn't answer, Tove responded enthusiastically, "Save the princess, cure Alanna, and rescue your family."

His eagerness proved contagious. Coran smiled as Fortan clapped his hands.

Jastyn, unable to stop herself, grinned. "Simple, right?"

"And here I was thinking I was better off staying behind. Whoever said humans don't know how to have a good time had no idea what they were missing." Fortan beamed, his eyes flashing playfully.

Jastyn shot him a look but reveled in the lightness of their ship's cabin for the first time all day.

She knew this wasn't going to be easy. Nothing ever was. Looking at Fortan, her father, and Coran, she willed herself to hang on to hope. She closed her eyes, picturing Aurelia. The princess wouldn't give up. She'd stand tall, optimism blazing in her blue eyes.

Holding on to that now, Jastyn made herself believe that she could do this. She had to.

There was no other choice.

CHAPTER TWO

Father!" Aurelia rushed into the dungeon cell, surprised by her own relief at seeing her father once again. She hugged him tightly, then stepped back, frightened by how thin he'd gotten. His handsome face—formerly defined and strong—appeared gaunt, his scarred arms frail as they shook.

"Aurelia," he cried, his voice thick with shock as his hazel eyes seemed like they were trying to see through her, as if she might not be real.

"Now you all are together again. How lovely," Baroness Enya said from the cell's open door. Its black, crisscrossed bars marred the torchlight that flickered from a sconce on the wall behind her.

"Your mother," her father started, worry creased throughout his face, "she went in search of you."

"I know." Aurelia glanced behind her, then stepped aside to reveal Dechtire's limp form in Drest's arms.

A choking sound came from her father, and he lunged forward, nearly falling over the end of his navy cloak. "Oh gods, no."

Aurelia kept him steady, tears in her eyes at the look on his face. She ached to tell him the truth—that her mother was only under a spell of her own conjuring—but didn't dare with the baroness so close.

"Well, we had better be off. It's our duty as representatives of the distraught and grief-stricken royal family we relay this terribly tragic news to the court." The baroness stepped behind her son, peering at the queen's body. "Poor Dechtire simply wasn't strong enough to withstand the arduous search for her precious daughter." Enya pouted, her thin lips scrunched. "It was so good I decided to accompany her on the journey to find you, or she would have been lost to the Wildlands eternally." Her sharp gaze fell on Aurelia. "That would have been awful."

Aurelia's red saol flashed between her fingers. She forced herself to keep her arm at her side, though the urge to aim it at the baroness was strong. "You won't get away with this."

The baroness only smiled, flicking a piece of straw from her red tunic sleeve. As she started to close the cell door, Aurelia called, "Wait. Please." She stepped closer, placing two hands on the iron bars. "Let us have time with her."

"She's to be prepared for the funeral pyre," Drest said, his chin high, and his barrel chest puffed. But the baroness held up a bony hand, her gaze lingering on Aurelia's father, who knelt, unblinking, on the dungeon floor as silent tears streamed down his face.

"Come now, Drest," she said, "we are Gulterans, not barbarians." She sighed, a giant ruby flashing on her right hand as she waved it, seemingly annoyed. "Very well. If you wish to spend one night with Dechtire's corpse, so be it. The guards will come to collect her at dawn."

Drest pushed the door open, unceremoniously using Aurelia's mother's legs to assist him. He looked ready to toss her to the ground as her father shuffled to him.

"Please, I'll take her," he begged, standing slowly. Aurelia shivered and pulled at the sleeves of her blue tunic; she had never seen her father so bereft.

Drest sneered but relented, passing her mother over. When the cell door clanged closed and Drest and Enya had gone, Aurelia and her father stood silently until the final creak of the dungeon's distant, heavy door rumbled to a close. Once it did, Aurelia helped place her mother carefully on a pile of dirty straw that sat next to the rear wall of the cell.

"She's not dead," Aurelia said quickly, her whisper rushed as she stepped back, boots sticking in something she tried not to think about. "It's a spell she cast over herself." She blinked, still shaken by her mother lying still. "It all happened so fast."

Her father knelt, stroking her mother's face. He pulled the cloak from his shoulders and laid it over her mother. The gesture felt so intimate, Aurelia looked away as she took a deep breath. "We were on the western shores, nearly to the cure." Her father shifted, still kneeling, to listen. "There was an attack, like the one here. The elves came after us. One of them…" She faltered, recalling the arrow lodged in Sif, who had tried to keep her and Coran safe on the beach. "One of them hurt my friend. I was fighting him when"—she sniffed, wiping her nose on her tunic sleeve—"when Mother appeared. She took out the elf. I didn't understand what she was doing there."

Her father's chin trembled. "She was looking for you."

Aurelia's sadness was replaced with frustration. "Why? Why was she following me?"

"She wanted to make sure you were safe."

"From Jastyn?"

He flinched at the mention of Jastyn's name but shook his head. "She knew something wasn't right here in the kingdom." He looked at her mother. "She knew it before any of us did. She tried to get you back, to protect you from the dangers inside this very castle."

Now frustration withered into confusion. Aurelia sat down, tired, her pants picking up dirt from the grimy floor. "That's why she sent so many fae after me."

"To bring you back. *Not* to keep you from the Odium. It was to protect you from the baroness. Enya was trying to hunt you down."

Aurelia rubbed her forehead, pushing strands of hair from her face. "I don't understand. How did all of this happen? How did Drest escape?"

He exhaled, one hand resting on her mother's arm while the other ran over his red beard, now filled with patches of gray. "Once we brought Drest back after finding you in the Wood six months ago, we interrogated him for days. He relinquished little in the way of information. It seemed as if he'd gone mad, speaking only in riddles when he did speak. He spoke of 'darkness' and 'retribution' and 'a cleansing of the land.'" He shook his head. "He was antagonistic but not a threat."

Aurelia followed his gaze to an empty cell across the room.

"Chains kept him in place until two weeks ago. I'd grown distracted. Between the invasion and…everything that had happened during the attack, my focus waned. Your mother was consumed with how the elves had penetrated the kingdom. She sought answers. When Louarn disappeared, she was convinced something more than a broken agreement between allies was happening."

He coughed, his face contorted as he tried to hold back a sob. When it proved useless, he cried into his wide palms, huddled over her mother. It was odd to watch her father cry in such a way. She remembered all the times she'd cried, mostly for trivial reasons, when she was young. Her younger self had shed the most hysterical tears while sitting on her father's lap, wrapped in his protective arms. Now it was him who cried like the world was ending. Maybe it was.

Slowly, Aurelia moved nearer, placing a comforting hand on his shaking back. She had no idea what to say. *What does a daughter say to her father when their roles are reversed?*

Eventually, he gasped for breath, still shaking as he spoke. "I should have paid more attention."

"You noticed Louarn was gone, though, didn't you?"

"Of course," he replied, wiping his eyes with the back of his hands. "I didn't understand it at first. Then the baroness came to us one night after dinner. She explained that it was Louarn who had convinced Drest to carry out his bidding. She told us it was the baron who orchestrated the elven attack, and that he'd tried to convince her to go along with this plan. She was a wreck, nearly hysterical, telling us that she couldn't keep it from us anymore." His eyes searched the cell as he recalled. "Then, when we received word that Louarn had fled, it only proved her words to be true. I thought his guilty conscious had become too much for him."

"But, Father, the baron was always so kind."

"He was my best friend. It was difficult to fathom." He took a deep breath. "Your mother convinced me to investigate. I admit, I was reluctant, too consumed by my own misery at being betrayed to be of any use. I sent guard parties into the Wood to find him. Soon after, Louarn's body was recovered."

Aurelia straightened, swallowing to quench her dry throat. "Enya killed him."

He nodded. "Another thing I didn't realize until it was too late. She'd had our ear since the attack, and she worked her misgivings into my mind. Her powers of persuasion are otherworldly. I knew Drest had manipulative wind powers, but she...she twisted my thoughts." He squinted, two fingers thumping against his temple as if to rid himself of whatever she had told him. "I was weak, and I listened to her."

When he glanced again at the empty cell, Aurelia's eyes went wide. "No, Father."

His silence confirmed her suspicions.

"You ordered Drest's release."

His chin fell to his chest against his dirty navy tunic. "By then, your mother had left in search of you. Enya convinced me that everything would be fine, that Drest had been under Louarn's influence and was merely following his father's orders. She would right his wandering ways, she told me." His face lifted in a sneer. "'Show him pity,' she had said. And I did." Aurelia could hardly believe what she was hearing. "That same night, Drest seized me from my chambers." He looked around at the grimy stone walls. "Dragged me in here under the cover of darkness."

After a moment of quiet, as Aurelia reeled, he added, "They probably constructed some story to tell the court, like they're going to do for your mother. Like we did for you."

"What have they been told?"

"Your mother and I had to tell them something when you didn't return." At this, he looked away, rubbing his hands together.

"What did you tell them?"

"That the Odium had kidnapped you and was in league with the elves."

Her heart sank. She looked at her mother, then back to him. Anger boiled inside her stomach, made her skin itch. But now was not the time to be angry. There was too much at stake.

"Does the court truly believe all of this? That I'm still missing and you've...what?"

"Taken a leave of absence from the throne in order to properly grieve my children."

Scoffing, Aurelia found no words for the preposterousness of the situation.

Her father's voice pulled her from her thoughts. "Evil has found its way into our kingdom. It's nestled here, burrowed deep under our very feet." His gaze fell to her mother. "And now I fear there may be no way of defeating it."

Aurelia, who had been lost in a haze of dreadful images, straightened. "Father," she said, "you don't believe that."

"We've lost so much, sweetheart." With one hand, he cupped her face, his eyes glistening.

She placed her palm on top of his hand but pulled it down. "There is a way out of this, Father. There has to be. We only need to figure out what spell Mother used on herself. Then we can bring her back and break out of here. We'll tell the court the truth about what's happened, and we'll spread the word throughout the kingdom. Everyone will know the true nature of the baroness and her son. From the royal guard to the farmers on the hill, they will know—" She cut herself off and swallowed.

"What is it, darling?"

"Jastyn." Her skin turned hot as she remembered how she'd ended up here in the first place. "Gods, where could she be?"

Her father was silent. He tucked part of the blue cloak he'd strewn over her mother beneath her leg as if to keep the biting cold of the dungeon at bay. Lost in her thoughts, Aurelia continued, "She doesn't know I forgave her. What if she's still in the caves? What if something happened to her when she tried to obtain the cure?" At this, she turned to her father, who searched her face.

"What cure do you speak of?"

She sat cross-legged. "Do you remember the business I told you Jastyn had to take care of? Her sister is ill. I fear it's life-threatening."

"The horse master's daughter. I remember your mother mentioning it."

"Jastyn was told that the cure lay in the western caves." Her mind raced with everything that had happened since she'd first left alongside Jastyn, Coran, and Rigo. "We were so close to getting it when…" She cleared her throat. "When things became complicated." She stared at the floor, not willing to recount her argument with Jastyn when she thought she'd been betrayed. Her heart still stung with the words they'd exchanged on the sand near the selkies' cove.

Her father reached out, resting a hand on her knee. "At least you're safe now, sweetheart."

Frowning, she lifted her gaze to meet his. "I wasn't the only one out there, Father. Jastyn was there, but so was Coran and our friend Rigo. What if they're still in danger?" She recalled the image of Coran falling unconscious at her mother's will.

"The stable boy? I've seen no sign of him here."

"They didn't bring him back, too?"

"I don't think so. I heard the guards bring in somebody, several people, I think, a few days ago. They must be on the other end of the passageway, for I haven't seen who they are. But I doubt it's Coran. Petty thieves, most likely."

Then maybe he's with Jastyn. Gods, I hope they're all right.

"We've got to get out of here." She looked around the dark chamber. There was only one window, no larger than her hand, near the passageway that snaked away between their cell and the one Drest had been held in. The torchlight was all they had to see one another. Aurelia had never visited the dungeons. She'd never even heard of what they were like. When she'd asked about them as a child, her mother had said, "Oh, don't worry about that, darling. We'll teach you everything when you're older."

Now, here she was, in one of those very cells beneath the castle with her mother and father. The entire royal family, imprisoned.

How were they ever going to get out of this?

CHAPTER THREE

Aurelia pressed back into the layer of grime between her and the dungeon wall, indifferent to the hardness of the stone and the uninviting smells of the prison.

She closed her eyes to the dim figures of her parents, her father sleeping with one arm over her mother's body. A few hours had passed, and night had fallen, drenching the cell in total darkness. Aurelia relished the faint flicks of heat from the dying torch on the far wall. Wrapping her arms around herself, she tried to think. She and her father had attempted to surmise which spell her mother had used to put herself in a temporary stupor, one that left her with every appearance of death save for one.

Aurelia had listened closely to her chest after Enya and Drest had taken them from the beach. Her heartbeat was faint and only happened sporadically, but it still beat.

Her mother had a reason for doing this to herself. The baroness was trying to kill her on the beach. Bringing her body back was of use to Enya, as it would prove her story to the court. Unbeknownst to her, it also gave Aurelia and her father a chance to escape. Well, only if they could figure out which spell had been used.

Picking dirt from her boot, Aurelia brought her knees to her chest, then pressed her palms into her closed eyes. Frustration rose in her throat. This all seemed too absurd. She and her family were imprisoned in their own castle, her mother was incapacitated, and—worst of all—Drest was free.

"Gods, when I see him again..." she muttered, dropping her forearms to rest on her knees. She stared out the cell between the iron bars to the torchlight. She wasn't certain what she'd do if she saw Drest again. She hated him, despite having been taught to not spend her precious royal energy on things like hate. "A princess has better things to do than waste her time hating somebody," her mother had told her when she was nine and claimed to hate her riding instructor because he wouldn't let her practice galloping. Aurelia laughed. The irony of her mother's words and her new knowledge of her lineage's hatred toward fae and women like Jastyn's mother didn't escape her.

Jastyn. Aurelia knew exactly what Jastyn would do if faced with Drest. The flash of Jastyn's dagger blazed in her mind. Licking her lips, she tried to imagine the feel of the hilt in her hand.

The hoot of an owl made her jump. She needed to focus, but there was so much running through her mind which, like her body, was exhausted. She and her mother had been transported by the wind magic of the baroness and Drest, which left her chest heavy, as if she'd run acres without stopping. Her shoulders still ached from the pooka's grip months before. Shaking back her shoulders, her mind conjured the image of Jastyn. Aurelia prayed to the gods that she was all right, wherever she was. Had she gotten her sister's cure? What had happened at the cove; had the selkies been able to keep the elves at bay? She shivered at the thought of the second elf invasion she'd witnessed in less than a year. Thinking of Rigo, she hoped he too was all right and able to find some sort of solace in all this.

She feared for him and for Coran and hoped they were reunited with Jastyn. Maybe Coran could explain that Aurelia understood why Jastyn had done everything she had. Of course, her mother's spell on him may have knocked his memory around a bit, erasing parts of the last conversation they'd had. Still, she hoped Jastyn knew, somehow, that Aurelia forgave her. She had been angry, furious even, but she'd had a right to be. The Red One's words were clever: "noble sacrifice." Aurelia had been fooled, too. But she knew it was a different sacrifice that Jastyn had to give of herself to get Alanna's cure. Her eyes traced the black ceiling of her cell. *I hope it could be given.*

The darkness of the cell overpowered the torch on the wall, and Aurelia fell asleep, tired to her core. Yet her mind remained restless, and in its wanderings, conjured an old memory.

Aurelia pushed aside more of the dining plates and climbed on top of the table. "I don't believe it." She sat opposite her brother and stared at his weak smile, his hunched shoulder, and the four-inch hole in his side.

"Neither do I," he breathed, looking around at the bewildered faces surrounding him. Brennus met their parents' gaze. "Did I miss dinner again?"

Their father wiped tears from his eyes, and their mother pulled Brennus into a hug. Aurelia jumped on top of them, embracing her brother with every ounce of strength she had.

"I can't believe it," Drest said, shaking his head. He smiled, and Brennus reached out. They shook hands. "I thought we'd lost you."

Brennus grinned. "You'll have to tell me all about it."

Sitting back, Aurelia sniffled. Everyone wiped their faces clean when the baron asked, "What do you remember?"

Brennus frowned. "I don't...I don't remember much." He reached up to rub his forehead, then pinched the bridge of his nose. "I'm sorry. My head...it aches so."

Their mother stood. "Of course, darling. We can save the investigation for the morning," she announced, shooting the baron a look. "You need to rest."

"That sounds like just what the herbalist ordered," Brennus said tiredly. "Aurelia," he added, "you owe me a duel in the morning, what do you say?"

She nodded. "Absolutely."

But when their father leaned down to lift Brennus from the table, he let out a string of coughs. Blood spat from his mouth and into his open hand. His eyes went wide, and his hand flew to his chest.

"Brennus, are you all right?"

He didn't respond. Instead, he fell onto the table, his body shaking once again with spasms.

"Brennus," their mother shouted. She and their father braced their hands on his shoulders to quell his movements, but it was to no avail. They stepped back and watched helplessly as their son's body shook with agonizing force. When blood trickled from his ears and nose, Aurelia cried out.

"Mother, what's happening? What's wrong with him?"

"I don't know," she cried. They both looked to her father, who shook his head, his eyes filled with terror. Her mother grabbed the arrow that had been cast aside by Drest. "Is this what was in his side?"

Drest, who watched, bewildered, only nodded. She lifted the arrowhead to her nose. Then she licked the tip of it and spat.

Aurelia felt sick. "What is it?"

Her mother's gaze was empty when she said, "Poison."

The air was sucked from the room. Her father took a knee next to his son. Blood ran from every orifice in Brennus's face, and the blood from his wound turned a sickly brown as it bubbled onto the table. Aurelia shuddered when his chest heaved one final time.

Aurelia jolted awake. Her breathing came in hurried bursts, and her forehead was slick with sweat. She wiped it on her tunic sleeve. "It was only a dream," she told herself, blinking as the dark cell came into focus. But the sound of coughing and pain continued, echoing in her mind and against the walls caging her in.

Then she realized the coughing was no longer her terrible dream but was coming from somewhere inside the dungeons.

"It's one of the other prisoners." Her father's voice made her jump, drawing her gaze to where he sat against the bars, still only inches from her mother. "She sounds young, too, poor thing," he said with a sympathetic look over his shoulder to the far wall.

Taking a deep breath, Aurelia pushed her palms into the ground at her side, their heels digging into the hard earth as she pushed away the remnants of her nightmare.

After a moment, her father said, "I dream of him, too."

"Dreams are the only time the dead can visit us," Aurelia recited Eegit's words automatically. They'd become a sort of mantra when visions of Brennus in his last agonizing moments filled her mind. "I shouldn't complain," she added tiredly, unable to mask the bitterness in her voice.

Her father shook his head. "I dreamt of your brother every night since his passing into the Otherworld. Every night. Until the gods bestowed upon me a new subject." Aurelia raised a brow, and he answered, "When you left us, I dreamed of the worst possible things happening to you out there in the Wildlands."

His words were those of a worried father, but Aurelia couldn't halt the resentment in her tone. "Father, I told you I would be fine." She gestured to her tattered pants, her ragged tunic, then glanced accusingly around. "I'm fine. I'm here."

"Aurelia, if something had happened to you—"

"It didn't." She glared, mildly guilty at the surprised look on his face. Softer, she added, "The Diarmaid heir is safe."

The tilt of her father's head told her the message she'd intended had been received. But she wasn't ready to discuss that further. The future where she was queen was impossible and daunting, so she gestured to the small window outside their cell. "It will be dawn shortly. What are we going to do? They'll be back soon."

He took the change of subject in stride. "I've been searching my mind for the spell your mother could have used." He sighed. "I can't seem to recall anything."

"Nor can I," she admitted. She watched her mother's figure. Her honey-colored hair fell partly over her fair cheek. Her riding clothes were dirty from what had been a long journey, combined with the filth of their cell. Her face rested on her left shoulder, as if she were only stretched out for a nap. Bits of straw and gods knew what else surrounded her tall frame. Half a year ago, such a sight would have shocked Aurelia. Now it only stoked her anger toward Drest and his mother.

Rubbing her temples Aurelia said, "She gave no lesson on any spell like this one." She ran through her mind, pulling up pages of books and scrolls of parchment overflowing with ancient ink that listed ingredients and the words needed for innumerable levels of magic. None of it matched the spell her mother had cast. No tutoring lesson in the confines of the castle had ever included a way to put oneself in a near-death state.

She threw back her head, exasperated. "I should have paid better attention."

Her father's bushy eyebrows shot up, followed by his lips curving in a smile.

"What?"

"I was remembering the number of times your mother had to chastise the two of you for not remaining on task during your lessons."

"It's hardly our fault," she replied. "Most of the lessons were dreadfully tiresome. Only when Mother returned from the village with her stories were my lessons of any excitement." She paused. "That's it!"

"Sweetheart, what is it?"

"The village." She hurried to her feet and paced around the cramped cell. "I remember. It was four, maybe five winters ago. Mother had gone into the village to tend to a family. I think they were herders? I don't recall." Her frantic steps paused as she collected her thoughts. "The father of the family was quite ill. He suffered from a common enough malady, one which caused him to be constantly cold, yet his body was wildly hot, and fluids flowed effortlessly from his nose and eyes. Since it was winter, Mother told the family that while the herbal teas were helping, the freezing cold would prove life-threatening. She proposed a spell that would put him to sleep." She glanced at her mother's figure, then resumed her pacing. "She said he could better fight whatever had taken hold of him in a state more akin to sleep." Her face scrunched in concentration.

"Something like being stronger if his body could attack the illness from within," her father said, straightening. His eyes lit with the same spark Aurelia felt inside. "I remember your mother telling me about him. He made a full recovery."

Aurelia bit her lip, scanning the ground. "Gods, I remember, but what was that spell?" She fell back into the memory of her mother explaining how she'd leaned over the villager in his bed to administer the incantation. Aurelia had pictured his wife and four children huddled near the corner, all watching with bated breath as her mother worked. Aurelia saw her mother's lips move, beginning the spell. Then she saw her mother returning from the village three days later, reporting the good news that he had come back to life when her enchantment had been lifted.

Squeezing her eyes shut, Aurelia imagined her mother's hands hovering over the villager's chest. Magenta flames glowed beneath her fingers. In the cell, Aurelia's hands grew warm with the fire from her saol.

"What was it she said?" she muttered.

A door creaked open down the passageway.

"Sweetheart."

Aurelia paused, listening. *They're coming.*

Resuming her hurried steps, her father pulled her mother closer, propping her up so that she lay against his chest and was as far from the cell door as possible. Staring at her mother's slack face, Aurelia willed herself back into her memories. Steps echoed on the other side of the cells, but she conjured the image of her mother at work.

She rushed forward, placing her hands over her mother's heart. Quickly, she recited the incantation, hoping it was the right one. Her saol glowed, awakening her mother's body.

As her mother's eyes fluttered open and she gasped the stale air, a pair of guards rounded the corner.

Her father's gaze met hers, swimming with tears. He nodded, and Aurelia hoped he understood her message. He shifted to conceal her mother from full view. Aurelia prayed to the gods for an idea.

Aurelia stood. Her mind buzzed as she placed herself between her parents and the guards. She didn't recognize these men, not that she had paid much attention to the guards when she was in the castle.

"Hand over the queen," one of them said, his mouth contorted in a nasty smile above a stubbly chin.

"Please," Aurelia said, "we need more time with her."

The same guard ran his tongue over his teeth, then spat. "We have our orders."

"Since when does the royal guard answer to anyone other than the royal family?" She pulled back her shoulders, lifting her chin. "It's you who should be locked in here for treason."

The guards laughed.

"Don't waste your time, darling." Her father spoke slowly. "These men have been bought. That's the lowliest kind of person." He raised his lip. "They're not worth it."

The second guard—taller with arm muscles bulging out of his leather armor—stepped forward, but the first one held out an arm. "Don't give them the satisfaction. We'll be rid of them soon enough."

Aurelia bit her tongue and took a breath, throwing a glance at her father. She turned back to the guards. "At least give us one last moment to say good-bye. Please."

The guards exchanged looks. "Make it quick." They stepped out of the cell but kept their eyes fixed on Aurelia, who nodded courteously despite every fiber of her being itching to wipe the looks from their faces.

She walked to where her father still sat and knelt so the guards had no view of her mother, who opened her eyes. A faint smile graced her chapped lips.

"Mother," she said, loud enough for the guards to hear, "I wish we could have been together outside of these walls once more. I wish Father could help you from this prison, and I could lead us back to the royal grounds." She held her mother's gaze a moment more, then looked at her father. He nodded. Then she dropped her voice. "Ready?"

Her mother blinked in acknowledgment. Aurelia stood. Slowly, she turned to face the guards. "Very well. You may carry out your orders."

Both men walked into the cell. They were fixated on her mother and didn't seem to notice Aurelia step behind them and conjure her saol. The red light was faint, but sparks flew from its edges as she summoned more spell-fire between her palms.

As the guards bent to pick up her mother, her father yelled, "Now!"

Aurelia let her saol go. It split from her hands, a massive flame hitting both guards in the back. The one who had spoken toppled forward, unconscious. The other staggered but grabbed his sword. He wasn't fast enough though, as Aurelia had already aimed another saol. It flew across the cell and hit him on the jaw. He collapsed, joining his partner in an unmoving heap.

Satisfied, Aurelia nudged one of them with her boot. "I would apologize," she said, "but I was raised to never tell a lie."

When she glanced at her father, his mouth was agape. Ignoring this, she helped her mother stand.

"Well done, my darling." She wavered but looked infinitely better than she had one minute before as she tried to keep her balance.

"I was hoping I stalled long enough to give you time to regain your senses."

Her mother cupped her cheek. "You did wonderfully." She turned. "Grannus."

He reached to push hair out of her mother's face, placing it back toward her disheveled braid. "My love." He grabbed her hand, kissing her knuckles. "I've missed you."

Aurelia shuffled her feet. As her parents pulled back from an embrace, Aurelia asked the question she'd been dying to. "Mother, Father, what is happening in Venostes?"

Her parents stood straighter as if remembering they were the queen and king and had a plethora of items to see to. Her mother said, "We have much to discuss." Then she grabbed Aurelia's hand. "But first, we must go. Now."

CHAPTER FOUR

As the sun rose, painting the sky vermilion, Jastyn and Coran tugged their rowboat ashore, dragging it to rest upon the sand. When it dug into the beach with one final, emphatic crunch, they stepped back, breathing hard.

"Boating is a lot of work," she said, half smiling as Coran bent over at the waist.

"You're tellin' me."

She followed the path their rowboat had taken from the larger ship still floating several lengths out at sea.

"Think they'll be safe out there?" Coran asked.

"These aren't friendly waters to selkies. But they're smart. Tove and Fortan are going to cast a cloaking spell over their ship once we're out of sight." She squinted at the ship bobbing lazily beyond the break in the waves coming into shore. "I like to think my father knows what he's doing."

She ignored Coran's raised brow. They turned to the rocky shore that slanted away from them in a steep uphill climb toward the mainland.

"Welcome back, Jas."

Shaking her head and adjusting the satchel carrying her sister's cure over her chest, she said, "Come on. We better get started."

"Where are we going?"

Looking over her shoulder, Aurelia's mother threw her an impatient glance. "Back to the castle, sweetheart. Where else?"

Aurelia stopped in her tracks. "No, we can't. It's not safe there."

Her parents slowed their hurried strides, retreating to Aurelia. The three of them stood outside at the base of the castle's western tower after having escaped miraculously unseen through an exterior door one floor above the dungeons. This was the same tower Aurelia had snuck into nearly nine months ago when she'd first learned of the unrest developing in her kingdom.

"Love," her mother said gently, though Aurelia could hear the strain in her voice, "our things are inside. Tools we can use to fight. And I am certain there are members of the court who remain loyal to our family. If I can speak to them—"

"That may be, Mother, but Drest is also inside. And the baroness. By now they have to have heard of our escape. It's too soon to go back. We'd be jeopardizing everything."

When her mother's face only pinched in deliberation, Aurelia threw a pleading glance at her father. He sighed. "Dechtire, Aurelia is right." He reached out, caressing her mother's dirt-smudged cheek. "We need to be patient."

Her blue eyes softened. "Very well." Then her gaze swept over the grounds, the high stone tower beside them, and the quickly lightening sky. "Where should we go?"

Aurelia bounced as an idea came to her. "The stables." She recalled Jastyn's stepfather. "The horse master, he's a good man. You've said so yourself." She turned to her mother. "He might be there. He may be willing to help us."

Her parents exchanged looks.

"It's the only chance we have right now," her father said.

Aurelia tried to ignore the emotions surging through her at the memory of the day she'd met Jastyn in the stables. That was the day her entire world had changed.

Taking a deep breath, she waited as her mother contemplated. Eventually, she nodded. "To the stables."

"You do have a plan, right, Jas?"

She frowned at the trepidation in Coran's tone. "Don't I always?" she asked, teasing as they ascended the last incline of the embankment before reaching the green grass of their kingdom's hillside. Pausing to catch their breath, they stared at the sprawling hills that stretched ahead of them. They'd come ashore at the southernmost point below the royal grounds. The castle loomed beyond, perched atop the highest bundle of hills, its gray stone looking more unwelcoming than Jastyn remembered.

"I can't believe we're back."

She glanced at Coran. "You should find your mum." She recalled the aftermath of the elf attack on Venostes. Coran's mum had been caught in the chaos, a victim of an arrow in her back that had left her with permanent impairment, though it was mild compared to some of the other victims from that day.

He stood quietly, the ocean's breeze pulling his tunic around his torso. Jastyn winced at how thin he'd become.

"She'd want to know you're all right."

When his silence dragged on, Jastyn pushed him forward.

"Are you sure?" he asked, though Jastyn knew he was dying to see her.

"Go," she told him.

"What'll you do?"

She patted her satchel. "I've got to figure out this cure. But my family is trapped." She motioned to the castle. "I've got to get them out. I'm sure my mother and Elisedd can help once we're together again."

"I'll go see my mum, then I'll come find ya."

Smiling, she held out her arm.

He blinked. "You're jokin', right?" He pulled her into a hug. Wrapping her arms around him, she buried her face in his shoulder. "You're not alone, Jas, ya hear? We'll get your family out. We'll find out what's goin' on in that castle, and we'll figure out the cure."

Sniffling, she wiped her nose and stepped back. "You forgot Aurelia."

"How could I?" He sighed. "We got our work cut out for us."

Waving him off, she said, "Go on."

Walking backward, he asked, "Stables?"

She nodded, watching him go.

"I'll see ya there."

Later, tying off the end of her braid she'd redone—not surprised at how tangled her hair was—Jastyn stepped carefully through the thin stretch of Wood that lay between the shore and the meadow leading to the castle grounds. A single step among the trees was all it took for her to feel like herself again. At least, that was how she felt at first, as the crackle of fallen twigs crunched beneath her boots, and she spotted the familiar gnome hills dotting the bases of trees. The farther she walked, though, the more something was different. No, not different. Missing.

Aurelia.

A hare scampered across her path. Everything seemed the same. The leaves were a lush green, at their peak before the autumnal equinox in two weeks' time. The fairy nests glowed dully in the daylight. The paths she'd walked hundreds of times were still there. Yet things were different.

Focus, Jastyn.

Shaking herself out of her musings, she walked on, inhaling deeply. She needed to get into the castle and free her family. She needed to make the cure. A tingling ran up the side of her calf. She grimaced. Tove and Fortan had started work on her new dagger—apparently, selkies didn't need half the equipment local blacksmiths required—but she was growing impatient. With the dagger, she could handle whatever madness had taken hold of the kingdom.

Speaking of madness. She paused against an ash tree, taking a sip from her flask. *I think I went mad on that journey.* She'd been completely fixated on the noble sacrifice being Aurelia, so she'd lost sight of the Red One's specialty: riddles. She had been set on the worst possible scenario being the only option because that was how things had always been. Aurelia had to have been the sacrifice because of her noble blood. She was also the one person Jastyn couldn't stand to lose.

Shaking her head, she poured water into her hand and splashed her face. Laughing, she could hear Coran's voice warning her not to go down this path. She couldn't allow herself to fall into a dark place. Not after a weight had finally been lifted for her in the western caves.

Had that really been her mother in that cave along the cove? The Red One was clever, but her mother had felt so real. Everything they'd said, everything Jastyn had confessed…she wasn't sure if she could have that conversation again.

A blue jay trilled overhead.

"I know, I'll go." She pulled up her tunic sleeves as the sun broke over the treetops. When she cleared the Wood, she stood gazing across the meadow. On the other side sat the outdoor pens of the castle stables. A flash of memory ran through her mind, and she watched Aurelia ride in on her horse the first time Jastyn had seen her.

A sudden wind broke the still air. Jastyn frowned. The Wood had grown quiet. Spinning around, Jastyn raised her arm, her saol ready. Immediately, she stumbled.

The Dark Fae stood twenty paces away, framed by the pale trunks of two ancient birch trees.

"How?"

Her question was answered with the phrase she'd grown to despise: "Odium Child."

Scanning the area, Jastyn saw no horse, no billowing mounds of dark clouds. The rider was alone and realer than ever before. He walked closer. Jastyn hurried backward, farther from the Wood.

"I know your name, Jastyn Cipher."

This time, when he reached out a hand, Jastyn saw rotted flesh on decayed bone. His voice didn't hold the same emptiness it once had.

Curious, Jastyn stopped. "Who are you?"

The Dark Fae only walked steadily toward her. Jastyn realized she'd never seen him in the light of day. She couldn't make out his tribe's colors since everything he wore was faded, like him. The cloak masking his face was nearly gray. The worn tail of a belt held faint traces of yellow. His fingers were only an arms' length from her now. Jastyn remained where she was, scrutinizing the rider who'd haunted her more than half her life. Each time they'd met, he'd seemed otherworldly, a phantom. Looking at him now, Jastyn thought he seemed more human than ever before.

When his fingers were inches from her throat, Jastyn snapped from his thrall. A bony hand, this one small and warm, grabbed her wrist.

"Move, child!"

"Eegit?"

The hedgewitch fixated on the Dark Fae. She reached out her other frail arm, her gnarled fingers extended to match his. "She's had enough of you." A blazing white light shot from the ground, forming a wall between them. It expanded, swallowing the Dark Fae in its glare. Jastyn shielded her face. When the brightness subsided, she looked around.

"Where is he?"

Eegit teetered as she replied. "Sent him back where he came from. Where that is, you'd have to gamble a guess."

Jastyn steadied her. "You're weak."

She slapped Jastyn's arms down. "You're too skinny." She stomped across the meadow, her animal-skin clothing swaying as she waved for Jastyn to follow. "I've recovered enough since I saw you at the beach." She squinted at the bright sun. "I'll regain my full strength soon."

"How did you know where to find me?" Jastyn kept pace with her, wondering at her sudden swift steps.

She guffawed. "The fae are watching everything these days with the kingdom being what it is." She gestured to the surrounding trees. "Water nymphs told the tree nymphs, who told me about a peculiar ship taking anchor off the southern shore."

"But the selkies...they cloaked it."

Eegit grunted. "To humans, maybe. They need to leave that cove of theirs more often."

"Wait." Jastyn held out an arm. Eegit grumbled but slowed. "Thank you, for helping me." She paused, thinking a moment. "He just told me he knows my name. Years ago, the first time we met, he told me I was lucky because I didn't know my true name." She felt flush creep up her neck. "He said I was *gan athair*."

Eegit pulled a leaf from her hair, staring at the veins in the faded green when she said, "Without a father."

"Do you think he knows?" She pointed to where the Dark Fae had stood. "Do you think he knows I've met my father?"

"Probably." At her frustrated sigh, Eegit added, "Some of us have the gift of Sight, child. You know that. Though he probably sold his soul for it. He's the Collector of Odiums. He knew your life as soon as you were born."

"The Mountains of Ionad...I didn't know Tove then, but he still got close." She reached up, rubbing her neck where the bruises from the Dark Fae's grip used to be. "How did he get to me, then?"

Shrugging, Eegit said, "Too much magical energy in one place."

Jastyn thought of Vreis. Could their being in the same place have drawn the Dark Fae there? Vreis wasn't an Odium, but he was a half blood like her. Then she remembered. "I didn't have my dagger." Eegit only grunted, and Jastyn shook her head. "I'm ready to be rid of him."

Eegit turned to Jastyn, her wide eyes roaming her face. "This will not be easy."

"I know."

Nodding, Eegit turned. Jastyn grabbed her shoulder, then pulled her into a hug. "It's good to see you."

Eegit's hands came to rest on her back. "Oh, child. It's good to have you back."

Stepping away, Jastyn looked at her dear friend. Even when she left Jastyn frustrated with more questions than answers, she couldn't not love her. Eegit's face, full of deep lines crisscrossing this way and that, the hunch in her back, and her tattered leggings were a part of Jastyn's life, and she wouldn't have it any other way.

Then Jastyn remembered the vision her mother had showed her in the cave, the one where it was her mother's doing that Eegit took her under her wing. Clearing her throat, Jastyn wasn't sure how to bring such a thing up. She met Eegit's dark, watery gaze. "Eegit, in the caves...I..."

"You got the cure, didn't you?"

"I did." She ran a hand down her braid, then anxiously patted the satchel. "But there's something else."

Eegit stepped back, glancing up as wisps of clouds formed overhead. "Your family. They're in the Diarmaid dungeon."

"Yes, but Eegit—"

"Stop blabbering, child." Eegit hurried forward, pushing Jastyn's back to get her moving again. "You've got to get in there."

Jastyn gave up on trying to talk about what she'd seen. "Are you coming with me?" she asked.

"Can't, child." She rummaged under the layers of her tunic, pulling out a drawstring bag. "I've got to see someone about some minerals."

Jastyn rolled her eyes. "Still trying to bottle luck?"

Eegit harrumphed. "Wouldn't you like to know." With a final shove, she sent Jastyn on her way. "Be careful, child."

When Jastyn glanced over her shoulder, Eegit was gone.

Jastyn shook her head as she made her way across the open meadow to the stables. No matter how much had changed, it was nice to know Eegit remained the same.

CHAPTER FIVE

"This way."

Aurelia led her parents through the back doors of the stables, tucked opposite an entrance into the southern tower. She closed the heavy wooden doors behind them, motioning them down a straw-laden aisle framed by chicken coops. Halfway down, her mother held up a hand.

"Wait," she said, her breath labored.

"What is it?" Aurelia wheeled around, scanning her mother for signs of distress.

"I only need a moment. I'm still recovering."

Nodding, Aurelia said, "Thank the gods we got out of there."

Her mother smiled. "I had faith in you, my darling."

Aurelia's father, pushing up his tunic sleeves in the warm, stagnant air of the stable, said, "You could have warned me of your plans, my love."

"Darling," she replied, one hand pinching her side, "you were unreachable. I had to act." She swiped away straw that had been kicked up into his beard. "Enya had you enchanted. If I'd told you what I planned to do, she would have found out and killed me before I could begin my search in the Wildlands."

Aurelia recalled her capture, when she'd first learned of Drest's betrayal. In the Wood, he had spun her mind into a frenzy. "She penetrated your mind's weak point in order to control you."

"I was already vulnerable. Torn apart by everything that had happened." He inhaled deeply. "She convinced me to release Drest." His eyes brimmed with tears. "I'm such a fool."

"It's not your fault," her mother said. "Their hearts and minds have been corrupted by greed."

"Speaking of corruption and evil things." Aurelia pursed her lips, trying to think of the best way to broach recent events. "That figure on the beach. The dark force. It seemed to be working with them, Enya and Drest."

"Yes," her mother said, throwing a look to her father.

Catching it, Aurelia leaned forward. "You know who it is," she said eagerly. "You know of this force."

"Sweetheart—"

"Tell me who he is. This force has wreaked havoc on my life for the past six months. It's torn people apart." Jastyn flashed through her mind. The image of her ensnared in his awful grip in the Mountains of Ionad resonated like discordant bells. "If you know his identity, you cannot keep it from me any longer." Her voice reached a fever pitch. Several of the chickens flapped their wings, disturbed. She was about to continue her argument when a familiar whinny made her pause.

"Aurelia—"

She held up a hand. Her mind was still whirring as she walked down the dirt path before rounding a corner. The horse pens came into view, their chest-high wooden walls laid out evenly in a row. In the closest one stood her beloved mare.

"Keller!" Speeding through the doorway, she greeted the horse, wrapping her arms as best she could around the horse's sturdy middle. Keller neighed, then snorted in acknowledgment. Her hoofs stepped in place. "Oh, Keller. You're all right."

"The baroness and Drest must have brought them along when they took us back here," her mother said, surprise in her voice.

Pressing her face into Keller's nose, Aurelia said, "Drest always wanted what never belonged to him." She patted her mare's strong neck. The elation of the moment faded when she turned to her parents. "Please, tell me who he is."

They stood outside Keller's pen, exchanging a worried glance.

"You're right," her mother said finally. "It's too dangerous keeping you in the dark. Look what it did to Brennus." Her father gave a small nod.

Aurelia's heart skipped a beat. *Yes, this is what I want. I want to know. I want to be able to help. To fight.*

Her father cleared his throat again. "Very well." When his tired eyes locked on Aurelia's, she swallowed. "The dark force is more than legend. He is more than the Wandering Man from your childhood stories. He is, I'm afraid, very real." He paused. "And he is also the first Gulteran King."

❖

As Jastyn carefully pushed through the doors of the royal stables—the same doors she'd walked through nearly nine months ago on a mission to speak with the queen—she was struck by the sounds of an argument. Leaving the door ajar, she stepped quietly down the dirt path bordered by troughs and littered with chicken feed. Heated voices drifted over the still air from somewhere near the horse pens.

Moving closer, she was careful not to kick a stray bucket or frighten the animals and give herself away. The poor beasts seemed frightened enough as the chickens squawked, and several horses brayed nervously as whoever was inside continued to bicker.

Jastyn peered past a stallion's broad body to find the source of the loud discussion. The ground fell out from under her. Aurelia stood a few yards away, gesticulating wildly and pointing accusingly at her parents. Relief overwhelmed her. Aurelia was here, in Venostes, and she was okay. Jastyn swallowed, hoping to suppress her emotions and kick the nagging desire to run to her. Questions quickly formed. What were the king and queen doing here? And why did they look like they'd just fled persecution?

Jastyn sidestepped, still half-hidden by the large horse. The royal trio stood two pens away, in the middle of a path separating two rows of stables and causing quite the commotion. If they were on the run, as she guessed they might be from their haggard appearances, why were they being so loud? Wondering at the sight before her, she fixed her gaze on Aurelia.

She's beautiful when she's angry.

Giving her own cheek a smack, Jastyn told herself to focus. Why did she want to know what was happening? Last time she was here, she couldn't have cared less about the royal family. She wouldn't have cared about how fatigued the king looked or how the queen seemed like she could hardly stand. And she absolutely would not have wanted to run to Aurelia, to hold her and never let her go.

Finally, Jastyn stepped out from where she'd been watching. As she did, new voices penetrated the barn's walls from outside.

"The guards are coming," she called to the still bickering trio, who froze mid-accusation and whirled to face her.

The king and queen's brows rose in shock, and Aurelia's mouth fell open, her blue eyes wide. She started to speak, but Jastyn cut her off. "If you don't want to get caught, follow me." She spun, racing back toward the front stable doors. When she heard no movement, she glanced back to see the three of them standing in the same spot, staring, dumbfounded. She frowned, then shouted, "Now!"

The Diarmaids jumped and hurried after her, Aurelia at the front.

Jastyn spoke as they ran. "The guards are coming from the back. I know a place in the market they won't look." She caught Aurelia's gaze and saw she was dying to talk to her, but Jastyn pushed them on. "Follow me. Stay low, stick to the base of the walls near the brush, and stay together."

Much to her surprise, neither Dechtire nor Grannus said anything, only nodding their acknowledgment.

"This way." She ran ahead, leading the royal family to safety, another feat she never could have imagined only a year ago.

A few minutes later, Jastyn extended an arm to halt their group. Aurelia ran right into it. The queen in turn collided with her daughter unceremoniously.

"Why are we stopping?" the king asked from behind them.

Jastyn held up a finger to her lips, silencing them. It was imperative they keep quiet. She'd thrown a disarming spell over them, one she occasionally used in order to avoid detection when swiping items from unsuspecting vendors. It made her movements nearly undetectable as long as she was silent. It was also an illegal enchantment, but she figured desperate times called for such magic. Nobody had protested thus far.

Scanning their group, she saw all three of them take in their unfamiliar surroundings. They were deep in the market, in an alley off the main road. It was filled with discarded carts hosting broken wheels, crates of spoiled fruit spilling onto the ground, and piles of pungent scraps she'd rather not identify. A drop of moisture hit her shoulder, one of several that fell from various items of clothing hung to dry upon lines of rope zigzagging overhead.

Aurelia's mouth opened to speak, but a troop of guards rushed by, and they pressed against the wall, crouching behind splintered barrels. The guards shouted at villagers to get out of their way as they pushed toward the market's edge that ran to meet the Wood. After a minute, Jastyn dropped her arm. "It's clear."

The queen and king pulled back their hoods.

"Thank you," the king said with a curt nod.

Jastyn ignored the queen's icy stare and asked, "Who exactly are you running from?"

"Our own guard, evidently." The king smiled through a shake of his head.

Jumping into the conversation, Aurelia added, "My family has been betrayed by a member of the royal court. Baroness Enya and her son are behind everything."

Jastyn listened but kept getting distracted by the movement of Aurelia's lips as she explained.

"They're working alongside the dark force."

At this, Jastyn met her gaze. "What?"

"He's a part of this, too. He has been for some time," she added, shooting a look that could wilt flowers to her parents.

Jastyn shifted uncomfortably. "I don't understand. The Dark Fae is after me."

"Because you're an Odium, yes," Aurelia said, "but I've only recently learned that my great-great grandfather grew lax in the banishment of the Wandering Man and fell under his influence."

Jastyn struggled to follow. "Wandering Man?"

"It's a rather long story and perhaps better told when we're not fleeing our own guard." Aurelia glanced past Jastyn's shoulder.

"Good point, darling. We should retreat to safe ground," the queen interjected, stepping closer. Jastyn's hand balled into a fist. To her surprise, Aurelia hesitated to respond.

Jastyn bit her lip. How was this real? Was she really helping the Diarmaids find refuge? Exhaling, she rubbed her forehead, which was beginning to ache. She needed to get started on the cure. She needed to help her family. So why did she care so much about the wellbeing of this one?

A gentle hand cupped her elbow. Jastyn looked to find Aurelia leaning down to pull Jastyn's gaze up to hers. "What's wrong?" Worry was set in a thin line between Aurelia's eyes, and Jastyn knew it was useless to not tell her what was happening.

"My family has been taken prisoner."

Aurelia eyes widened. "They've *what*?" She spun so fast, her long hair flew out around her like a lion's mane. Her words even came out in a roar Jastyn never imagined she could possess. "Who ordered this? What could they possibly have done?"

Jastyn, taken aback, watched the king and queen cover their shock at being spoken to in such a way by their own daughter by pulling back their shoulders stiffly.

Dechtire stammered an answer, but Grannus said, "Darling, we couldn't have."

While Aurelia glared, Jastyn remembered what Coran had told her at the cove. Reluctantly, she said, "I think they're right." She ignored the incredulous look Aurelia gave her. "If your mother was searching for you, the order couldn't have come from her."

"She could have ordered it before she left," Aurelia countered, crossing her arms. Jastyn tried not to smile at the exact thought she'd had the day before.

"Darling," Dechtire said, looking completely out of her element, "please, I wouldn't do such a thing."

Jastyn appreciated the accusing look Aurelia gave her mother, knowing full well the royal family was capable of such things and had done so before.

"And I was already locked up," the king chimed in, drawing his daughter's vicious glare.

Aurelia shook her head. "Then who?" To Jastyn, she asked, "How do you know they've been imprisoned?"

"Eegit found me at the beach. After…" She faltered, glancing at the king and queen. "After we talked."

"Oh." A small flush flew to Aurelia's cheeks.

"She transported me back here, showed me a vision that had come and gone. The royal guard came into my home and arrested my mother, stepfather, and my sister."

"Elisedd?" Dechtire, for the first time, sounded alarmed.

"That's why he wasn't in the stables," the king said. "He was in the dungeons with us that entire time."

"With you?" Jastyn's headache burst down the back of her head, tensing her shoulders. She faced Aurelia. "You were in the dungeons?"

She bit her lip. "Only temporarily."

Jastyn raised her brow, amazed at Aurelia's nonchalance. She studied her face, which seemed deep in thought.

"It was the baroness, then, who ordered your family's arrest. She's taken over the castle."

"There's not a lot of time," Jastyn said, her body practically vibrating with the need to move. "I need to help them."

"Of course." Aurelia looked as if she wanted to say something but only stepped back toward her parents.

"In that case," her mother asked, "where are we to go? There are hidden rooms inside the castle, but it doesn't seem like the best time to return."

The question hung in the air between all of them. Jastyn adjusted her satchel, feeling for the vials inside, comforted by the weight of them. Every moment she went without making the cure was more time lost on her sister's life. Yet she hesitated. She knew Aurelia would let her go to her family. But she didn't know if Aurelia would ever forgive her for the betrayal from their time together on the journey. Jastyn couldn't leave things badly a second time. Not after everything.

"Come on," she finally said, stepping past the Diarmaids to peek out into the market. "I know a place you can hide until it's safe to return."

Looking startled Aurelia said, "But your family—"

"They are strong." Jastyn willed herself to hold tight to her own words. "I'll return for them. First, you need to follow me."

CHAPTER SIX

A urelia wanted to leap for joy. She wanted to shout into the tops of the tattered vendor roofs, dance across the lush grass, and sing among the trees as Jastyn led them into the Wood.

Jastyn was alive. Aurelia, a few steps behind, took a moment to scan her figure. The worn tunic looked dirty, much like her own, but her old boots had a shine to them. She desperately yearned to pull Jastyn aside, talk to her, tell her that she understood why she did what she had done. She also had a dozen questions. Where was Coran? Gods, she hoped nothing had happened to him. How did they get back to the kingdom? What happened at the cove with the invasion? Where was Rigo?

She longed to take Jastyn's hand, to talk to her about everything, but this was not the time. She threw a glance over her shoulder, impressed to find her parents keeping pace as they splashed across a babbling brook. Her mother's riding clothes needed a wash, and Aurelia knew her mother was dying for a hot bath. Her father looked almost gleeful, a small smile hidden beneath his grizzly beard as they each leapt over a large fallen log.

"Where are we going?" Aurelia asked, more for her parents' sake than her own. She trusted Jastyn and perhaps naively, hoped her parents might, too. She wished that they could see Jastyn as the wonderful person she was and hoped they would change their minds about Odiums. Alas, since following Jastyn's lead, her mother had kept her distance, and such a change of heart didn't seem promising.

"I'm taking you to Eegit's meadow."

"Who is Eegit?" her father called, his voice intrigued. "Someone from the village?"

When Jastyn looked back, Aurelia caught her grin. "She's a friend of mine."

Her father gave a curious pout. Her mother did not look amused. Aurelia tried to give them a reassuring smile, but even she felt anxious.

After navigating through several layers of apple trees, they cleared the final line of tall ash trunks to find themselves in a lovely open meadow surrounded by hawthorn trees and scattered with bilberry flowers.

Her mother was at her side, speaking under her breath. "Darling, what is she getting us into?"

"Mother, Eegit is a friend." At her mother's wrinkled forehead, she added, "This is a safe place. Trust me."

Aurelia winced at her mother's scoff and threw an apologetic look to Jastyn, but she was already halfway across the open space, the ankle-high grass parting with each purposeful step she took. She motioned for her parents to follow, but they lingered instead, scrutinizing this new place. The king lifted his chin to sniff the air. Aurelia, too, could smell the salt on the breeze and realized they were near the coast.

"Why does the air feel...peculiar?" her father asked, his deep voice carrying on a light breeze.

"Cloaking spell," Jastyn called over her shoulder.

Aurelia's mother crossed her arms, still not moving. "Your friend doesn't trust many if she feels the need to cloak her home from the rest of the world."

Jastyn, who had crouched to rummage through a pile of old pots, stood. Aurelia swallowed as her mother's gaze bored into Jastyn's, who stepped around the firepit. "I could say the same about you, Your Majesty."

"Me?" Her lips raised in a smile. It was the smile she used when the conversation in the dining hall broached a topic she didn't care for.

Jastyn pointed between the three of them. "You don't cloak your home like Eegit does. The royal family hides behind giant towers of impenetrable stone, crawling with layers of guards." She walked over as she spoke, never breaking eye contact with Aurelia's mother, who stood several inches taller than her. "What are you afraid of?"

Aurelia squeaked, meeting her father's frantic gaze with her own. Her mother seemed unperturbed. "We hide from nothing. Our home is one of fortitude." She gestured around the meadow. "What drives your friend to such an isolated part of this realm?"

Jastyn smiled. "You do."

Aurelia felt as if the strings of a harp were tightening inside her chest as she blinked between Jastyn and her mother. "Well, shall we start a fire? I feel the air growing colder, don't you all?" When her mother and Jastyn continued to stare one another down, Aurelia said, "Jastyn, care to help me?"

To her relief, Jastyn turned to assist her but not before saying, "And you're wrong, Your Majesty. This place isn't one of isolation. It's freedom."

Jastyn felt light. She'd never spoken to the queen like that. Growing up, she'd had no desire to. Occasionally, in moments of frustration over her sister's health or the terrifying moments following one of her nightmares, she had pictured herself shouting at the royal family. In her mind, she stood over them, berating them for her miserable life. Those moments, passionate as they were, had been brief. Generally, she didn't think they were worth her time.

But ever since she'd watched the queen bare her controlling teeth after the attack in the Wood six months ago, unwilling to let her daughter go, Jastyn had been dying to speak to her. She hadn't had a plan or thought about her choice of words. She certainly hadn't imagined speaking to Her Majesty in a situation like this. Still, their exchange left Jastyn feeling pretty pleased.

"You look amused," Aurelia muttered as they knelt on opposite sides of the firepit, facing the charred logs.

As Jastyn conjured her saol, Aurelia doing the same, she said, "I have begun to understand your attitude toward your mother." Aurelia's saol flickered, then leapt from her hands toward Jastyn, who fell back. "What was that for?"

Aurelia's eyes shimmered with anger. "She is frightened, Jastyn." Lowering her voice, she added, "We all are."

Frowning, Jastyn let her saol linger on the scraps of wood until it caught. Standing, she placed her hands on her hips. "They could be a little more grateful."

Scrunching her face, Aurelia tilted her chin up. "You're correct on that front." For a moment, she held her gaze, and the longing Jastyn thought she saw in it sent a chill down her back. They had so much to talk about. Aurelia glanced around. "Where is your dear friend Eegit, anyway? I assumed she'd be here."

"She's off somewhere. No doubt she'll be back soon." Then she smiled as Aurelia scanned the ground and pulled two larger dry logs closer to the fire. Jastyn shook her head; Aurelia's habit of making seats remained endearing.

As if feeling her gaze, Aurelia looked up as she adjusted one of the logs with the toe of her boot. "What?"

"Nothing."

Jastyn found herself mesmerized by Aurelia's eyes. She wanted to walk around the fire and pull her close, beg her forgiveness for what she'd done on their journey. She knew all of this back-and-forth now was simply Aurelia being, well, Aurelia. She had to make things look all right, even if they weren't.

A loud pointed cough broke the silence. King Grannus stared at the ground near them, moving a small rock with his foot. The queen held a look in her eyes Jastyn couldn't place but didn't like having aimed at her.

"Eegit will come around soon," she said to break the awkward silence. "There's extra squirrel meat in the hut. I checked. And it looks like there's some water in this cauldron." She gestured to the one at her feet. "Like I said, nobody can find this place, so you're safe."

The queen and king nodded, and Jastyn wished she could stay to watch Venostes' royalty fend for themselves, but she had to get back to the castle.

Adjusting her satchel—too afraid to take it off for even a second—she started for the meadow's edge. When she was almost to the trees, the queen shouted, "Aurelia!"

Jastyn turned. The princess sprinted past her parents. When she did, Aurelia called back, "I'm going to help her."

The queen raised her hand, magenta flames shooting out from her fingertips. In seconds, they engulfed Aurelia, trapping her in a bubble of her mother's own saol.

"Aurelia." Jastyn rushed to her. The flames seemed to only impede her ability to break free, as Aurelia demonstrated through a series of pounding with her fists against the bright light, shouting furiously.

"Let. Me. Out."

The queen stormed forward, and Jastyn stepped back.

"Aurelia Diarmaid, if you think we are letting you run off with her *again*, then you seriously misunderstood."

Up close, with the magenta light dancing over her face, the queen looked fearsome. Her hair was loose in the braid that ran down the center of her head, and strands flew wildly across her fair face.

"You cannot keep me here against my will."

"I am your mother. I most certainly can."

Aurelia pounded harder against the saol. The frustration on her face, in her fists, made Jastyn want to leap in the fire after her.

"You can't keep me in here." Aurelia stopped her fruitless efforts to escape, her mother's saol clearly too strong.

The queen stood face-to-face with her, the flames crackling in the air between them. "Aurelia," she said, her voice serious, "when will you understand that everything your father and I do is for your benefit? We only want to keep you safe."

"All you've done is stifle me. I knew nothing before I left the castle."

"You were taught so much—"

"Of ancient stories and figures and numbers but not of our own realm, Mother." Aurelia threw up an exasperated hand. "You and Father kept us ignorant of everything that mattered. And look where it got us. Look where it got Brennus."

Dechtire stumbled, her light eyes lit with their own fire. Jastyn was certain the flames of her saol intensified with her shock.

Aurelia looked down. "I'm not a child anymore. And Brennus is gone. I have to be out there, Mother." She seemed to steel herself before adding, "As future queen, what good am I to our people if I am ignorant to the world they live in?"

Her chest rising and falling quickly, the queen's outward agitation dimmed, her saol with it. She gave a final flourish of her hand, and the magenta flames vanished, releasing Aurelia.

"Thank you," she said. Then she stepped closer, placing her hands on her mother's forearms. "You have to trust me. We're going to be all right."

The king walked over now that the wrath of his wife had subsided. He raised a hand to Aurelia's cheek. "We don't want to lose you, too."

Jastyn shifted, uncomfortable at what had become an intimate family moment.

"You won't lose me." Aurelia caught Jastyn's gaze. "Jastyn knows what she's doing."

A swell of gratitude filled Jastyn's chest. *Maybe there's hope after all.*

Aurelia released her parents' hands, which reluctantly fell to their sides. "We'll be back once we've secured Jastyn's family." The king looked ready to say something, but Aurelia spoke first. "Please, stay here. We'll discuss matters upon our return."

Jastyn gave a small chuckle at her decisiveness, then at the queen and king's compliance as they took seats on the logs Aurelia had arranged.

When Aurelia walked by without a passing glance, Jastyn hurried to catch up. Unsure what to say, she finally asked, "Are you okay?"

"I'm fine." Aurelia seemed to focus on her footsteps. "Let's go save your family."

Jastyn followed, awestruck. The queen's saol may have raged with power moments ago, but it was Aurelia whose fire burned brightest among the Diarmaids.

CHAPTER SEVEN

After throwing another disarming enchantment over herself and Aurelia, Jastyn headed back toward the castle. Even without the spell, she doubted they would be recognized. Aurelia, in her torn, dirty tunic and pants, her long hair filled with tufts of dandelion and grass, looked the opposite of regal as she lifted her hood to mask her face. Meanwhile, Jastyn tried to lose herself in the buzz of villagers milling along the midmorning market streets on a sunny day. She strained to hear the discordant bells under the carts or even the glaring shouts of people screaming over one another to be heard by customers. Anything but the voice in her head telling her to talk to Aurelia.

Glancing sideways as they rounded a corner, heading toward the final strip of market road before the dirt paths gave way to rolling grass, Jastyn found Aurelia wearing a look of determination.

"You didn't have to come," she said, but regretted it at the look Aurelia shot her.

"Not your best choice of words, given our history," Aurelia replied, her voice laced with anger. "Besides, do you even know where to find your family?"

"They're in the dungeons."

Aurelia sighed. "I mean, do you know how to get down there?"

"I…" Jastyn grimaced. "I guess I don't. I'm sure I could manage."

"I'm sure you could."

Biting her cheek, Jastyn decided it was better to not talk. Not now, anyway. She let Aurelia take the lead once they passed the castle's main gate, then over the hillside where the prince's Remembrance ceremony had been held. From there, they hurried around the eastern tower.

"The stables?" Jastyn asked as they came into view.

"We'd just left the dungeons when you found us earlier. Cutting through the stables into the castle will be the most discreet way."

Nodding, Jastyn followed. When they were near the stables, a few paces from the doors leading inside, Aurelia slowed.

"What is it?"

Aurelia pointed. "The door is ajar."

Jastyn shrugged. "I think I left it that way."

Looking skeptical, Aurelia leaned through the open space, which was just large enough to fit through. She jerked backward, wide-eyed.

"What?" Jastyn hurried beside her.

Aurelia put a gentle hand on her sternum, stopping her progress. Her response came in stammered bursts, and a flush emerged in her cheeks. "It seems there's someone...there's several someones...I fear we are intruding..."

Confused, Jastyn nudged her aside. They didn't have time for games. "Intruding on what?" She shoved through the doorway only to skid to a halt. Beneath a loft only a few yards from where she stood, Coran and Roisin nestled atop a bed of straw. Averting her eyes from having to witness another moment of Coran indulging in amorous affection, Jastyn gave a loud cough.

Mid-kiss, Coran and Roisin looked up.

"Gods almighty," Roisin cried, shoving Coran. He tumbled awkwardly onto the ground, rolling down the straw. Standing, he adjusted his tunic while Roisin seemed to dig deeper into the pile of hay.

"Jas," he said, "hiya." He shot Roisin a pleading look. "I was comin' to find ya when I ran into Roisin."

"Quite literally, I presume." Aurelia, recovered from her initial shock, sauntered in to stand beside Jastyn.

"M'lady!" There was a flurry of hay and dirt, and Roisin was on her feet. "You're here."

Jastyn stepped aside so Roisin could tackle Aurelia in a hug.

"I'm not sure what to make of your doubts, Roisin." Aurelia smiled despite her remark, and she met Jastyn's gaze over Roisin's shoulder. Jastyn cleared her throat and turned her attention to Coran.

"Sorry to interrupt," she teased while he ran a hand through his hair. She helped him pick out a few pieces of hay. "You saw your mum, I hope?"

"I did. She insisted on feeding me, but I told her I had to meet ya. She was worried…said there's been all sorts of talk in the village about what's been happenin' in the kingdom. Says the Diarmaids have disappeared since the prince's death. People are scared. They don't know what to think." His face fell in seriousness. "There was a slew of guards here earlier, just as I arrived. They left, though. Seemed like they were lookin' for someone."

Aurelia, holding to Roisin's waist, sighed. "They're looking for my family."

"What?" Roisin looked aghast.

"It's a long story, Roisin. One I'm afraid we don't have time for."

"Are you headin' to the dungeons?" asked Coran.

"My family's down there." Jastyn's skin itched. She needed to get to them. She needed to get to Alanna.

"Gods." Roisin walked over to Coran, pulling Aurelia with her. Jastyn ignored the pang of jealousy at Aurelia's hand in someone else's grasp. "There really is trouble brewing, isn't there?"

"We should get a move on," Coran said, but Jastyn shook her head.

"Coran, it's too dangerous."

He looked incredulous, then faced Aurelia. "Did she try that on you, too?"

She scoffed. "Of course she did."

Jastyn, embarrassed, threw up her hands as they both crossed their arms. Roisin pouted in confusion. "With all respect," she said, "I don't recall volunteering for…whatever this is," she finished, making a circle with her finger around their group.

Coran smiled and squeezed her hand. Aurelia looked at Jastyn expectantly.

Jastyn said, "You mentioned there were guards earlier."

Coran's brows went up as he caught on. "We'll keep a lookout."

"Thank you." Jastyn exhaled.

"Just hurry, will ya?"

A short while later, Jastyn crept a step behind Aurelia along a cramped passageway that descended beneath the castle's main chambers. They'd proceeded into the depths of the massive castle in silence, Aurelia pointing or nodding directions when needed. The dark, quiet hallways only amplified Jastyn's uproar of emotions, and she struggled to focus, running into the wall as she and Aurelia turned another dark corner down a passageway that resembled all the others. Jastyn smiled to herself; Aurelia had been right; there was little chance Jastyn could have found her way through this maze of winding tunnels. Cutting her gaze sideways, she tried to see past Aurelia's resolute face. What was she thinking about? Would Jastyn be able to explain herself, given the chance? What would she say? Were there any words worthy enough to beg forgiveness for keeping such a secret for so long?

Jastyn chewed her cheek, her eyes on the back of Aurelia as they hurried through an archway and down a winding staircase. Aurelia was too good of a person not to help her now, but would she be as kind when they finally had a moment to talk?

Aurelia stopped at the base of a staircase where a separate hallway shot out to one side. After peering around a corner, she motioned for Jastyn to look.

Two guards stood at the end of a long hallway in front of what Jastyn presumed was the door to the dungeon. The look Aurelia wore told Jastyn she hadn't considered this as part of their rescue mission.

After thinking a moment, Jastyn rummaged through her satchel. She ignored Aurelia's confused look when she pulled out an apple she'd plucked upon leaving Eegit's meadow.

Locking eyes with her, Jastyn motioned for her to wait. Then she tossed the fruit around the corner and pressed Aurelia against the wall.

The guardsmen's footsteps hurried toward them. Jastyn conjured her saol. Catching on, Aurelia followed suit. Holding up her fingers, Jastyn counted down from three. Then they rounded the corner, catching the two men off guard and knocking them out easily with their spell-fire.

"We'd better hurry," Aurelia said, leaping over them and running for the end of the hallway. "They won't be out long."

Upon reaching the heavy wooden door, Aurelia muttered a spell, and Jastyn watched, wide-eyed, as the door's lock clicked open.

Trying unsuccessfully to hide a smile, Aurelia shrugged. "I had to keep myself entertained somehow in this place," was all she said before leading Jastyn into the darkness of the dungeons.

Jastyn's eyes swept the space, taking everything in. "Why are there no guardsmen in here?" she asked as they passed two empty cells.

"I imagine they're all out looking for us."

When they turned a corner, a new set of cells were just visible in the feeble torchlight. Jastyn's heart beat so loud at the sight of her mother, Elisedd, and Alanna in their iron cage that she couldn't hear herself think.

Alanna saw her first.

"Jastyn!"

Running over, Jastyn gripped the bars of the cell door. Her mother and Elisedd stood quickly. Her sister's cold hand found hers, and Jastyn felt a wave of relief so strong she didn't care that tears filled her eyes.

"We've come to get you out," she said, her voice thick with emotion. Her gaze went from Alanna to Elisedd. He looked the same, his sinewy arms hanging tiredly out of his tunic. His fine beard was in need of a shave, with tufts sprouting along his cheeks in patches. Dark circles sat beneath his dark eyes, which brimmed with surprise at the sight of her.

Her mother's hands joined Alanna's, resting atop Jastyn's. Slowly, she forced her gaze to meet her mother's. Neither of them said anything, but Jastyn knew her mother could hear what she couldn't manage to put into words.

"Your Highness." Elisedd bowed his head.

"Horse master. Branna," Aurelia said, nodding.

Alanna looked as if she'd just discovered a rare bird upon realizing it was Aurelia who stood behind Jastyn. "Princess Aurelia?" She gaped. Jastyn raised an amused brow but felt a blush rise in her face when her mother looked utterly unsurprised.

"You're up," Jastyn said to Aurelia. "Go ahead."

She frowned. "I fear I don't follow."

"Do that spell, the one you used before."

It was Aurelia's turn to blush. "That spell only works on doors manufactured from wood. It's elemental." She wrung her hands. "I thought you had a spell of your own. I thought that was why you didn't look for keys on one of the guards."

Swallowing, Jastyn asked, "But how did you escape earlier?"

"We ambushed the guard."

Elisedd made a noise resembling a snort, but Alanna began to tremble. Jastyn placed her hands atop her sister's. "It's okay." She lowered her gaze, turning to Aurelia and dropping her voice. "What are we going to do?"

Jastyn's mother interjected. "The guards have to return eventually."

Aurelia nodded. "Those two upstairs will be conscious at any moment."

"So, what," Jastyn said, glancing between them, "we take out multiple guardsmen again? Isn't that pressing our luck?"

"We've got to try," Alanna chimed in.

Jastyn smiled weakly. Reaching through the bars, she said, "I've missed your optimism."

Alanna squeezed her hand. "We can help." She glanced eagerly between her parents. "Can't we?"

Her mother pursed her lips to hide a nervous smile, but Elisedd nodded, looking determined. He grabbed a cup of water sitting on a tray filled with stale breadcrumbs. He walked to the back of the cell, emptied the water on the floor, then kicked some of the straw that littered the cell over it.

"Well, we are out of water. They have to refill it. Unless they're complete monsters."

Jastyn exchanged looks with Aurelia. "It's the best plan we've got."

Shouts echoed from outside, and the dungeon door opened.

"Get back, girls," her mother instructed, pulling Alanna away from the bars. Elisedd, cup in hand, took a seat on the floor while Jastyn tugged Aurelia into the shadows along the opposite wall.

"Where are they?" one of the guards shouted as he and his partner—both sporting well-trimmed red beards and strong upper bodies—rounded her family's cell. One grabbed a torch from the wall, shoving it toward the bars to better see, casting an orange glow over the black and gray space.

"Where is who?" Jastyn's mother asked, a convincing line between her brows.

"Don't play stupid," the first guard said. He lurched forward, and Jastyn noticed a soft jingle coming from his hip. Aurelia placed a cautious hand on Jastyn's arm as she leaned forward eagerly.

"Two women came in here. One of 'em was the Princess Diarmaid." The guard speaking continued to flash the torchlight, waving it to light every corner of her family's cell. His partner scanned the rest of the room. Jastyn held her breath when he squinted into the dark where she and Aurelia stood.

"If we saw anyone, we would tell you," Elisedd said, drawing the guards' attention. "Why would the princess be down here?"

Jastyn didn't miss the look between the two men. She was sure they weren't supposed to be spreading word of what was happening to the Diarmaids. Her stepfather spoke again. "Please, since you're here, would you give us some water? My daughter isn't well." The guard who had started across the room paused. He sneered, turning back to the cell.

"That sounds like a personal problem to me." The guards guffawed.

"Please," Elisedd said. Alanna coughed. Jastyn knew she was giving a performance, but she didn't like the crackling sound behind her sister's staggered breaths. Elisedd gave the men a pleading look.

The one holding the torch sighed. To his partner, he said, "Maybe they ran back out when we were on the other side of the cells."

Nodding, they turned to leave.

"Wait," her mother cried, "the water. Please."

The way the guards smiled at one another made Jastyn's stomach churn. The one not holding the torch approached the bars, and Jastyn's heart sank when, rather than reach for the cell door, he merely stuck his hand between the bars. Her mother's gaze snapped to where Jastyn and Aurelia stood, panicked. Elisedd stood slowly, handing the guard the cup.

"You need water?" the guard asked. He tilted the cup toward his chin, then spat into the opening.

Aurelia gasped softly, but Jastyn hardly heard it over the rush of blood surging in her ears as she sprang out of the shadows.

"Jastyn, no!" Her mother's voice echoed off the cell walls as both guards whirled, but Jastyn already had her saol aimed and fired it at the guard. The spell-fire hit his hand, and he dropped the cup. A red saol shot past her right shoulder, hitting the same guard in the side and taking him to the ground in a groaning heap. The other one drew his sword and waved the torch in a menacing show.

Jastyn looked up at his overbearing stature, noticing he kept himself in front of her family's cell. Smart, she thought. If she fired on him and missed, she risked hitting one of them. On the ground, the other guard moved but only barely as he lay on his stomach.

"The baroness will be thrilled when I tell her I captured the princess." He gave his narrow blade a spin and jabbed the torch closer.

"You're a traitor to the royal name," Aurelia said, her saol hovering over her open palm. He sneered and dove forward. Jastyn and Aurelia dove to opposite sides. Jastyn shot her saol at his back, hitting him between the shoulder blades. Aurelia gave a cry that surprised Jastyn so much, she stumbled when Aurelia kicked the guard's hand, forcing his sword out of his grasp. She fired her spell-fire, hitting the guard in the back of the head. He fell face-first onto the ground, unmoving.

Breathing heavily, Jastyn blinked at the guards straining to even roll over.

"Jastyn," her sister called from the cell. She hurried to the second guard and swiped the keys off his belt. At the cell door, the third key proved the charm, and she pulled open the iron bars.

Alanna bulldozed her. "I knew you could do it," she said, muffled into Jastyn's shoulder. Jastyn held her tight, hating how feeble she felt since she'd seen her last.

Not finding her words, Jastyn stepped back. Alanna's face was thin, her cheekbones frighteningly prominent. Her dark eyes were sunken, but they somehow still had the spark in them Jastyn remembered. Pulling up her satchel, Jastyn said, "I did it. Alanna, I've got it."

Her sister's eyes widened, but behind her, their mother pointed, shouting, "Your Highness, behind you."

Aurelia ducked to avoid being hit with the still-flickering torch now in the firm grip of the second guard, who was back on his feet. Jastyn's heart sank when he kicked Aurelia, sending her to the ground with a nasty thud.

Before she could think about how best to retaliate, a berry-red flame flew by and knocked the guard onto his stomach. The torch fell from his grip, hitting the ground in an unceremonious clatter. Elisedd, another saol ready, rushed through the open cell door, Jastyn's mother and Alanna behind him. His eyes flashed as he took the guard's sword from the ground, then knocked him out for good with a swing of the pommel to his head.

Jastyn helped Aurelia to stand; she clutched her stomach as she gulped for air. "Are you okay?" she asked warily at the queasy look on Aurelia's face.

She nodded, stepping toward Jastyn's stepfather. "Thank you."

He bowed. "I'm at your service, Your Majesty."

She extended an arm. "Please, call me Aurelia."

Jastyn, hurt at Aurelia moving away from her, was distracted by Elisedd's bemused face. He glanced at her mother. Finally, he shook Aurelia's arm. She smiled. Teary-eyed, Jastyn looked between her family members finally free from their cage.

Elisedd, unsurprisingly, reminded them of the present situation. "We should move." He reached for Alanna. Aurelia motioned for them all to follow her. Elisedd tugged Alanna along, but she paused by Jastyn.

"Is that really her?" she asked, gawking at Aurelia.

Grinning, Jastyn said, "That's her, all right."

Her sister remained wide-eyed as Elisedd pulled her along.

Jastyn watched her for a moment. Her mother came up beside her. Jastyn felt as if the air had been sucked from the room. She wanted to tell her mother everything that had happened on her journey. But the idea of doing so left her reeling, like she was rocking on the waves out on the open sea. She wanted to ask about the caves and tell her that even though she had Alanna's cure, there was still work to do. Jastyn wondered how to bring up the fact that she had met her selkie father and that he was floating aboard a ship just offshore.

Her mother pulled her into a hug. Jastyn wrapped her arms around her. "Mother, I—"

"Come on." She squeezed Jastyn's shoulders as she stepped back. "We've got a lot to discuss. Like why her royal highness just helped us escape."

The laughter surprised her. Jastyn wiped her nose, tears mingling with her smile.

CHAPTER EIGHT

Aurelia silently led their group up another staircase. She smiled, remembering all the times she and Brennus had slipped through these corridors and passageways unbeknownst to their parents. As quickly as the happy memories came, they were chased out by the image of her brother lying still, his blood-soaked tunic sticking to his unmoving chest.

She tried to focus on her feet. Jastyn's stepfather followed a few paces behind. Branna walked behind him with Alanna. Jastyn trailed at the end. As a flurry of court members ran past, she held up a hand, and they lingered in a corner near the opening of a southern archway.

"Any mother would have done what Dechtire did," one of the ladies said hurriedly, her pair of braids swinging side to side like her furtive gaze.

"Of course," her companion, a harried looking maiden, replied. "But to leave Grannus behind and place the castle in jeopardy? What will the villagers think when they hear what's happened?"

The women vanished around a corner. Aurelia waited another moment to be sure they were gone, wondering what the baroness had said about her family. Surely someone was concerned enough to take action. A dreadful counterthought emerged: what if they were all complicit in Enya's scheme? What if the entire court wished to see the demise of the Diarmaid line?

Aurelia ushered everyone forward, quickly moving out of the archway, down one more hall, then out a doorway and into the bright afternoon sunlight. They sprinted past the outdoor stables. Glancing over her shoulder, Aurelia caught Jastyn coaxing her sister along; she looked dreadfully pale as she worked her long legs. At the same time, Coran and Roisin—true to their word and keeping watch through a stable window—hurried to join them. When they all reached the Wood, everyone paused to catch their breath.

"I'm all right," Alanna said, answering the question that had formed on her family's faces.

"You need to rest." Jastyn's stepfather had a deep, concerned tone. Aurelia noticed the similar, sharp features between him and Alanna. Even her long arms moved the way his did when she spoke. Alanna had the same fair complexion as Jastyn, but her eyes were darker, unlike either of her parents, and Aurelia wondered if the darkness around her pupil was an effect of the curse. She was nearly as tall as Jastyn, the latter having inherited the shorter stature of their mother. Branna helped steady Alanna's shaking frame. The pain in Jastyn's eyes made Aurelia's heart ache.

Branna said, "We should get you home."

Aurelia was about to say something when Jastyn said exactly what she was thinking. "The guards will probably already be there. I'm sure they're combing the village in search of us. Our house will be the first place they look." Jastyn met her gaze, and Aurelia agreed.

"Where should we go?" Elisedd asked, leaning into Alanna, who let out a cough.

Coran spoke next. "My mum can help."

"No," Jastyn replied swiftly. "It's too dangerous to involve her." He seemed to agree, grimacing and wrapping an arm around Roisin's shoulders. Her cheeks were flushed from running. "Eegit's meadow is our safest option."

Nearly everyone nodded, Alanna even smiling. Elisedd, however, stiffened.

"I know you don't care for the Wood," Jastyn said. "But I promise you'll be safe there."

Jastyn's mother placed a comforting hand on his arm. Curiosity sprang through Aurelia's mind as she tried to imagine what made him so anxious.

Reluctantly, he said, "Very well."

"My parents are already there," Aurelia said, feeling the need to add her sentiments. But Jastyn winced as if in pain. Alanna stared.

Jastyn's parents shrank, moving closer to their youngest. "No, it's all right," Aurelia said, trying to be encouraging. She licked her lips, turning to Jastyn's mother. "I know what my family did to you. I'm so sorry for the pain we caused." Searching for something else to quell the fear on Branna's face, she stammered, "I'll speak with them. It will be okay."

Jastyn stepped closer. "I don't like it either," she said to her mother. "But we haven't got a choice."

Aurelia nearly missed it, but some secret deal was struck between mother and daughter as their eyes locked. Aurelia knew it was a promise they'd made many times in the life they'd fought through to survive.

Eventually, Jastyn's family consented. Feeling awkward in the presence of a family forged from her own family's bigotry, Aurelia glanced pleadingly to Jastyn. Thankfully, she seemed to understand.

"This way," she said, taking the lead as they started for the depths of the Wood.

When they passed the brook that lay only a few minutes from Eegit's meadow, a nervous knot tied itself in Jastyn's stomach. On one end of that anxious bundle sat relief that she'd managed to get her family out of the dungeons alive. The guards were swarming the village and marketplace, but she wasn't concerned about them. She knew that, if they had to, her family could handle themselves. It was the other twisted strand in her gut that had her worried: her mother had never come near the castle since her banishment to the kingdom's edges twenty years ago. Now she was about to come face-to-face with the Diarmaids who'd locked her up. The unease inside Jastyn was a sign of something bad to come. Added to that constant knowledge was that her window to make the cure was shrinking, and her body was so tight with worry, she felt stiff.

Furthermore, they'd all been so busy since she and Coran had rowed ashore that she had no idea when she and Aurelia would be able to talk. Since being reunited, they had been working together fine, yet their exchanges and actions had seemed automatic. It was like the sun rising and falling each day; they were simply doing what they needed to continue onward.

Still, something was missing between them, and a new, foreign tension had taken its place. Aurelia was sharp in her responses, though she exuded civility in front of everyone else. She averted her gaze when Jastyn looked at her, and she seemed to put every effort into not standing too close. Jastyn ached to think that what was missing, what she'd felt vanish between them on that beach, might never return.

Gripping the strap of her satchel, Jastyn led everyone between a set of large apple trees to Eegit's meadow. Her throat went dry at the sight of the king and queen sitting right where she'd left them.

"Aurelia!" The queen ran over to wrap her daughter in a hug.

Aurelia gave a small laugh as Jastyn and her family huddled together, Coran and Roisin standing a few feet off. "We weren't gone long, Mother." She gestured skyward. "The sun is still high."

The king walked over. Jastyn had noticed that he always seemed to do things a step or two behind his wife, as if he needed to know what she would do before he decided which way to move. Jastyn pulled her shoulders back but felt very small as she and the others faced the Diarmaids, the only sound the soft buzz of fairy wings from nearby nests.

Jastyn didn't know what to do as the Diarmaids stood across from her mother and stepfather. Both parties seemed to be having a silent conversation with furtive glances and shuffled feet.

Alanna spoke first. "Your Majesties." She bowed low but straightened when a fit of coughs overtook her.

Jastyn saw a flash of something in the queen's eyes...concern? But she remained still.

"Forgive her," Elisedd said. "She is not well."

The king looked sympathetic. "We've known of her ailment's severity for some time." While he spoke, the queen's eyes roved over Alanna, reminding Jastyn of a farmer inspecting a withered crop.

"That's why we left." Everyone turned to Aurelia. "Jastyn and I," she said under so many pairs of eyes. "She...we...she was told to journey west for her sister's cure. That's the business she needed to take care of," Aurelia finished, blinking rapidly in a rare show of nerves.

Jastyn felt self-conscious as the king's gaze landed on her. "Were you successful?"

She placed a hand over her satchel, feeling the vials within. "I was."

"Oh, Jastyn." Aurelia clasped both hands over her mouth. Tears sprang to her eyes, the blue in them shining.

Coran grinned, and Roisin hid a smile behind her hand. Jastyn pursed her lips, uncomfortable as her and Aurelia's parents stared between them. In all of the commotion since arriving, she hadn't realized she'd never told Aurelia that she'd gotten the cure.

Aurelia wiped her eyes, adding, "That is wonderful news."

Jastyn's parents looked amused while Aurelia's seemed perplexed. Alanna beamed.

"We should probably start from the beginning," Jastyn said slowly.

"Perhaps that would be best," King Grannus said before holding out his arm. Alanna, wide-eyed, took his cue, holding Elisedd's hand as they walked with the king toward the fire. Coran and Roisin scurried after them.

Aurelia stood beside the queen, mirroring Jastyn and her mother. Both Queen Dechtire and Aurelia were taller than them by several inches. Despite the royal women donning simpler tunics and cloaks and looking weary, there was still no denying their nobility in the way they held themselves.

Jastyn knew Aurelia was eager to speak, to fill the silence radiating between their mothers. She opened her mouth, but Jastyn raised a finger, telling Aurelia to give them time. Aurelia frowned, looking ready to burst when Jastyn's mother spoke.

"My condolences, Your Majesty, regarding your son."

The words seemed to hit the queen, an actual force that knocked her backward. The two women held one another's gazes.

"And my condolences for your daughter's health."

Her mother took in the queen's words with a face that revealed only the slightest hint of gratitude. She began to move past her when Queen Dechtire added, "If I can help in some way, with the cure…" Her words stopped as if stuck inside her chest.

Jastyn felt as shocked as her mother looked upon hearing this. Her brows shot up; her mouth opened. Blinking, her mother composed herself quickly and gave a small nod. She joined Elisedd and Alanna by the fire. The queen watched her go, then followed a few paces behind.

Reeling from that exchange, Jastyn didn't notice Aurelia standing next to her. "I think that went well." Her voice was pitched in a question, but Jastyn didn't have an answer. She only stared at her mother sitting opposite the Diarmaids in Eegit's meadow: a sight so baffling she thought maybe she was in a dream or perhaps still lost inside the western caves, witnessing a vision of the Red One's conjuring.

A cool hand touched her wrist. She jumped. Looking down, she stared at Aurelia's fingers. They trembled. Moving her gaze to the ground, Jastyn felt unable to look up, though she knew Aurelia was searching her face. When Aurelia reached out, pulling Jastyn's chin up so that their eyes had to meet, Jastyn let her. She stared into the eyes she could lose herself in for days, the eyes that, to her surprise, stared back at her in a way Jastyn didn't dare hope was real.

"Aurelia—" She braced herself as Aurelia fell forward, throwing her arms around her. Jastyn wrapped her own arms around Aurelia's waist, pulling her close. Aurelia buried her face against Jastyn's neck.

"I'm so glad you're all right," she muttered, and Jastyn shivered at the closeness of her lips. She closed her eyes, letting the words seep into her skin.

They would have to talk about everything. Jastyn knew that. But right now, in this moment, Jastyn let herself enjoy the feeling of being in Aurelia's arms. She let herself relish the fact that they were both here, both alive.

Jastyn let herself relax in this good moment because she knew all too well that good moments didn't last.

CHAPTER NINE

Aurelia leaned forward on the log she shared with Coran and
Roisin. Her father sat to her left on his own seat. She eyed
his share of squirrel meat, mostly untouched, as Jastyn recounted the
harrowing events of the fight against the Dark Fae in the Mountains of
Ionad.

Thus far, their tale had been met with inquisitive silence and the
occasional gasp from Roisin or Alanna. Across the fire, Jastyn's sister
was cross-legged on the soft grass next to her mother. Both had finished
their food quickly. Jastyn, on the other side of her sister, had offered
Alanna some of her own dinner, but her sister had declined, not taking
her eyes off Aurelia when she'd told them about the stretch of land
before the mountains.

Jastyn left out several details about her near-death experience
with the Dark Fae. She downplayed how close they'd both come to
perishing had it not been for the sudden appearance of the Uterni twins.

"Uterni?" Aurelia's mother asked, holding a squirrel leg carefully
between her thumb and forefinger. "They'd sent guards to Ionad?"

"They claimed it was part of their training regimen," Aurelia
explained with a shrug.

"How peculiar," her father mumbled behind his fingers, his elbows
resting on his knees.

Jastyn continued with their story. "They were different, those two.
But helpful." For a moment, she seemed to lose herself in the flames
throwing light over the encroaching shadows as the sun faded behind
the trees. When her silence dragged on, Aurelia spoke.

"Thankfully, we managed to escape."

Jastyn was rubbing her neck as if searching for the bruises that used to be there. Aurelia looked to Coran.

He swallowed a bite, then set his food down. "Right. We, uh, left the mountains and continued west after that."

"Gods," Roisin said, tossing a bone into the firepit. "What a time you all had."

Coran, Jastyn, and Aurelia all exchanged looks. Aurelia knew what they were thinking. Their tale had several missing parts. If their families were truly listening, they would notice that certain aspects didn't align. Aurelia also knew Jastyn didn't want to share much of what had happened after leaving Vreis's cave. And the selkies were not Aurelia's story to tell.

As Aurelia anticipated, Jastyn skipped ahead. "Once we reached the caves, we found ourselves near a cove." She glanced toward Branna, who had been leaning against Elisedd, listening intently. "It looked like a ship graveyard." For a second, she met Aurelia's gaze, no doubt remembering the beach. That day had started so wonderfully. Aurelia recalled the pure bliss she'd woken up in that morning, then how quickly her entire world had crumbled upon learning Jastyn's intentions.

Wanting to push things along, Aurelia jumped in. "We got separated. Once Jastyn entered the cave, the elves attacked."

"That was when I found you," her mother said, meeting her gaze.

She nodded, replaying the terrible image of an arrow shooting through Sif's chest. She looked down, wiping her hands on her pants then tracing the torn material on her knee.

Roisin asked, "That's when your friend…Reegan…left?"

"Rigo," Coran corrected. "He took a stand against his own kind."

"He sounds brave," Alanna said.

Aurelia and Jastyn shared a look. Aurelia was hopeful that Rigo was out there somewhere.

Elisedd, who had been chewing thoughtfully, asked, "That's when you got the cure?"

All heads swiveled to Jastyn. She still had the satchel she'd been carrying since she'd found them in the stables. A sense of anticipation filled the air, mixing with the thin line of smoke curling skyward from their fire.

Jastyn reached inside the bag and pulled out three small vials. "These were in a box inside in the cave." She held two in her left hand, one in her right as she extended her open palms. Aurelia leaned in, dying to learn more about what Jastyn had to do to obtain these. If the Red One had a part in all of this, things hadn't been simple. Jastyn had thrown timid glances at her mother since the dungeon escape, as if Branna knew something about the caves that Jastyn wasn't eager to discuss. That seemed impossible, but then again, their journey had possessed a slew of improbabilities.

Alanna turned one of the vials over before passing it to her mother. Aurelia could see the liquid shimmering from where she sat across the fire. It reminded her of something, though she wasn't sure what.

The vials continued around their group until Elisedd held all three. Jastyn didn't take her eyes off them. Her stepfather held up the one containing what looked like a tiny collection of leaves and sprigs.

"May I?" Aurelia's mother held out a hand. Jastyn's feet shifted as if she wanted to dash over and reclaim the vials. But she remained seated, the muscle along the side of her jaw tightening.

Aurelia's mother raised the vial to the fading daylight, her thumb and forefinger holding the length of the glass while she examined the contents.

Alanna glanced expectantly between her parents, who exchanged hopeful looks but said nothing. Aurelia's father was looking across at Jastyn, his bushy brows low.

"What d'ya reckon it is?" Coran asked.

Aurelia's mother threw him a quick look, as if she'd forgotten he was there. "It looks to be a combination of wormwood, pineapple lily, and…" She squinted, giving the vial a small shake. "Umazifisi."

Aurelia frowned. "Are you certain?"

Her mother stared more at the sprigs and roots mixed with bits of petals. "Yes. How peculiar."

"Peculiar?" Elisedd asked.

Both Aurelia and her mother nodded. "None of those are native to these lands. They're from the East."

"Not just the East, sweetheart, the Southeast. The tribal lands in the southern seas."

"How did they get to our realm?" asked Coran.

Her mother took on a tone Aurelia knew well from their studies. "Pirates. Merchants. There are a great many people who travel the world, bringing with them their native lands' goods."

"Or the fae." All eyes turned to Jastyn. "Fae could have brought it here."

An uncomfortable silence befell their group. Aurelia said quickly, "Mother, I'm having trouble recalling the third one you mentioned."

"The...uma...uzu...," Alanna stuttered, her face puckered in concentration. Branna smiled at her efforts.

"Umazifisi," Aurelia's mother corrected quickly but kindly. "It's known in our tongue as the 'restoration plant.'"

Before she could explain further, Elisedd said, "What does Her Majesty make of this?" He passed her the vial holding the splash of liquid.

"Oh, how interesting." The edge of her lips crinkled in a smile. Then, seeming to remember the purpose of the liquid, she turned her head, straightening. "I can't be certain, but this could be one of two things." She handed it back. "I'd rather consider it for a time before saying anything."

Aurelia snorted. Her parents' gazes snapped in her direction, but she pretended to be busy discarding scraps into the fire. She couldn't help it. The last time she had been unaware of a vial's ingredients, its contents had brought her brother back to life only to make him relive excruciating pain before succumbing to death's snare. Gods only knew how much her mother hadn't taught her.

"What does that say?" Roisin's question was directed at Branna, who had pulled a small scroll from the third vial and unfurled it. Grateful for the distraction, Aurelia turned her attention to the parchment. It was surprisingly lengthy, almost as long as her forearm, but incredibly narrow.

"It looks almost like...like a recipe." Her face pulled tight as she read silently until Elisedd placed a hand on her knee. She cleared her throat then read:

"Combine contents with one cauldron of water. Must be done on the first new moon of the autumnal equinox.

"Add blood, mixed and boil.

"Let simmer for one day.

"Upon sunrise of the next day, drink immediately."

"That's not a recipe I've ever heard." Roisin looked at Coran, who shook his head.

Aurelia also had to admit the wording was odd. She'd read many spells in her lessons and memorized hundreds of varieties of potions and remedies, but none resembled this one.

"Why blood?" Elisedd reached for the scroll, reading again, "Add blood, mixed and boil." Creases lined his forehead.

Aurelia's mother stared over at the parchment, deep in thought as her father said, "The wording is muddled."

"And specific," Jastyn added.

"The timing is specific, yes," Aurelia's mother replied, her eyes still on the paper. "In other ways, it isn't."

"Like whose blood they mean," Roisin said, looking more overwhelmed by the minute. She shuddered.

They all sat quiet, pondering, until a shrill shout sounded behind Aurelia.

"Out! Too many. Out."

Whipping around, Aurelia found Eegit hopping madly near her hut, hurrying toward them.

"Eegit?" Jastyn stood, running around to collect the vials. Branna quickly rolled up the scroll, slipping it back inside the third glass before handing it to her.

"The guards are on my heels," Eegit shouted to all of them before rounding on Jastyn. "What were you thinking, child?"

Jastyn's neck flushed. "What do you mean?" she asked as Elisedd helped Alanna to stand. Aurelia's parents sat looking astonished at the sight of Eegit's hunched, frail figure gesticulating wildly.

"My protection spell is good for three, maybe four souls inside my meadow." She waved at their large group. "But nine? Nine." She made a noise like something between a laugh and a choke. "Child, this is too many to conceal. The guards saw your fire from two miles out, and even a nymph could sniff out the slew of magical energy bubbling around in here."

"What do we do?" Aurelia asked.

The fire seemed to blaze brighter as Eegit's chapped lips parted. "Diarmaids." At this, Aurelia's parents stood, circling the fire to stand behind Aurelia. Eegit's face turned up in a smile. "They're coming for you."

Her tone made Aurelia feel like she'd stepped in an icy river. "We need to move."

Coran and Roisin were already standing near Jastyn and her family on the opposite side of the fire. Looking across the orange sparks and curling smoke, Aurelia felt overwhelmed at the sight. Their fear was evident, but there was something else. A familiarity to such a situation, as if they'd stood here before, ready to flee, ready to fight.

The ground trembled, and Aurelia glanced toward the trees, panicked.

Eegit poured a handful of dirt over the fire, stifling the flames. Through the choking mist, she shouted, "Get out of here. Now."

CHAPTER TEN

The moments that followed were a blur but were somehow orchestrated with such precision, it seemed to Jastyn they had all known on some level that this was going to happen.

As the low rumble of hooves neared, their group scattered like mice, reforming into three separate, unexpected clusters. She heard the king say something to his wife, whose response had been a wide-eyed look of dismay as she clutched Aurelia amid the commotion inside Eegit's meadow.

But when the princess said with certainty, "It's safer this way, Mother. Just for a short while," Queen Dechtire fell awkwardly behind Roisin and Coran, who called out to Jastyn.

"We'll head to the oak." Coran grabbed Roisin's hand and motioned for the queen to follow. With a final glance at Aurelia, the queen fled into the darkening wood and disappeared.

Aurelia started toward Jastyn, and though she ached to have her near, to know she was safe, she turned instead to the king. "Come with me, Your Majesty."

Grannus—his hair and beard as frazzled as the look in his eyes—stumbled over a log while Eegit pulled her charred pots and bone piles into her hut. "Mother, Elisedd..." Jastyn couldn't finish the sentence, couldn't bring herself to send Aurelia away. Luckily, her mother nodded in understanding.

"This way, Your Highness," she said to Aurelia, who stood between the two as if she was lost. When their gazes met, Jastyn could only swallow the words she wanted to say.

"We have to move." Elisedd said urgently, reaching for Aurelia.

"Go," Grannus said.

"We'll reunite at dawn." Jastyn kept her attention on her mother, though she could feel Aurelia staring her down.

Finally, Aurelia followed Jastyn's family toward the trees. Her sister called, "Be careful, Jastyn," as they ran away from the oncoming troupe of guards and back toward the village.

Gripping tight to her satchel, Jastyn glanced back at Eegit when the king asked, "And us? Where shall we go?"

Taking a deep breath, she said, "Follow me."

A short while later, as Jastyn and King Grannus scrambled down the rocky bluffs toward the shore, a modest wooden rowboat appeared on the water. One moment, the dark horizon sat undisturbed. Then, as if a curtain had been drawn back, Fortan sat thirty yards from the sand, rowing swiftly inland. The dark waters carried him closer as the deep purple sky began to glitter with stars.

"Gods, where did that come from?" the king asked.

Landing with a thud on the soft sand, Jastyn waited for Grannus to join her before answering. "He's here to help. Unless you'd rather go back and face the guards?"

His face shifted from shock to scrutiny, but Jastyn held his gaze. He was the least intimidating of the monarchs. His haggard appearance made it clear the last several months had taken their toll. His rich blue tunic was worn, though it still looked like it was worth the price of the entire village with its intricate golden threads tracing the frayed cuffs and collar. Despite his nice clothing and poise, something about him felt approachable. Regardless, he remained a Diarmaid, even if at this moment, they were on level playing field. And while Jastyn couldn't believe she was helping him, she wasn't going to give a Diarmaid the satisfaction of her fury. At least, not yet.

His stunned silence said he didn't object to her leading him toward the water. When Fortan bobbed a few yards away, she and Grannus hurried out, kicking up tufts of foam and seaweed before scurrying aboard.

"Welcome." Fortan extended one arm while rowing with the other to turn their boat back toward the wide width of ocean. "My, who do we have here?"

Jastyn settled across from Fortan so they faced one another. King Grannus eyed the small space next to her and sat only after a wave nearly knocked him into the water. His pupils shrank to pinpoints as they roved over the selkie's sleek, dark skin and black eyes, their deep vastness unsettling at first but now a comforting sight. When Grannus stared at the sealskin atop Fortan's head—its legs hanging over his chest and framing his long black hair—Jastyn said, "Fortan, meet the king of Venostes, Grannus Diarmaid."

Fortan's smile fell. He looked between them. Leaning close, he said to Jastyn, "My dear, it seemed you were in trouble upon the shore, which is why Tove insisted I come fetch you." He threw a glance to Grannus. "But what in realm's name are you doing with the king?"

"I'm right here, you know. I don't appreciate being spoken about as if I weren't present."

Jastyn smirked, and Fortan sat back, looking around at the mild dark water.

"We were in a hurry," Jastyn explained. "The Diarmaids are being hunted in their own kingdom."

"Oh, yes. The unrest you all spoke of." Fortan didn't even try to mask the intrigue in his voice.

Grannus shifted, and Jastyn could feel his unease at being ignored. "We'll go ashore at sunrise." She scanned the lazy waves drifting under their boat. "That should give us enough time to wear out the search parties." She glanced sideways at the king. In such close proximity, she could see the lines in his forehead and around his eyes. His beard, which she remembered being full and red six months before, was now a rusty shade with silver peppered throughout. His hair, long enough to tuck behind his ears, featured the same aged coloring. Jastyn saw Aurelia in his cheekbones and the way he tilted his chin. She would much rather have Aurelia sitting next to her now, but she was in safe hands with her family.

"And Her Highness?" Fortan's question made Jastyn wonder if she'd said her thoughts out loud.

"She's with my family. The queen is with Coran."

His face lifted in a smile. "Your speckled friend. I am quite fond of him. What a dancer he is."

Jastyn snorted. Grannus held up two pleading hands. "Will one of you *please* explain to me where we are going?"

With a flourish of his hand, Fortan said, "Isn't it obvious?"

The selkie ship appeared, bobbing in greeting as if it had been expecting them. Grannus started back in surprise. He gawked at the wooden sideboards running the length of the ship's hull, which compared to their rowboat, seemed towering. The white sail flapped happily against the night sky.

Slowly, the king's gaze fell to Fortan. "Who are you?"

"I am Fortan."

"A selkie."

Fortan stood, grabbing one end of a rope that had been left hanging against the ship's side. "Not just any selkie, I promise."

Grannus blinked like a fawn unsure how to take its first steps.

Jastyn grinned. "Don't mind him, Your Highness."

After tying a tow rope to their boat's gunwale, Fortan quickly climbed onto the ship. Jastyn followed. When she leaned over the side to toss the king a rope, she found him standing, staring up at them. The look on his grizzled face was somewhere between bewilderment and fright.

"Selkies aren't allowed in these waters," he said in a monotone. He continued to stare while Jastyn and Fortan exchanged glances.

"Trust me, Your Greatness, I would rather not be here, but when ones loved ones are in trouble, one doesn't hesitate to lend a hand." Fortan shook the rope in encouragement.

Grannus stammered, "The treaty—"

Rolling his eyes, Fortan said, "Yes, the Fae-Diarmaid Treaty, I know. We can only go as far as Gultero." He squinted mischievously. "I'd be happy to sail us over there now, though I fear that wouldn't be very helpful to your situation."

Grannus's eyes went wide, and he looked around the rowboat as if only now realizing he was alone. Hurriedly, he shimmied up the rope and climbed aboard.

"Why have you brought me here?" he asked. She closed her eyes, suddenly weary. Was the king always so skeptical? The sea breeze felt like relief on her face. It held a crisp bite as it blew through her braid. Autumn was approaching, and their window of time to make the cure for Alanna was slimming.

"Young lady," Grannus said, apparently thinking she hadn't heard him and tapping her on the arm.

"It's Jastyn."

He stepped closer warily, as if the barrel of fish sitting nearby might spring to life and threaten him. She wondered at his reluctance. Had he already forgotten how much she'd helped him?

"We needed a safe place to go. Drest and whoever else is after you want all three of you. This is a safe place," she repeated, watching him glare at Fortan. "Besides," she added, following Fortan as he headed through a door that led belowdecks. "Nobody knows there's a selkie ship floating offshore. You had no idea." She smiled at the offended look on his face.

She was being smug, she knew. But she didn't care. She might be in love with Aurelia, but she had no qualms giving the king a taste of the apathetic treatment the Diarmaids had given her.

CHAPTER ELEVEN

Is it true you get to choose between venison, lamb, and pork every night for dinner?" Alanna asked.

Aurelia frowned. "Well, yes."

"Is it true there are tapestries of pure silk from the East hanging on castle walls?"

"There are."

"And is it true—"

"Alanna, sweetheart," Branna said, "we need to be quiet."

"But, Mother—"

Branna held a finger to her lips, warning her daughter, who frowned and fell silent.

Crouching behind a trio of old boysenberry shrubs near a line of birch trees, Aurelia gave Branna a grateful smile. She had spent the length of their run through the Wood and around to the far side of the village answering a series of rapid-fire questions from Jastyn's sister. "How many dresses do you own? Is riding a horse difficult? It looks difficult. How long have you been taking riding lessons? Is it true the castle is full of secret passageways?" The inquisition had only paused when, near the market, they had to duck behind an abandoned meat cart as guards ran past, heading toward Eegit's meadow.

Now, they all waited in a stretch of wood that was unfamiliar to her. Elisedd had insisted they wait while he climbed over a low stone wall and disappeared down a hillside. It was too dark to make out anything else, and she didn't dare conjure her saol for fear of bringing attention to them.

Alanna, despite looking frighteningly pale in the half moonlight, bounced eagerly on her toes. Aurelia smiled at the young girl who had been staring at her as they huddled close. She shared Jastyn's tenacity, only Alanna's was a tamer sense of earnestness, no doubt from a life of caution and quiet.

"It's clear." Elisedd appeared in the shadows, making Aurelia jump. His tall, lanky frame reminded her of a banshee, only bearded. No wonder she had hardly noticed him in the stables all those years. He moved with the stealth of a wolf.

Single file, they followed him between the trees and out into the open hillside. Climbing over the wall, Aurelia discovered they were above a group of homes, each dark and still.

They came to a stop beside one, a home that resembled all the others: quaint, the door slightly off-kilter, and its thatched roof uneven. Aurelia glanced at the chickens wandering aimlessly near the back. She studied the pocked stone exterior, then the patches of dirt forming a well-worn path leading to a well up a separate hillside. A distant, soft bleat of sheep caught her ear when Branna opened the wooden door.

"Like we thought, the guards have come and gone here," Elisedd said before wandering in.

Aurelia blinked as a candle flickered to life within. "Here?"

A pair of hands pushed gently into her back, ushering her forward. "Our house," Alanna said, her voice giddy.

When she entered, Elisedd was righting an overturned table in the far corner. It was clear the guards had indeed been here. Bowls were strewn near an upturned washbasin next to the door, the hearth was littered with cauldrons thrown haphazardly atop the ashes of charred logs, and sacks of food hung sadly, their contents splayed across the floor.

Quickly, she leaned down to collect a handful of potatoes when Alanna, who had disappeared through one of two doorways, cried out.

"What is it?" Branna called as she swiftly reassembled her kitchen at a speed that left Aurelia wondering if she'd used a spell to help.

"They've shredded our quilt."

In the doorway, Alanna stood clutching what looked like a bundle of faded, multi-colored rags. Her dark eyes brimmed with tears.

"We'll mend it, sweetheart, don't worry."

Despite the encouragement, Aurelia caught a hint of resignation in Branna's voice. Even the best seamstress would have trouble reassembling the uneven pieces of fabric the guards had left behind. Aurelia's stomach twisted as Branna wrapped an arm around Alanna. She was furious at what Enya and Drest had done to the minds of the guardsmen. They would have never done such a cruel thing under the eyes of her family.

She hesitated, considering if that would in fact be true. She wasn't sure anymore. Standing awkwardly in the middle of the room after righting an overturned chair, she said, "I'm sorry."

"You didn't do this, Your Majesty." Elisedd gave her a reassuring nod as he moved to the hearth to clear it.

Branna didn't say anything, only continued to hold her daughter, who was whimpering against her shoulder. A look flashed in her eyes that was so similar to a look in Jastyn's that Aurelia felt dizzy. It left her wondering just how deep the scars ran that the Diarmaid name had left behind.

Once everything was tidy and Alanna had been sent to bed over fervent protests, Aurelia sat near the hearth with a cup of chamomile tea. Branna had lit the fire with her saol but kept the flames dim. The guards had probably retired their search for the night, but it was still best to keep a low profile.

Stretching her legs out on a rug, Aurelia faced Jastyn's stepfather and mother. She thought about the contents of the vials for Alanna's cure while Elisedd was speaking about the upheaval in the kingdom.

"There was talk, of course, in the village and inside the castle. I ignored it for the most part. Not one for gossip." He fiddled with some sort of tool. Aurelia imagined it was meant for his work with the horses. "People always find something to complain about. But I had no idea of the dissent within your court." He shook his head, running a hand down his untrimmed goatee.

She sighed. "I was unaware, too." She recalled the hushed meetings behind closed doors between her father and Brennus in what seemed like another lifetime. "We had heard of the unrest, but we thought it was the fae who were unhappy. We thought it was they who spoke of anarchy." She caught a look between Branna and Elisedd. She bit her lip. She'd been treading carefully with her words since arriving at their home. Even her actions had been meticulous. She didn't want to say or do anything to offend them.

She took a sip of tea. She had a hundred questions. She wanted to know everything about this place, about Jastyn's parents. Specifically,

Branna. Who was this woman deemed fit for the dungeons more than twenty years ago?

When no one said anything, Aurelia cleared her throat. "We did eventually figure out the fae were a ruse by people within the castle. Well, 'we' being myself and Jastyn and the others." She added, "Somebody was using the fae, manipulating them."

At their stares, she explained, "The elves may have been the ones to kill my brother, but it was the baroness and her son who orchestrated the events. With the help of that…that figure." She shuddered at the image of the Dark Fae.

"Jastyn's nightmare." Branna watched the soft yellow flames. She frowned. "He's followed her for years."

"How is he connected to what's happening in the castle?" asked Elisedd.

Aurelia finished the last of her tea and took a deep breath. "I believe the man who has haunted Jastyn is more than a phantom. I believe he is the first king. King Taranis."

Hurriedly, she recounted the pieces of this grand puzzle she had slowly put together over the course of the journey west. The Wandering Man. The first, sinister reign of the early king. His desire to oppress and wipe out not only Odiums but all of fae-kind.

"How can you be certain they are one and the same?" Branna sat very still in her chair, her eyes trained on Aurelia.

She considered this, running a finger along the edge of her chipped cup. "Well, I suppose I can't be completely certain." She cocked her head. "Consider the evidence: the 'Dark Fae,' as Jastyn calls him, roams these lands like the Wandering Man. He is after Jastyn, an Odium child. I've come face-to-face with him, and he certainly seems like he's been to the Otherworld and back." She raised a finger for emphasis. "And when I was with the baroness on the beach, she called him 'grandfather.'"

Pulling one leg up to hold her knee, Branna said quietly, "I see."

Elisedd rubbed his forehead. "What does that make him, then, this former king? Is he man or fae?"

Aurelia shrugged. "It makes him our enemy."

The hint of a smile graced Branna's lips. Elisedd stood. "You have our support, Your Highness." Stretching, he stifled a yawn.

"Please, call me Aurelia."

He bowed. "We have a few hours until dawn. A bit of sleep would do us all good. We can form a plan in the morning. And ensure we have everything we need to begin the cure for Alanna. The equinox will be upon us in two days." He reached out to Branna, who took his hand and squeezed it. Aurelia focused on her empty cup, allowing them a moment. Once he retired to the other room, Aurelia felt a shot of pain go through her knee, and it spasmed.

"Apologies," she said at Branna's surprised glance. "Lingering effects of an old wound." She played with the frayed edges of the tear that framed her scar. She traced the new, pink skin, and she recalled the feeling of Jastyn's fingers working delicately to spread the calendula herb.

Branna's voice interrupted her thoughts. "It must be difficult." Aurelia lifted her head, still hazy with memories. "To not know who to trust within your own home. To be betrayed by somebody you believed to be a friend."

The warm sensation her memories had given her dissipated. Uncertain how to interpret Branna's words, Aurelia said, "Yes." Then, as her mind cleared, she understood. "Much like how difficult it is to be unwanted in the kingdom you call home."

Branna's gaze snapped to hers, one eyebrow quirked. "And how does such a situation make you feel?"

"Wretched. And low."

Nodding, Branna folded her hands in her lap. She sat quietly, as if waiting for Aurelia's next words.

"Nobody deserves to be persecuted for who they are. For loving who they love."

"Your laws say differently."

"They're not my laws."

"Are you not a Diarmaid?"

"I am, but—"

"But what?"

Frustrated, Aurelia placed the cup down harder than she intended. Branna's gaze flickered. Was she amused? Aurelia caught a glimpse of Jastyn in her face. Finally, Aurelia said, "What would you like me to say? That I don't agree with my family's laws? That I didn't understand the pain being caused or the years of torment people and fae were subjected to? Would you like me to say I'm sorry? I'm sorry for the fact that my family's legacy is built on the back of hate. I'm sorry that you and hundreds of women before you had to give birth to their babies in chains. I'm sorry that because of my family"—she gripped her tunic over her chest—"my family is the reason Jastyn grew up with hate in her heart for anyone bearing my name. I'm sorry she had to face impossible choices her entire life. I'm sorry."

Aurelia didn't know when the tears started. Her face was hot, and she inhaled sharply, acutely aware of how loud she had gotten. Taking a deep breath, she wiped her cheeks with the back of her hand.

They sat quietly for a time.

"I grew tired of hating the Diarmaids a long time ago." Branna leaned to rest her chin in her upturned palm. "No good can come from hate. And my daughters deserved a mother who could move forward despite everything."

Aurelia listened, swiping hair from her perspiring forehead.

"I'm not proud of every decision I made, but I did it all to protect my girls...to give them a chance."

Is that why my parents lied to me? To keep me safe? She nearly asked the questions out loud. But Aurelia sensed a different drive in Branna. Something ingrained, something so feral and desperate that Aurelia started to see the woman Branna was and where Jastyn had learned to be strong.

Then she recalled something else. "Something happened before Jastyn left for the cure." She let the words hang between them, still as the air in the room. "You told her about her father."

Pursing her lips, Branna closed her eyes. "She had a right to know. I had no idea if I'd ever see her again."

Aurelia hadn't considered that, but it was entirely plausible, she realized now. Her parents had probably felt the same when she'd refused to go home with them. But there had been no doubt in her mind that Jastyn would succeed, that they would make it back.

Itching to bring up the selkies, Aurelia held herself back, knowing it was Jastyn who should broach that topic.

"I did have one dream," Branna said, her eyes unfocused and a V between her brows. "When Jastyn was gone. I dreamt she made it to the caves. I was there, and I was so relieved to see her, but it was like...I couldn't be both there and here. As much as I ached to throw my arms around her, I couldn't. Something was holding me back. I could only listen and respond."

Her heart beating fast, Aurelia listened intently. Jastyn hadn't said a word about what had happened in the cave. Could this have been part of it?

"I'd felt sick inside for months, not knowing where she was or what she was thinking but sure she hated me. Don't pretend she didn't." Branna smiled sadly at Aurelia's protesting hand. "I know my own daughter. I was so afraid the last conversation we had would be that awful fight."

Aurelia was quiet, knowing exactly how she felt. The image of Jastyn crying in the sand burned in her mind.

"I tried to show her," Branna continued. "I tried to show her what I'd done...why I'd done what I had."

"What did she say?"

The first full smile graced Branna's face. "She forgave me." Wiping away tears, she said, "Then it was like I could see the anger lift from her shoulders, like a heavy cloak falling away."

Aurelia sat mystified. "The noble sacrifice," she muttered.

"What?"

"That's how she got the cure." Aurelia scooted closer, her body tingling with understanding. "Jastyn was told she needed to make a 'noble sacrifice' in the caves to obtain the cure. I thought it was me, well, we all thought she intended me to be sacrificed." She waved a dismissive hand at Branna's confused look. "But I was wrong. We all were, thankfully. She'd been harboring anger and resentment in her chest since the journey had started. That's what she had to give up. It makes so much sense. Gods, the Red One is clever."

Sensing Branna's bewilderment, Aurelia grabbed her teacup and stood. "I apologize for rambling. My mother always says I can get carried away. I will wait until Jastyn can explain things herself."

She returned the cup to the washbasin and was about to retire to Alanna's room, which had been joyfully offered earlier, when Branna said, "How was she...on your travels? Jastyn, was she okay, all that time?"

"She was more than okay." Aurelia smiled, her heart beating fast. "She was magnificent."

CHAPTER TWELVE

T hank the gods you're all right."
      Tove set his cup down, some of the wine spilling out as he hurried across the cabin. His steps faltered, however, when he noticed the king enter behind Jastyn and Fortan. "Jastyn," he spoke slowly, the jovial glint in his eyes gone, "what is a Diarmaid doing on my ship?"

"You know him?" Fortan asked, pouting. "I forget you've been around longer than I have."

"He's under my watch until dawn," Jastyn explained, one hand raised to calm her father, whose fingers twitched, no doubt for the dagger tucked against his boot. "The royal family is in danger."

His incredulous brow told Jastyn he believed she had to be joking. Before she could explain, the king interjected.

"Believe me, this is the last place I expected to be dragged for refuge." He glanced skeptically around the cabin, his bushy brows leaping at the fish piled waist-high in one corner, then at the dozens of dripping candles scattered across the lone table and trio of barrels carrying the selkies' preferred drink: red wine. "Nevertheless, this young lady seems to think this is the best place to pass the night."

"It's Jastyn," she said, taking a seat near the table. "My name is Jastyn."

He eyed her but said nothing. He only rolled up his tunic sleeves now that they had escaped the cold night air.

Fortan poured himself a drink, then sat. "He's harmless, Tove. All pomp and circumstance." He gestured dismissively, and Jastyn smiled at the king's frustrated harrumph while he remained standing just inside the doorway.

"Do all selkies speak about others as if they weren't there?" he asked heatedly.

"Oh, not all of us." Fortan smacked his lips. Jastyn, enjoying this banter, stole a sip from his cup. He swatted her away.

"Only councilmembers, apparently," she teased.

"Councilmembers?" Grannus stepped into the room.

"Yes," Tove replied. "You're in the presence of two of them."

Tove and Grannus stared one another down. While the king was taller, broader, and generally stronger in appearance, he looked weary and old compared to Jastyn's father. Whether it was the magical elements from being fae or otherwise, Tove looked eager and to her dismay, ready to pick a fight. She tossed Fortan a look as the silence dragged on.

"Yes, yes. The king and I have already had our own conversation regarding the treaty. We shouldn't be here. He shouldn't allow the continued persecution of fae throughout the realm and so on," Fortan said before taking another drink.

Jastyn cleared her throat as Grannus said, "I beg your pardon. I said no such thing about—"

"The unfair treatment of fae? Who originally owned the land and sea you stand upon?" Fortan fired off.

"I never spoke a word of—"

"Why you continue to punish Odium children like Jastyn for simply existing?"

"Now see here."

"Or how, right now, you wish you could snap your kingly fingers and pretend none of this is happening or none of it ever had, so that you can go back to living as an ignorant tyrant who follows the rules his parents laid out for him, as submissive as a little lap wolf."

"Enough!"

Jumping, Jastyn turned to gawk at Tove. He moved deliberately around the table, his fists clenched. Glaring, he said, "Fortan, this conduct is abysmal."

"Though not undeserved." Fortan seemed unfazed by Tove's outburst, but Jastyn swallowed nervously. Maybe this hadn't been such a good idea after all. She'd jumped at the chance to drop the king into an unknown situation, to see him flounder. But the tension in the cabin was so thick, a blade could slice through it.

"If Jastyn believes your coming here to be the best thing, so be it." Tove's gaze softened when it fell to her. "I trust my daughter's judgment."

Fortan mumbled his agreement into his cup.

"Daughter?"

Jastyn glanced over her shoulder. She was well aware that the Diarmaids didn't care for her. Ever since they'd learned who she was that night in the Wood, their disdain had been evident. No, she reasoned, watching the king now, it wasn't just that. The Diarmaids didn't care to even acknowledge her existence. It seemed that, if they ignored her, they could will her away into oblivion. She was "young lady" and "you there" and somebody the queen refused to even look at.

Maybe learning this would make them see her.

"Your Majesty, meet my father, Tove."

Grannus went pale. His jaw fell open. Stumbling, he sat on the edge of a barrel, looking quite lost.

Fortan slid a cup of wine across the table. "Here," he said, "this will help."

The king framed the cup with his large hands, staring. Then, in one go, he downed the wine, dribbles of bright red resting in his beard. Tove slowly sat and joined them.

After a refill and a healthy gulp, the king said, "I'm on an illegal ship with two selkie councilmembers and an Odium."

Jastyn wasn't sure what to make of this. She glanced at Tove, who kept a blank face.

"Yes," Fortan said, nodding, "and the gods haven't struck us down with lightning, can you imagine?" He grinned, and Jastyn bit her cheek to keep from laughing.

Grannus, still looking shocked, turned to Tove. "I should have you arrested for trespassing."

"I should use my dagger to avenge what you've done to Jastyn's mother."

She felt like she was witnessing a standoff between predators, each vying for the opportunity to sink their teeth in for the final, triumphant kill. The energy of the room prickled at her fingertips, her saol itching to take part in this battle of wills.

Eventually, Grannus ran a scarred hand down his face. "Gods, what a mess this is." His shoulders fell, his body turning within itself much as it had done on the day of the prince's Remembrance.

"Tell me, what has the great Diarmaid king done to warrant his own people turning on him?" Tove asked delicately, but his voice was firm. While his posture remained vigilant, Jastyn could see the angry spark dwindling in his eyes.

"It's not that," Grannus said, shaking his head. "It would be simple if that were the case, something we could set right." Glancing at each of them in turn, he explained, "The Baroness Enya, originally from Gultero but with ancestors who hail from Venostes, has somehow brought back the ancient King Taranis. He was a brilliant man whose views were rigid. His beliefs were extreme, and he showed little mercy to the fae, whose land he stole, drawing kingdom lines and writing the laws that govern us to this day."

"What is the baroness's purpose in resurrecting him?" Tove asked.

The king took a deep breath. "I believe her reasoning is twofold. First, it seems she and her son wish to bring back the old ways, when humans extinguished any fae they came across." His fingers shifted uneasily beside his cup. "Second, the ancient king has his own agenda: to collect the last surviving Odiums, thus ensuring they, like the fae, are wiped out for good."

Tove leaned back in his seat. "The Dark Fae on the beach," he said, looking to Jastyn, "that is the same being…this king?"

Jastyn's throat felt dry as tree bark, and her head spun at this new possibility.

"That's why he's been after you?" Fortan asked. "Because you're an Odium?"

"Yes, but my dagger protected me," she said, gesturing to her father. "The one Tove made. Until I lost it," she added, rasping her knuckles reluctantly atop the table.

"On your journey?" the king asked, keeping his eyes on his cup.

"Yes, the one that started in the search for your daughter," she replied, unable the keep the sharpness from her tone. Didn't he remember she'd been part of the effort to bring Aurelia home?

Grannus laughed. "You seemed perfectly content keeping her from us."

"Aurelia is not an item to be passed around," she said through gritted teeth.

"You took my only child across the realm, forced her through unimaginable dangers."

Her voice, like her anger, rose. "I never forced Aurelia to do anything." At the same time, Jastyn itched with the guilt at the sudden memory of her words to the king months ago. "I will do what I can to bring your daughter home." She'd only been speaking half of the truth. The journey had made things more complicated than she could have ever imagined.

Tove raised a hand as if to create a wall between Jastyn and the king, both of which sat in fuming silence. "Back to the current situation," he said, looking at Grannus.

He took another drink, running a hand down his beard. "The baroness and her son have orchestrated all of this. I don't know how long this plan has been in place, but..." His voice faltered, and he cleared his throat gruffly. "It was they who murdered my son in an effort to gain control of the castle." Fortan nodded solemnly. "And if she can get to the rest of us, there's no stopping her from taking over completely."

Tove swirled his wine. "Why should we help you?"

The king frowned. "I have not asked for your help."

Fortan snorted.

Jastyn couldn't help but hear Aurelia in the way Grannus responded. "So like a Diarmaid," she said. "You're all too stubborn for your own good."

He finally met her gaze. "Excuse me, young lady—"

Pounding her fist, she shouted, "My name is Jastyn." She couldn't take it anymore. Was he truly acting like this, even now, even with her helping him? "I am Jastyn Cipher, the Odium child you and your wife abhor. But I am the Odium who ensured your daughter's safety for months. Not because I care at all what you or the queen think of me, but because Aurelia is the singular light in your dark reign as Diarmaids. She is someone who cares, somebody who could fix the awful mess you"—she pointed across the table—"and Dechtire have made of our lives. Aurelia is the one who deserves our help." She took a breath, her shoulders shaking. "She is why we will help make sure the royal family doesn't fall."

She stared hard across the table. It was like something lit itself within the king's gaze. It flickered to life, though he blinked rapidly as if to contain this newfound spark of knowledge.

She'd lost her temper, yes. But she couldn't stand the inane rebuffing Grannus insisted on. They didn't have time to go around in circles, accusing one another of missteps they already knew they were guilty of. Alanna, most of all, didn't have time for this. Jastyn's father had been right the first night she'd met him. Hate got them nowhere.

"Well, then." Fortan pushed back from the table, then collected several fish from the corner and headed toward the door. "That's settled. The selkies will aid the Diarmaids. Not in a hundred years could I have predicted it." He laughed on his way out of the room. "Wait until Revna hears about this."

CHAPTER THIRTEEN

Aurelia was half-asleep when Jastyn wrapped an arm around her waist. She intertwined their fingers and brought their hands up to her chest. Jastyn pressed herself closer, her smaller frame flush against Aurelia's. Completely content, Aurelia sank deeper into blissful slumber.

When a strange clattering jolted her awake, she glanced around. Sadly, Jastyn wasn't there. Instead, Alanna slept beside her, facing the opposite side of the bed. The faint light of dawn slipped through the closed shutters in the single window to her left. When a second crashing sound came from the next room, Aurelia sprang to her feet.

She checked to make sure Alanna was still asleep, then slowly stepped into the main room. Abruptly, she tripped over something large.

"Elisedd?"

Eyes closed and flat on his back, he lay unmoving. His arms were splayed awkwardly. Quickly, she knelt and held her knuckles beneath his nose. He was still breathing. She looked to find all of the furniture once again upended. Branna stood near the hearth. Aurelia saw the frightened look in her eyes as she backed away from a barrel-chested man with wild blond hair.

"Drest."

He turned with one palm up, a yellow orb poised above it. "Aurelia. I've been looking everywhere for you." His smile was sickening. "It's rather selfish, don't you think, using these poor people to hide behind?"

With his attention focused on her, she tried to motion to Branna, signaling her to run. She shuffled sideways.

"Not that this one is innocent," Drest was saying. "She is a particularly nasty woman. Fell in love with a fae. Bore an Odium." Sneering, he wheeled around. "Where do you think you're going, you wretch?"

Before Aurelia could raise her saol—which burst forth in her hand, fueled by rage at Drest's words—he caught Branna in a raging wind. She fought against the tunnel, but it was no use. Within seconds, she fell to the ground, unconscious.

Aurelia flew forward, anger driving her steps. She hurled her saol, but as he always did, Drest deflected it easily, sending the flame into the hearth.

"Come now, Aurelia. Is that any way to treat an old friend?"

"You may no longer call yourself my friend. I can't believe you ever were." She gestured to Branna. "And you have no right coming here, torturing this family."

He swiped his hands on his tunic. "As the future king of Venostes, I have every right to do as I please."

She laughed. "You're delusional."

He stepped around Branna and the chair she'd been sitting in, now overturned on the rug. "It pains me, Aurelia, truly, that you insist on resisting this transitional time."

"Do you hear yourself, Drest?" She shook her head. "Your mother has completely warped your mind."

His gaze was glassy and unhinged. "My mother has the kingdom's best interests at heart. Change is never easy, Aurelia. There is always a cost."

"People's lives are not yours to play with." Her breath came unevenly. "You murdered Brennus. For what, power?" Her saol simmered at her fingertips.

Drest grinned. "He had to go, I'm afraid. The Diarmaid reign will come to an end."

She swallowed, wanting to cry but filled with so much rage, it took all her concentration just to speak. "Then why haven't you struck?" She held out her arms, dimming her spell-fire. "What are you waiting for?"

He made his way around the room, near the front door, facing her. "Oh, Aurelia. Don't you know I've always had a soft spot for you? You're like..." He paused, searching the ceiling. "A pestering little sister." He smiled as if he'd paid her an actual compliment. "Mother doesn't approve, but I want to offer you another opportunity."

"Opportunity…what for?"

"To join us."

Scoffing, she said, "I'd never join you."

"You haven't heard my offer yet."

"It doesn't matter. My answer is no."

"Even if that means losing your precious Odium?"

The floor fell out from under her, but when she glanced down, somehow, her feet remained on solid ground despite the feeling that she was falling.

"If you help in bringing about the new regime, I can guarantee your lover's protection."

Aurelia's head swam. How did he even know about Jastyn? How did he know how she felt about her? They'd seen him only a handful of times. Had the baroness found out somehow?

"You're lying," she finally said. "Your grandfather is hunting her as we speak. Why would he spare her?"

"Having a Diarmaid on our side will quell the concerns that many of the villagers will no doubt have once my mother takes control. Our union will provide a sense of familiarity. If you promise your allegiance, I will make sure the Odium lives."

But Aurelia was stuck on something else he'd said. "Our union?" Her stomach roiled.

He waved as if swatting a fly. "Oh, come now. It would be for show, nothing more. To ease the transition," he repeated casually, as if everything he was proposing didn't mean the entire world was turning upside down.

Feeling sick, Aurelia stumbled, staring at the man she'd known her whole life, wondering at the horrible person he had become. She tried to reconcile this individual with the boy she'd played with in the halls of the castle. The young man who'd helped her and Brennus escape the iron fist their parents always held over them. Had this version of him always been there, waiting for the perfect moment to reveal himself?

"Was this your mother's plan all along?" she asked, glancing toward the other room, hoping Alanna was still asleep.

"Yes," he said matter-of-factly. "My father was always hesitant but went along because he loved Mother. His adoration of Grannus, however, proved to be his downfall. He cared too much about your family. Ultimately, he was more of a hinderance than a help."

"Your own father." Aurelia remembered Louarn's kind demeanor over the years, his friendly dinner conversations in the main hall every night.

"We can't have anyone standing in our way, Aurelia."

"What makes you think I'd ever side with you?"

"I told you." He dug through the kitchen and bit into an apple. "I will spare the Odium."

"How?"

He sighed. She knew he was growing exasperated, but she didn't care. She needed to understand. "My grandfather is under our command. Since his banishment, the consequences of his eternal life come with a stipulation: he works for those who control him. When my mother's father died, that honor passed to her. I've only just started learning the process."

"Enya? She commands him?"

"We both do. So." He tossed the gnawed core across the room. It landed unceremoniously next to Elisedd. "If you pledge your loyalty, we can make sure he leaves your Odium unharmed."

Aurelia pictured Jastyn, heard her screams echoing that night in the Wood. She saw Jastyn's very life being drained from her body, heard Jastyn's cries during another sleepless night. Could Drest really bring an end to all of that? Could Jastyn finally have the life of peace she deserved?

Then she thought of Vreis forced into hiding deep in the mountains. "What about the others?"

"Other Odiums? Or other half bloods?" He quirked an eyebrow. "Don't be greedy, Aurelia. We can't very well start with a clean slate if we allow all of them to live."

Her stomach turned. "By 'clean,' you mean 'pure.' You'll wipe out everyone who's not human."

His silence confirmed her fears, and she knew there was only one way forward now. She hated that she had even considered his offer for a moment.

From the corner of her eye, movement stirred from the doorway of Alanna's room. The edge of Alanna's nightshirt poked out from behind the wall. Aurelia tried to say something to keep Drest's attention on her, but it was too late. He leapt sideways, leaning hungrily toward the doorway.

"What do we have here?"

Aurelia sprinted, putting herself between him and the bedroom. Her saol sprang to life, hovering over her palm. When he didn't stop, she threw it, hitting him in the shoulder. He took it in stride, chuckling.

"Stay back," she commanded, conjuring more spell-fire until it burned as wide as the doorway. He paused, but his eyes were clear.

"You've tried my patience long enough," he said. "I gave you your chance. Step aside, or meet your end."

Her legs trembling, Aurelia forced herself to stand tall. Silently, she prayed Alanna would stay back, stay behind the wall where it was safe. Her saol glowed brighter, vibrating to life as a barrier formed as high as the ceiling between her and Drest.

She glanced over her shoulder to find Alanna close behind her, her hair sticking up from sleep. "Aurelia?" Her face was pale, and she trembled terribly.

"Get back," she shouted. "Alanna, it's not safe."

"The horse master's daughter?" Drest's eyes were completely clear now, a wind spell starting to form in both hands. "Oh, what a shame that will be. One hates to kill a pure blood, but sacrifices will be made."

Alanna scurried back into her room. Aurelia faced Drest. "You will not touch her." With all the strength she had, she pushed her saol forward. It smacked into him as he stood transfixed in the thrall of his building spell. He fell back, his magic dissipating. She conjured another fist of spell-fire and hurled it at him. He clutched his side where it sizzled into him, and Aurelia took the few seconds he stared to run after Alanna.

"We need to move," she said, pushing Alanna toward the window before shoving open the shutters.

"But my parents..." Alanna looked ready to burst into tears as Aurelia urged her backward.

"They're not dead. Only stunned." Aurelia hoped she wasn't lying as Alanna finally climbed through the window. Right as she did, a yellow orb narrowly missed her right knee. The spell-fire smoked and hissed where it landed against the wall.

Once Alanna was outside, Aurelia turned back to Drest. He seemed too big for the room with his hair on end and his arms outstretched. She knew the spell he was trying to conjure, and she didn't want to stick around to be its latest victim.

"You won't win." She reached up, feeling for the window, hoping she'd given Alanna sufficient time to start running.

His voice was as hollow as his gaze when he said, "You're going to die just like your brother. And as with his death, I'm going to enjoy every agonizing moment of it."

Her stomach tightened. Bile rose in her throat. Squaring with him, she lifted her hands, each of them blazing brighter than she'd ever seen. Fury like she'd never felt coursed through her veins. This was not the man who had once been her friend. This person was evil and nothing else.

A strange sound filled the room as she reared back, ready to strike. Was that her screaming? Then something else caught her ear, high-pitched and light, like a harpsicord being pulled tight.

She jumped when an arrow zoomed past her left shoulder. It landed with a satisfying *thwump* in Drest's thigh. The spell vanished with a howl as he wailed, gripping the shaft and falling to the ground.

"Your Highness."

Aurelia gasped at Rigo framed in the small window. His long silver hair was tied back, and his gray eyes were dark as steel.

"Rigo!"

"We must move, Your Majesty."

Bewildered, she stammered, "Jastyn's sister, Alanna—"

"She is safe."

With one more glance at Drest still shouting as blood bubbled around his wound, Aurelia hurried through the window and out into the harsh light of day.

CHAPTER FOURTEEN

Jastyn was more than ready to row ashore the next morning. A sense of thrilling relief filled her once her boots hit the sand, and the king climbed out of the rowboat after her.

Tove met her gaze. "You know where to find us if you need anything. We should have the last of the materials needed for your dagger soon. I'll get it to you the moment it's ready."

"Thank you." Jastyn situated the satchel over her chest, the vials within resting against her hip.

"Be safe."

Her father turned and rowed back out to sea. For a moment, she stood peacefully on the beach as his figure retreated toward the horizon. The air around her shifted, and Jastyn imagined her mother standing beside her, one hand shielding her eyes from the bright sun, watching Tove sail away.

"Thank the gods. I knew I'd seen gooseberry shrubs along here." The king's voice tore Jastyn from her reverie, and the vision vanished. Turning, she found Grannus already up the embankment, kneeling and eagerly popping handfuls of berries into his mouth. When she scaled the incline to join him, he added, "If I had to smell all of that unsalted fish a moment longer..." He shoved more fruit into his mouth, chewing rabidly. Jastyn, bemused, handed him her flask. He eyed it but accepted the drink and washed down his breakfast. "Thank you."

She nodded, grateful he'd started to come around since their night on the ship. "I thought kings were immune to seasickness." She relished the regretful look on his face.

He squinted, standing and regaining his height advantage. "It's been a few years since I've sailed."

Shaking her head, Jastyn plucked some berries for herself and motioned for him to follow. As they walked, clouds formed overhead, covering the blue sky in mounds of white edged in ominous gray. Jastyn tried to ignore the feeling of dread at the sight of the darkening sky. She didn't feel ready to face the Dark Fae after a night spent dealing with the king, even if he had begun to treat her like a regular member of his kingdom.

They stayed along the edges of the Wood until Jastyn dipped between several ash trees that led to an oak grove north of the village. She spotted Coran's red-orange locks first, but Dechtire hurried out of a cavernous old trunk upon seeing them.

"Grannus." She, unlike her husband, didn't look worse than the day before. In fact, aside from more dirt on her riding clothes and face, she appeared well-rested as she embraced the king.

"Jas!" Coran sat cross-legged on the ground inside the massive, hollow trunk. Roisin stood beside him, hunched at an angle due to the twisting bark as it stretched skyward. Coran passed her a half-eaten crust of bread before hurrying to meet Jastyn.

"How was everything?" she asked, her eyes cutting to the queen.

"Fine, Jas. Fine. We got some sleep. It's a solid spot."

She looked past him to the old tree. It was there she and her mother had spent an entire winter huddled together, starving and cold but out of the harsh, biting wind.

"Any activity from the guardsmen?" she asked, hands on her hips.

He shook his head, but Roisin answered, "Nothing yet."

Dechtire and Grannus had fallen into a hushed conversation. Jastyn and Coran exchanged glances.

"And your night?" he asked.

Rolling her eyes, she replied, "Ask His Majesty."

Puckering his lips, Coran said, "That good, huh?"

"And the others?" Dechtire stepped back toward their group, her light hair swept behind her ears. Jastyn continued to be startled by her eyes, the same as her daughter's, bright and inquisitive. Glancing skyward, Jastyn tracked the sun as it began its journey west. More clouds gathered.

"They should be here soon."

"Don't worry, Your Majesties," Roisin said, pushing back strands of wavy hair that had fallen from the braid twisted into a knot atop her head. "M'lady will be here in no time."

The king and queen smiled, but Jastyn saw the worry behind their eyes. Even she felt anxious the longer they had to wait for her family and Aurelia to join them. She knew her parents could handle themselves against the guards, but Aurelia always managed to find herself in troublesome situations.

"Come on," Coran said, nudging her. "We can form a plan while we wait. Keep ourselves busy, eh?"

She smiled and wandered to lean against the wide mouth that formed an arch in the oak. Coran stood with Roisin while the Diarmaids lingered nearby.

"Do you think it's safe to return to the castle?"

Jastyn knew the answer to Roisin's question before the queen answered. "I'm afraid for us, no. As much as I wish we could. I know there are members of the court, my ladies for instance"—she cast a hopeful glance to Grannus—"who remain loyal. I know they would come to our aid. But it's too soon."

The king nodded. "We would be putting them at risk."

Roisin looked around their group. "Then, what do we do?"

"The guards will search again. Enya will want to find us, I've no doubt."

"You'll need to stay in hiding," Coran said.

Jastyn mumbled her agreement, but she was only half listening. Her ears were trained on the surrounding Wood for the familiar tread of her mother's steps or even Elisedd's. Where were they?

"Maybe Eegit could take them in again?"

When Coran's question went unanswered, he gently kicked Jastyn's shin. "Hey, Jas, you okay?"

She glanced up. "Eegit? Sure. As long as we don't make her angry again."

Dechtire adjusted the collar of her tunic while Grannus shuffled awkwardly. When Jastyn scanned the trees, Coran asked, "What is it?"

"Something's not right." She stepped away, one hand on the satchel's strap over her chest. She was so afraid of losing the cure, she'd slept with the bag on board the selkie's ship. There was no way she was letting the vials out of her sight.

"Perhaps I could help prepare that for you. If you'd like."

It took a moment for Jastyn to realize the queen had been talking to her. She refocused on Dechtire. She stared, replaying her words, then glanced at the king. Blinking, Jastyn started to respond when the distant snap of a fallen branch made her turn.

"Jas, what's going on?"

She hurried toward the sound, peering between the tall trees and over their exposed roots and the low, rolling gnome hills. Figures emerged from the shadowy depths.

"Alanna!" Jastyn ran to her sister, confused to find her wearing her nightshirt and carrying a satchel of her own. After sharing a hug, Jastyn stepped back, scanning her sister from head to toe. "Why do you look like you rolled out of bed?"

Alanna shrank, her shoulders turning inward. "Something happened at home."

Jastyn's stomach dropped. She swallowed the bile of fear in her throat and reached out, gripping Alanna's forearms. "Are you okay?"

Her sister nodded as Aurelia appeared moments later.

At the sight of her, the tightness in Jastyn's chest loosened, but her stomach remained uneasy.

"Jastyn." Aurelia pulled up beside them, breathing hard. "Your parents…"

"What happened?"

Aurelia bent over, one hand on her knee, the scar from her old injury pink against her pale skin. The king and queen hurried over and framed their daughter protectively.

"Sweetheart, are you all right?" Dechtire placed a hand on Aurelia's back as she straightened.

"I'm fine." She gulped at the air. Grannus fetched a flask. Aurelia waved it off. Jastyn took it, handing it to Alanna.

"Please," Jastyn said, "tell me what happened. Where is my mother and Elisedd?"

Aurelia's heart raced as she struggled to regain her breath. She loathed the frightened look in Jastyn's face. Even more, she hated what she was about to tell her. Slowly, she started again. "Your parents—"

"Are they dead?"

The matter-of-factness of Jastyn's tone shook her but also helped pull her from the traumatic stupor she'd succumbed to since leaving Jastyn's home. "No. Gods, no. They're alive. But..."

"Aurelia, what happened?" Jastyn's gaze was pleading. One of her hands gripped Alanna's tightly. The other twitched anxiously at her side. Coran and Roisin stood a few paces away, listening.

"They've been taken," Aurelia said carefully. "We were all asleep when Drest ambushed your family."

The hazel in Jastyn's eyes turned dark.

"Drest?" her father asked. "You're certain?"

She spoke quickly. "It was him. He took out Elisedd first."

Alanna's eyes brimmed with tears, though she seemed to try to keep a brave face.

"That was when I woke up. I tried to tell your mother to run but..." Her voice caught in her throat.

Jastyn's jaw clenched when Aurelia's mother interjected. "Drest stupefied them with his wind spells?"

"Yes. They were still alive when I last checked them. But Drest..." She faltered, considering if now was the best time to mention the deal he offered her. Deciding against it, she said, "He went after Alanna."

Jastyn's eyes burned bright, but Alanna chimed in. "Aurelia saved me." Jastyn squeezed her arm assuredly, her gaze cutting back to Aurelia, who felt self-conscious.

"I only did what any sensible person would have done in that moment." Her cheeks warmed under everyone's gazes. "We escaped through your bedchamber window."

A slight rise in Jastyn's eyebrow caught Aurelia's attention, but Alanna cried, "He's the one who shot that man."

"What?" Jastyn turned to her. "Who shot Drest?"

"He did." Alanna pointed, and they all followed her finger to find Rigo standing next to a stalwart oak ten paces away.

"Rigo!" Coran ran to him. He smiled and held out an arm in greeting. Ignoring this, Coran tackled him in a hug.

"That's the elf who helped us escape," Alanna whispered to her sister, who looked from Rigo to Aurelia.

"It was rather good timing, I must say."

Coran steered Rigo to join them. He shook Jastyn's hand.

"It is good to see you," Jastyn said. "Thank you for helping save my sister." He bowed. Jastyn frowned, then asked, "Wait, how do you know they've been taken?"

"We went back," Rigo said. "Her Highness wished to ensure your family was all right."

Swallowing, Aurelia avoided Jastyn's gaze. Her mother's hand came to rest on her back, pressing hard. "Sweetheart—"

"I know." Aurelia shook her off. "It was dangerous to go back. But I couldn't leave them there. Not like that." She faced Jastyn. "But when Rigo and I returned, no one was there." She pictured the trail of blood that led from Jastyn's room to the hearth, small pools gathered near where Elisedd and Branna had lain. Aurelia hoped to the gods it was Drest's blood and no one else's. "I think he took them when he fled," she added, trying to sound hopeful.

"To the castle?" asked Jastyn.

She shrugged. "To the dungeons, I imagine."

For a time, the only sounds were the soft buzz of fairy nests and the distant rushing of the river. Aurelia bit her lip. She wanted to help, wanted to do something to ease the pain Jastyn was feeling.

Rubbing her forehead, Jastyn paced. Aurelia glanced at Coran.

"Let's sit, eh?" He led Jastyn to a hollowed oak tree. A pile of leaves covered half the interior.

Her mother leaned close. "This was our sanctuary for the night."

Aurelia was surprised at how casual she seemed about that fact. *Is this how Alanna knew to run here?* Then she wondered how Coran knew about this place. Even though she didn't want to think about it, Aurelia had a feeling it had to do with Jastyn's childhood.

Taking a seat between her parents, who had stayed close since she'd arrived, Aurelia wasn't surprised when Rigo remained standing. Smiling, Aurelia realized how much she'd missed his stoic presence.

Jastyn knelt next to Coran, Roisin beside him, while Alanna plopped tiredly down on the other side of her sister. From where she sat, Aurelia could feel the tension radiating from Jastyn's body.

"I'm sorry," Aurelia said, breaking the silence.

Jastyn didn't seem to hear her. She didn't move, one hand protectively over the satchel, her gaze glassy.

"What can we do?" Coran looked around their group. Aurelia caught her parents throwing furtive glances toward Rigo leaning on his bow a few paces from where they sat.

Jastyn spoke softly. "We need a plan."

A series of coughs burst from Alanna, who turned, trying to mask them as Jastyn leaned over her. Her entire body shook, and Aurelia was reminded of her brother and his horrible shaking spasms as he fell into the Otherworld.

Meeting her father's sympathetic gaze, Aurelia was about to speak when her mother said, "We need to get started on your cure. The equinox is tomorrow."

One hand on her sister, Jastyn shifted, putting her shoulder between Aurelia's mother and the vials.

"Your sister's time is running out," Aurelia's mother said.

They all watched as Alanna wheezed, then accepted a drink from a flask.

"I am an excellent remedy-maker. I've already deciphered most of the recipe," Aurelia's mother added, gesturing to the satchel. "I can be of great help." Her father nodded, but Aurelia saw the distrust in Jastyn's eyes.

"Why do you want to help?"

Aurelia felt her lungs tighten as Jastyn and her mother held each other's gazes.

"Because I am a healer. It's who I was before I was queen. It's who I am and what I can give. If you'll let me."

After another moment, Jastyn caught Aurelia's eye. She nodded, trying to give her a reassuring smile. Finally, Jastyn's shoulders relaxed. "Very well."

Aurelia felt their entire group collectively exhale. Alanna leaned, exhausted, into Jastyn.

"That still doesn't help my mother and Elisedd."

"No," Aurelia's father said, frowning.

Her mother, looking suddenly at ease, turned to Roisin. "Dear, you're still living and working in the castle, aren't you?"

Roisin, who had been staring in alarm at Rigo's looming presence and seemed generally bewildered by everything, blinked, stammering at being addressed. "Y...yes, Your Majesty. The ladies of the court have assigned me to several of their daughters since my charge is..." She stared at Aurelia. "Well, still missing, according to the baroness." She dug the toe of her shoe into the ground. "I had to spin a tale for my returning late last night. And I snuck out before dawn this morning."

"You must go back." Her mother had taken on the tone Aurelia knew well from their study sessions. "You must act as if nothing has changed."

Roisin practically fell backward. "But, m'lady, Aurelia is alive." She pointed enthusiastically. "She's here. You all are."

Catching on to her mother's idea, Aurelia said, "Roisin, no one can know that we're together, that I'm not captured. Or that my mother is alive. Not yet."

"I don't understand, m'lady."

"You will return to the castle. Carry out your duties as you normally would. But as you do, bend your ear to the goings-on inside the court."

Coran grabbed Roisin's hand. "It's brilliant. You can listen for news of Jastyn's parents. Find out what happened to 'em."

Roisin's eyes were so wide, Aurelia feared they might be stuck. "Roisin?" She patted her knee gently.

Roisin lowered her chin. "I'm not sure I can do that."

Aurelia glanced around, noting the glisten of hope in Jastyn's eyes. "Please, Roisin. It's only until we can learn what has become of Branna and the horse master."

"I believe in you." Coran pressed his forehead to her temple. Roisin smiled and took a shaky breath.

"All right. I'll do it."

Ripples of relief coursed through their circle.

"Thank you," Jastyn said, and Aurelia didn't miss the gratitude sitting in the corners of her smile.

"You're doing your kingdom a great service." Her mother beamed. Roisin flushed and leaned into Coran, one hand over her face.

"I'll do what I can, Your Majesties."

Sighing, Aurelia rested her hands in her lap. She smiled, gazing across at Alanna, who looked worn but happy as she held her sister's hand.

Aurelia despised Drest for what he'd done to her brother. But now he was going after others, going after Jastyn and her loved ones. Watching the two sisters now, Aurelia determined then and there that she would do whatever it took to stop Drest and Enya's wretched tirade across her kingdom. They would not harm anyone she cared about anymore. She wouldn't let them.

CHAPTER FIFTEEN

Roisin left with Coran soon after, the pair clutching one another as they went. Jastyn had pretended to be busy making a small fire as Aurelia said good-bye to her maiden. They'd embraced, and a flash of jealousy flared in Jastyn's chest, but she ignored it, focusing on wrapping her cloak around Alanna. Her sister sat shivering near the fire. The sky had transformed to a sheet of eerie gray. The wind was sharp, cutting between the trees. Summer was ending, Jastyn could feel it. The autumnal equinox was near.

"How much longer are you going to wait before giving Queen Dechtire the vials?"

Jastyn tossed more dried leaves on the flames. They wouldn't stay here long, but Alanna wasn't well, and she needed to keep warm before being forced to move again.

"Once we're in one place."

"Why don't you like her?"

"Alanna." Jastyn sighed. Slowly, she took a seat. Across the fire, Aurelia was speaking to her parents, the king and queen crouched in the tree trunk. Aurelia gestured sporadically to Rigo standing guard nearby.

Stoking the flames, Jastyn wondered how much her sister knew. She thought back to the quiet nights at home in front of the hearth, listening to stories from their mother. What had Alanna been told of their past? How much had she shared?

"Things with the Diarmaids are complicated," she finally said.

Her sister coughed, her narrow shoulders shuddering as she struggled to regain her breath. Through uneven gasps, she said, "They are good monarchs."

Snorting, Jastyn tried not to laugh. "What do you know of their reign?" She regretted her words at the hurt look her sister wore. "I'm sorry." She pressed two fingers to her temple. "There's a lot going on right now."

"The queen wants to help us, Jastyn."

Glancing over at Dechtire, Jastyn wanted to believe that. She recalled her own desperate plan to speak to the queen nearly a year ago, to plead her sister's case in hope of some assistance. Why then was there still this barrier of distrust Jastyn couldn't seem to overcome?

Because they were responsible for everything, she reminded herself, eyeing Grannus and Dechtire. How could she throw aside a lifetime of resentment after the pain they'd caused her family?

Of course, it wasn't just the Diarmaids who had made things difficult. Jastyn was still trying to come to terms with the awful work of her selkie grandfather, the one who cursed Alanna with this illness. Was there no good anywhere in this world?

Aurelia laughed at something her father said. Jastyn's heart fluttered at the sound.

"Do you feel the same way about Aurelia?" Alanna lowered her voice. "After all, you did travel across the realm together."

"With Coran and Rigo, too."

Alanna smiled. "I think she's wonderful. And brave."

A series of memories flashed before Jastyn's mind. Aurelia—green with shock—offering to prepare the buck she and Rigo had hunted for dinner. Another flash: Aurelia tending to Vreis's wound in the cave after the run-in with the pooka. Finally, the way she'd danced with her palm pressed to Jastyn's, their eyes locked and the music seeming to lift them above the selkie ship.

Dipping her chin, Jastyn said, "Aurelia will make a fine queen one day."

"Jastyn—"

Unable to think about Aurelia a moment more, Jastyn changed the subject. "You should eat." She searched her satchel and handed Alanna an apple and some berries. "Once you're done, we'll have to move again. The guards will be searching."

Her sister nodded, quietly munching while Jastyn tried not to focus on Aurelia. Perhaps she'd been wrong about their need to talk. She jabbed a stick into the dull fire. Maybe it would be better if they simply let things settle the way they were. What was the point of mending things between them if after they got through this—*if* they got through this—she and Aurelia would go their separate ways. It was inevitable, something Jastyn had known was going to happen since the beginning.

There had never been a chance in the realm for them. The princess and an Odium, there was nothing more impossible than that.

❖

"Are you certain this is a good idea?"

Jastyn rolled her eyes. "Yes, Your Majesty." She was glad the king continued to speak to her, but he remained one of the most perturbing individuals she had ever known with his need to question everything. "Eegit is probably not even there. Plus, there's fewer of us now, so the protection spell will work fine. Besides, I'm not staying long."

"You're not?" Aurelia's steps faltered where she walked between Alanna and Rigo on their way to Eegit's meadow.

"I've got to find our parents."

At this, both Aurelia and Alanna stopped in their tracks. Their simultaneous protests bombarded Jastyn, and she threw up her hands. "They could be in trouble," she insisted.

"It's too dangerous," Alanna cried. "That man." She looked to Aurelia. "He's not right. He'll hurt you, Jastyn."

Aurelia added, "Your parents are most likely in the dungeons. Which, oddly enough, is one of the safest places for them to be right now." Jastyn started to object, but Aurelia cut her off. "We have a plan, remember? Roisin will find out what's going on." Then she stepped closer, placing a hand on Jastyn's elbow. Alanna looked between them. "Be patient. I know it's difficult. But we have to take all of this one step at a time."

Relaxing her clenched fists, Jastyn nodded, though she was aching to take action, aching to do something to help her mother and Elisedd. What if they weren't just stunned like Aurelia thought? What if she never got a chance to talk to her mother about the cave?

When they arrived at Eegit's meadow, the fire from the day before was still out, and a few new charred cauldrons and squirrel skulls were scattered near her vacant hut.

SAM LEDEL

"See?" Jastyn said, gesturing around. "She's gone. We'll be fine here for a while."

"I'd like to meet this hedgewitch." Rigo smiled, holding up a frightening mishmash of bone fragments.

"I'm sure she'll pop up when we least expect her," Jastyn replied. Alanna sat near the firepit, yawning widely. "You should rest," Jastyn told her before collecting leaves. Rather than use them to start the fire, she arranged them near her sister. "Lie down. Sleep if you can. We may need to move again soon."

The dark circles under Alanna's eyes lifted with her smile. "Perhaps I'll close my eyes for a little while." Stretching out, she rested her head atop the leaves. The Diarmaids stood watching Alanna, whose breathing slowed as soon as she closed her eyes.

"Poor thing," Grannus muttered.

Gripping the strap of her satchel, Jastyn took a deep breath. There was no reason for dwelling in disdain anymore. Her sister was sick and needed help. Jastyn was only hindering her recovery by remaining stubborn.

Holding out the satchel, she said, "Here. If anyone can prepare this in time, it's probably you."

The queen took a seat on one of the logs encircling the fire that now glowed nicely thanks to Aurelia. "I'll do my best."

"You got what you were searching for?" Rigo's melodic voice drew Jastyn's attention. She felt strange without the satchel, and it took her a moment to respond.

"I did. The caves held the cure like the Red One said they would."

His gray eyes peered into her. "I am glad."

"Rigo." Aurelia must have sensed Jastyn's unwillingness to elaborate as she turned the conversation to him. "I've been meaning to ask...what happened, exactly, at the cove?"

The queen and king stopped stoking the fire to listen. Jastyn wondered what Aurelia had told them about Rigo. They still seemed anxious in his presence but not as much as this morning.

He passed his bow from one hand to the other, then knelt. "My queen sent two clans to attack the selkie cove. One of them my own."

"Gods." Aurelia sat, her hands clasped under her chin.

"We had never actually fought the selkies before. It was strange, seeing two proud members of fae clash." The slightest frown creased his forehead. "I was able to speak to some members of my clan and make them understand. Made them put down their arms. It is difficult to go against our queen's orders." He glanced down. "One third of my brothers and sisters were lost that day."

Shocked, Jastyn said, "One third?" She hesitated, then asked, "Daylor, your mate, he wasn't one of them, was he?"

"No, he wasn't there."

She nodded, relieved at some good news.

"The selkies were ruthless. Brilliant, tenacious warriors. Their skin is nearly impenetrable to our arrows unless there is a clear shot."

A vision from the caves rushed back to Jastyn, and Aurelia's next words confirmed her fears. "'Nearly impenetrable.' Tell that to Sif."

"I saw her being carried out to sea," Rigo said. "Though what became of her, I cannot say."

Jastyn felt ill. She hadn't liked Sif when they'd first met, but the tough selkie had grown on her.

Aurelia wiped a tear away. "I hope she's all right."

"Once it became apparent that their desired target was no longer present, the clans retreated."

"Do you think the elf queen will call off her invasions?" Dechtire asked, the satchel resting in her lap, one of the vials in her hand.

"I sent word back with those who believed me when I told them that our queen is being manipulated like your kingdom is." The Diarmaids eyes widened, but to Jastyn's amusement, Rigo didn't seem to notice. "However, I fear it will be difficult to make her see reason."

The king was staring at Rigo as if he had two heads. Dechtire cleared her throat. "Well," she said, fumbling with the satchel. "I had better get started on this."

Aurelia stood. "You need a cauldron of water, don't you?"

"Yes, sweetheart, but—"

"We'll fetch you some." Aurelia wore a determined look, and Jastyn faltered when she turned and said, "There's a brook nearby, isn't there?"

Jastyn could only nod.

"Wonderful. Jastyn and I will fill the flasks so you can begin."

Confused, Jastyn stammered, "But, Alanna…I don't want to leave her alone."

The Diarmaids shifted awkwardly when Rigo said, "I will keep watch."

"We'll only be a little while." Aurelia grabbed both flasks, careful not to disturb Alanna.

"Do hurry," Dechtire called as Jastyn, still baffled by Aurelia's behavior, hurried to catch up.

CHAPTER SIXTEEN

Standing beneath an ash tree, all Aurelia could hear was the monotonous hum from a fairy nest overhead. She grinned, recalling one of the many times she'd stumbled into one, needing to be rescued by Jastyn's quick thinking.

Now that they were alone, something Aurelia had been dying for since they were reunited, she found herself at a rare loss for words. Jastyn knelt beside the slow, trickling water, one flask dipped into the clear brook. Aurelia tried to think of the best thing to say first. The last two days had been tumultuous, to say the least. She had so many questions, but more than anything, she needed Jastyn to know that she had forgiven her. But how to say all that?

Anxiously, she crouched, grimacing at the faint pain in her knee. She wasn't as subtle as she hoped in concealing her discomfort because Jastyn said, "You should apply more calendula to that."

"I fear the time for that has passed. The pain is strictly internal now. It will probably accompany me for many days to come."

Jastyn's eyes were trained on the water flowing over her hand.

Perhaps if Aurelia simply kept talking, eventually, the right words would surface. "I learned something from Drest in our last encounter." Jastyn's brows rose, and Aurelia knew she had her attention. "He told me that the Dark Fae, his great-grandfather if you can believe it, is under his control. Well, his and Enya's."

Recapping the flask, Jastyn faced her. "What?"

"The Dark Fae. Actually, I'm not certain he's entirely fae, nor is he human. I don't know exactly what he is…"

"Aurelia."

"Sorry. What I mean is, I think this information provides us with an opportunity." Her heart sped at the prospect of giving Jastyn something hopeful to hold on to. "He's under their command, so once we stop Enya and Drest, we stop him, too."

Jastyn stared. "All this time, somebody has been telling him to kill me?"

Aurelia swallowed. "Well, when you put it that way…"

Running a hand down her braid, Jastyn exhaled and fell back to sit with her legs stretched out. She stared into the water.

"I thought…I thought this was helpful news." Aurelia tugged the cuff of her sleeve.

"Only if we can defeat the baroness and her son."

"Jastyn." Aurelia could see her slipping away, her mind falling to some dark place. "We will get through this. I know we will."

Rather than look optimistic, Jastyn grabbed the second flask and filled it silently. Aurelia didn't want to lose this chance. Gods knew time was more precious than ever.

"I forgive you," she blurted, biting her lip and watching Jastyn, who slowly pulled the flask back. She closed her eyes as if she was in pain.

"Aurelia."

"Please." She sat straighter, willing herself to go on. "I need to say this. I need you to know that I understand. I understand everything. I know why you joined the search to find me. I know why you felt you had to keep everything a secret." Jastyn moved to stand, but Aurelia held out an arm, keeping her in place. "It's all right," she said. "I know it was necessary to keep me in the dark. I understand why you did it. And I know it must have been so difficult. All of it. It must have been so hard in the caves to give up what you did." Jastyn's gaze swung to her, wide and startled. "But I knew you could do it. I knew you would get the cure."

Jastyn's swallow was audible, her eyes trained on the water. Why wasn't she saying anything?

"I forgive you," Aurelia repeated. "Jastyn, look at me, please." She tugged Jastyn's chin toward her.

Slowly, she lifted her gaze. Her voice was thick when she said, "Why?"

"Why? Why do I forgive you?"

"I lied to you for months. I was willing to do anything to save my sister."

"I know you felt as if you had no choice. You've had no choice your whole life. But I know you wouldn't have let anything happen to me."

Shaking her head, Jastyn said, "You don't know that."

"I do." Aurelia searched her face. Why was she fighting this so much? "Jastyn, I know you. I know the life you've endured, the hate you've faced, and the terror you've had to overcome." Tears filled her vision. "I forgive you."

Again, Jastyn tried to stand. "I don't deserve your forgiveness." She was on her feet. Aurelia stood and moved to face her, holding up her hands.

"You've got to stop this, Jastyn."

"No," she fired back, the sharp tone making Aurelia step back. "*You've* got to stop. Aurelia, we can't do this. Your saying all of this only makes it harder." Tears ran down Jastyn's cheeks, creating a pool of dread Aurelia knew it would be impossible to pull her out of.

Gripping her arms, Aurelia pleaded, "Listen to me, Jastyn."

"I can't."

"Why not?"

"Because." Her voice cracked. "If I listen to what you have to say, I won't be able to let you go."

The words hit Aurelia like an arrow. "Let me go?"

"There's no future for us, Aurelia." She gave a sad laugh. "You're the future queen of Venostes. Once all of this madness is through, if we make it, you'll go back to your castle. You'll go back to your life, and I'll go back to mine. And that'll be it."

Aurelia searched Jastyn's eyes. During their journey west, this fear had slept in the back of her mind. She wasn't completely naive; she knew who she was. She knew Jastyn was an Odium. She had no idea what would happen when all was said and done, but Jastyn was the woman Aurelia knew she couldn't live without.

Aurelia clutched her hands. "Jastyn, you coming into my life was the best thing that ever happened." She gripped her tighter when she tried to pull away. "Please don't walk away from this." She thought of that night aboard the selkie ship, and her body grew hot recalling

Jastyn's touch. A surge of emotions had coursed between them, shared in ways Aurelia had only ever imagined.

"Aurelia—"

But before she could protest again, Aurelia said the words she'd yearned to say since that night. "I love you, Jastyn."

Her hazel eyes brightened. Aurelia cupped her cheek, catching some of her tears. Now that she'd said it, Aurelia wanted to shout it for the whole realm. "I love you. So you don't get to walk away." She sniffled, feeling as if she was floating above the earth. "Because wherever you go, I'll be by your side. Whether you like it or not."

Jastyn laughed, the sound exploding in waves that washed into relief that enveloped Aurelia. She thought her heart might burst when Jastyn said, "I love you, too, Princess."

Grinning, Aurelia pulled her close, flinging her arms around her tightly. She'd felt happiness many times in her life, but this feeling? Aurelia wanted it to last forever. Leaning back, she found Jastyn's lips. Aurelia kissed her slowly, deeply, hoping she could feel how much Aurelia loved her. How much she would fight for her forever.

Jastyn pulled back, her breathing heavy. Aurelia opened her eyes to find her smiling.

"Does this mean you accept my forgiveness?"

"I guess it does."

After another kiss, Aurelia scooped up the flasks and took her hand. "Come on. We'd better get back. We've got a cure to make."

CHAPTER SEVENTEEN

The rest of the day passed with the queen huddled near one of Eegit's borrowed cauldrons, squinting at the cure's recipe and muttering under her breath. Alanna slept most of the time, waking only to eat a crust of bread Coran had left her or when coughs shook her body. Rigo, true to his word, kept a steady watch over her sister, for which Jastyn was grateful.

Of course, Jastyn wasn't sure anything could ever be as utterly heart pounding as Aurelia's confession by the brook. Half the day, Jastyn kept pinching herself, sure she was in a waking dream. But the longing glances and pure, open smiles Aurelia gave her as they sheltered in Eegit's meadow were real. They were the truest things Jastyn had ever known.

As much as she had been afraid to let her in, Jastyn couldn't *not* open her heart to Aurelia. She was persistent, another attribute Jastyn adored. And Aurelia had been right. All her life, Jastyn had been forced into a certain way of doing things, forced to choose survival and nothing else. But with Aurelia, she had been given an opportunity for something more. She had somebody to hold on to, somebody who wasn't afraid of who she was but actually loved her for it. Jastyn didn't understand how. Part of her was terrified. Still, she'd fallen for Aurelia months ago, and she'd slowly began to accept that it was fruitless to fight her feelings.

This morning, Aurelia had given Jastyn the greatest gift: the ability to believe in the future. Maybe even one where they could be together.

When they'd returned hand in hand with the water for Dechtire, Jastyn had seen the king stop mid-bite into his apple and stare at their intertwined fingers. The queen had either pretended not to notice or really was too preoccupied with the cure. Either way, Jastyn was glad neither monarch had felt the need to bring it up.

Later, as they sat around the fire, night bringing a cold wind only partially blocked by the protection spell, Jastyn pulled her knees close to her chest. She'd draped her cloak over Alanna, who lay sleeping near the fire since sunset.

"More tea?"

The king held out a ladle of boiled water. Nodding, Jastyn let him pour more into her cup of loose chamomile. Rain fell steadily overhead and on the outskirts of the clearing, dissipating once it hit the shell of protection. Jastyn wasn't sure if the royal family could have handled a night in both the cold and the rain but had to admit they were handling being on the run better than she'd expected.

Jastyn leaned back, taking in the dark blanket that was tonight's sky. The rain clouds marred any starlight, but they would have been cast in shadow as the moon was nothing but a thin waxing crescent before autumn's arrival.

"I can begin the process for the cure tonight. Then it will need three days to settle before she can drink it." The queen kept her eyes on the vials in her lap.

Taking a sip of tea, Jastyn replied, "Alanna is strong. She will fight to hold on."

"I remember seeing her once, years ago." Dechtire's gaze flickered to Alanna. "At a summer solstice festival."

Jastyn frowned. She didn't remember Alanna ever leaving the house, least of all to visit royal grounds.

Aurelia sounded as surprised as she was. "You did?"

"She was just as pale, though not nearly as tall. Clearly, she has her father's stature."

Confused by the fond smile, Jastyn asked, "You met her?"

Shaking her head, Dechtire said, "I only saw her in passing. Elisedd had waved to us across the grounds. Alanna was at his side, all elbows and big bright eyes." At Jastyn's incredulous look, she added, "I knew your stepfather when I was young. We grew up only a few hillsides from one another."

Jastyn caught Aurelia's wistful smile, but she wasn't sure how to take in that information. Elisedd and Dechtire were friends? "I didn't know," she finally said.

It was quiet for a time until Grannus said, "Aurelia was right earlier." His shoulders hunched under his cloak. "If Elisedd and your mother are in the dungeons, it's the safest place they could be."

Unsure what to say, Jastyn stared into her cup, drumming her fingers lightly against the side. She hoped they were right. She desperately wanted to speak to her mother. Even more after this morning's revelations.

"Mother." Aurelia's voice broke the silence. "Did you ever have a bad feeling about the baroness? Has she really been plotting this betrayal for years?"

The queen delicately replaced a small amount of restoration plant in its vial. She sighed. "Enya was a part of our lives. Since marrying Louarn, when was it?" She turned to Grannus. "Twenty-five, twenty-six years ago? She carried herself proudly and seemed to get along with the other ladies and members of the court." She paused, seeming to comb her mind for memories. "She was a respectful member of the castle."

Aurelia added, "Drest had his moments. But I've struggled to reconcile who he is now with who we grew up with."

The king and queen nodded. Jastyn glanced at Rigo, who sat cross-legged on the other side of Alanna. Suddenly, Dechtire cried out into her hands, making Jastyn jump.

Aurelia leaned forward. "Mother, what is it?"

Jastyn squirmed but couldn't take her eyes off the queen's rare show of emotion. When Dechtire lifted her head, Jastyn saw a look she knew well, one worn often by her own mother.

"The number of times we left you and Brennus with her...gods, its unbearable to think about."

Grannus pulled a handkerchief from somewhere inside his cloak and handed it to his wife. Aurelia reached out a comforting hand.

"But you didn't know."

"Looking back, it's hard to think that there weren't signs." Her head tilted. "Enya pulling Louarn from dinner early, claiming he had some matter to attend. Drest not being allowed out of his chamber some days." She blew her nose. "What if we could have done something?"

The queen's gaze had grown wide, wild even, as she seemed to search the meadow for answers. After another choked cry, Dechtire clutched the hem of her tunic as she held Grannus's gaze. "I let Aurelia go with Enya. During the invasion, I let that woman take our daughter." Tears fell from her eyes, and Jastyn was surprised as sympathy flared in her mind.

Aurelia started to speak. "Mother—"

The queen kept her focus on Grannus as if unable to look at her daughter. "What if we could have stopped all of this? What if we could have saved him?" More tears fell, and Dechtire leaned, exhausted, into the king.

Jastyn didn't have to ask to know who she meant. It was as clear as the pain in Aurelia's face. Jastyn considered saying something. A year ago, she wouldn't have had much sympathy for the agony the Diarmaids were clearly in. Now, she felt her own heart aching for what they'd lost.

"You can't think about that," she said. The queen's eyes flew to her, surprised. "I know it's easier to dwell on the way things went wrong. Trust me." She glanced at her sister. "But we have to at least try to look ahead, try to keep moving forward." She felt Aurelia's eyes on her. "Even if it feels like the hardest thing in the world. We have to try."

Still sniffling, Dechtire exchanged looks with Grannus. Right as Aurelia's hand came to rest on Jastyn's knee, a series of distant shouts echoed beyond the trees.

"The royal guard." Rigo was already on his feet.

"The protection spell," Grannus said, one arm around Dechtire. "We're safe here."

Standing, Jastyn listened to the oncoming beat of footsteps. "Yes, but we should spread out. At least until they move on."

The others stood. Aurelia put out the fire as Jastyn knelt, gently shaking Alanna awake. Her sister muttered, rubbing her eyes. "We need to move, Alanna. Just for a little while."

Aurelia was at her side, smoke from the fire curling skyward behind her. "Jastyn—"

"Stay with your parents on the north end." At Aurelia's blank stare, she smiled and pointed. "Over there on the other side of Eegit's hut. Stay low and keep quiet."

Nodding, Aurelia kissed her cheek, then led her parents to the far side of the meadow. The guards' voices were closer now. Jastyn helped her sister stand and ignored the knowing smile she wore. "Rigo," she called, "help us."

Together, they hurried to a tall patch of grass hosting bright purple flowers.

"What do we do?" Alanna asked in a frightened whisper.

Jastyn clutched her hand. "The protection spell will hide us, so for now, we stay here. And we wait."

CHAPTER EIGHTEEN

Once they huddled together behind Eegit's hut, Aurelia's mother waved, uttering a quick spell that encased them in a soft magenta shell.

Startled, Aurelia gaped. "*Another* protection spell? You know Eegit's cast one for us already. The meadow is secure."

"It's merely a precaution, darling."

In a huff, Aurelia crossed her arms. "But only for those you deem worthy of helping."

"I am helping, sweetheart."

Glaring, she replied, "You're only helping Alanna."

Her mother's pointed look told Aurelia to be careful. But she wasn't an obliging, well-mannered little girl anymore. Too much had changed. She had changed.

"Mother, you're acting ridiculously."

Her mother's brows shot up. Strands of hair flew over her face. She brushed them back, an intimidating glint in her eyes. Aurelia could feel her father ready to step between them.

"I'm acting ridiculously? Here I was thinking I was helping that poor girl."

"That's not what I mean, and you know it."

"Aurelia," her mother said, stooping at the sound of rustling brush several yards away. "Now is not the time to discuss this."

"There is no time, Mother. That's the point."

Her father said, "If I could just—"

"Not now, Father."

"Grannus, please."

With that, he waved a defeated hand and fell quiet.

Pouting, Aurelia said, "Father at least speaks to Jastyn. You hardly look at her, still. After everything she's done for us."

Her mother's voice was hard when she said, "She is an Odium."

"Why does that matter? Mother, there is nothing to fear from her. 'The bearer of any kingdom's end.' It's not Jastyn who is trying to tear apart Venostes."

Even in the dark, Aurelia could see the flush in her mother's cheeks. They'd had spats before, but this held a different kind of roiling tension beneath each word. Only now did Aurelia understand the meaning of fighting for what, or whom, she believed in.

"The laws were written for a reason, sweetheart."

Exasperated, Aurelia struggled to keep her voice low. "Please don't start with that again. The laws were written ages ago. Only incredibly conservative members of the court believe them. Half the kingdom is fae." She took a breath, remembering the night in the Wood when, after healing Jastyn, her mother had stared at her hands in disbelief upon learning who she was. "What are you so afraid of?"

Her mother's gaze was steady. They sat in silence, the only sound the thunderous pounding of her own heart. Finally, she said, "It is not easy, my love, to change the way things are."

Aurelia blinked. Was that it? Was that why her parents were so distant toward Jastyn? It wasn't that her mother and father *couldn't* act kindly toward her? Or that they couldn't bring about a new way of life.

It was because they simply weren't willing to try.

Unable to fathom this, Aurelia turned her cheek. She couldn't believe it. The rules, the stories, the fear, all of it concocted out of her family's unwillingness to stray from the familiar. Their lack of initiative was easier than taking action, their apathy a comforting hand that held their kingdom in a vise, an unrelenting grip.

When her mother placed a timid hand on her knee, Aurelia said hotly, "I love her, Mother. I love Jastyn. And if you are too busy clinging to your outdated thinking, I'll be the one to bring our kingdom into the light."

Stunned silence fell over them.

Voices echoed in the distant Wood. Aurelia felt as if she was spinning helplessly down a river, caught in the endless rush of water.

When the guardsmen's shouts grew faint, her mother spoke. "Aurelia, there can be no future for you and her."

Fuming, she faced her mother. "If we don't defeat the baroness, none of us have a future."

Her mother gripped her hands. "Darling, you are the future queen."

Unable to keep the indignance from her voice, Aurelia replied, "And as queen, I am free to love whom I choose." Her mother's face contorted as if trying to keep her composure as she and her father exchanged looks. "What, Mother? What are you not saying?"

Her mother glanced across the meadow to where Jastyn and the others waited. Finally, when her mother's eyes met hers, Aurelia was startled at the distress in them.

"Your father and I have only ever wanted to protect you." She continued quickly. "However, I am beginning to understand that no matter how much we want to or how hard we try, you are the one who governs your life now. The gods have a path for you, one only you can walk."

Her voice low, Aurelia replied, "I want to walk life's path with her, Mother."

Emotion brimmed in her mother's eyes. Her father leaned forward. "We want the life you lead to be safe, sweetheart." He glanced fretfully behind Aurelia. "Choosing her will bring endless obstacles. Targets will be placed upon your back."

"Like the ones you've placed on hers? And her mother's?" Her parents sighed, but she pressed on. "If we defeat Enya, we can fix everything. Jastyn won't have to live in fear."

"Darling, even if that happens, it will take years for people's minds to change about Odiums."

Aurelia leaned back on her heels, scrutinizing her parents in the dim, magenta spell light. Her father's face creased with worry; her mother's eyes were wide and pleading.

"You don't want Jastyn and I to be together because you're afraid of what people will say."

Her mother gripped her hands tightly. "We're afraid of what people might try to do...to you."

Aurelia let that sink in. She pictured herself when she was young with somebody always walking behind her. Roisin accompanying every moment of her day. Not allowed to leave the castle grounds until she was thirteen. Begging to join her mother's trips to the village. Knowing little about the world despite having everything at her fingertips.

Now, Aurelia had finally found someone she wanted. Yet her parents were telling her it was the one thing she couldn't have.

"That's not fair," she finally said, her face hot with frustration.

"Sweetheart, I know it's difficult."

"No." She faced her parents, looking between them. "Jastyn has fought her entire life. She's fought for her mother, fought for her sister. She's fought to simply live. You're afraid I will have to do that, too, if I tie my life to hers?" Their silence fueled her words. "Well, this may surprise you both, but contrary to your efforts, I am not afraid to fight." She gestured toward the opposite end of the meadow. "She is who I want. I will fight to be with her. I'll fight for her. I don't care how difficult it is. She's worth it."

The quiet night air trilled with energy. It filled the sky and the spaces between her parents' silent figures. Even her fingertips prickled with whispers of spell-fire. She'd never felt anything quite like this. A wonderful new sense of certainty settled in her chest, nestling between her lungs and wrapping its warm hands around her heart.

When she met her mother's gaze, Aurelia was taken aback at the reflection in her eyes. She saw herself, and it was like a cloak she'd been wearing for years fell from her shoulders, exposing a woman surer of herself than she'd ever been before.

Rigo appeared from out of the shadows.

"Your Majesties, it is safe to reconvene. The guards have moved on."

Aurelia stood. With her chin high, she walked toward the other side of the meadow to find Jastyn.

CHAPTER NINETEEN

Jastyn was conflicted. Part of her was thrilled about finally letting go of her reticence and allowing herself to feel love for Aurelia without hesitation. Yet she felt guilty for doing so because there was still so much to worry about.

Her sister's condition was worsening. When Alanna wasn't asleep, she struggled to go an hour without succumbing to a coughing fit. Her appetite was nonexistent. Once, before their midday trip to the brook to wash their hands and faces, Jastyn caught her sister scrubbing a blotch of blood from her chin after coughing. The queen remained diligent in her work on the cure, but Jastyn couldn't help worrying if they'd get it made in time. On top of that, she had no idea what sort of condition her mother and Elisedd were in. She hoped they were all right. Her mother was strong, but how long before even her will began to falter?

With all of this bouncing around like a tree-dweller in springtime in her mind, Jastyn struggled to let her unbridled happiness with Aurelia shine. And Aurelia seemed distant, angry even, at her parents. Jastyn knew their relationship was complicated, but since last night, she'd noticed Aurelia giving the queen and king a particularly cold shoulder.

Rigo, on the other hand, was a welcoming presence. His calm demeanor was like the steady flow of the river. It kept their group in a functioning, even mildly optimistic state. He gathered fruit when Jastyn slept during the day after a fitful night spent worrying about Alanna or battling visions of the Dark Fae. He helped Aurelia keep a second fire going for warmth so the queen could focus on the cure. Once, Jastyn had come back from the brook after filling their flasks to find him singing to Alanna, his melodious voice making her sister smile as she drifted to sleep.

"I must say, Rigo is my most surprising friend." Aurelia leaned down to rearrange a log next to Jastyn. Glancing sideways, Jastyn let her eyes linger on the exposure of skin at the loose part of her collar. Forcing her eyes back on the fire, Jastyn cleared her throat.

"I would have to agree." She watched Rigo, bow in hand, walk the perimeter of Eegit's meadow, scanning the trees. She recalled her first encounter with him and the sense of confusion when, in the leprechaun lodging, he'd attacked Drest, then his companion, allowing them time to escape.

"We've all come a long way since that public house." When Jastyn glanced at Aurelia, their gazes met, soft and warm. The look in Aurelia's eyes made her forget about the constant chill from the cool wind. When Aurelia turned toward her parents, Dechtire steadily churning the contents of a cauldron, her face fell. "Well, maybe not all of us."

Jastyn tugged her down to sit beside her. "Your parents are worried. A lot has changed." She hesitated before adding, "They lost their son. I think they're doing what they think is right to keep from losing you, too."

Aurelia frowned, focusing on a bundle of berries she'd fetched. "I'm not afraid to stand up to Enya. And I'm certainly not afraid of Drest."

Jastyn couldn't help but smile at her tenacity. Bumping her shoulder as she tossed a berry into her mouth, she said, "I know. I think they know that, too, which is what scares them."

With a sigh, Aurelia leaned into her. "Your mother let you go. She let you leave to find the cure. She didn't keep you from traveling as far as you needed to." She tossed a berry in the direction of her mother. "She wouldn't let me visit the shore...less than a mile from the castle. I'm so tired of living under their thumb."

Knowing she needed to tread lightly, Jastyn spoke slowly. "Aurelia, I never told you what happened in the caves."

Aurelia sat up to face her, the berries seemingly forgotten.

"When I was in there, the leprechauns presented several visions. At least, I think they were visions, some felt frighteningly real." She swallowed, remembering the horrible image of Sif with an arrow in her chest. Then the prince, his pale skin as lifeless as his eyes. Aurelia took her hand as she continued. "I saw my mother in the caves. She was the final conjuring. I didn't understand at first why she was there."

Aurelia was listening carefully, one knee bouncing like she was eager to speak.

"Eventually, I realized what was going on. I realized the Red One's meaning." Shuddering, Jastyn could practically feel her mother's hands cup her face to show her all the secrets she had kept. Secrets she'd guarded to keep Jastyn safe, to give her a chance at a life.

Jastyn didn't know she was crying until Aurelia wiped a tear from her cheek. "Forgiving my mother gave me the cure, but it did more than that. It helped me see everything that had happened in my life through my mother's eyes." Placing her hand atop Aurelia's, Jastyn kept her gaze on their interlocked fingers. "Part of me will never fully understand what she sacrificed. But she sacrificed for me and for Alanna because she loves us. I can disagree with the way she did things, but I can at least respect her point of view because it came from a place of love."

Aurelia stared, her eyes glistening. When she only smiled, Jastyn asked, "What?"

Aurelia grinned. "I think that's the most I've ever heard you speak at one time."

Jastyn laughed, bringing Aurelia's hands up to kiss her knuckles. Grannus, she noticed, watched them from the corner of his eye. "Your parents love you, Aurelia."

She sighed dramatically. "I know." Then she shook out her shoulders. "Even so, you're saying I don't have to agree with them? Because I most certainly do not."

"I'm saying...give them time."

Grumbling, Aurelia nuzzled into Jastyn's neck, who blushed when her lips found skin.

"Aurelia." She squirmed, acutely aware of the king and queen only ten paces away.

After a protesting groan, Aurelia sat up. "Fine. You win." She kissed Jastyn's cheek. "For now."

The following night, Jastyn paced around the meadow. She was restless and growing increasingly anxious the more time passed. A familiar sense of dread had uprooted the happiness she'd felt earlier. The lack of guard activity and absolutely no appearance of the Dark

Fae seemed like a bad sign, a sign that something terrible was lying in wait.

She was so wound up that she practically leapt out of her boots when a hand touched her arm. She was doubly surprised to find the queen standing next to her, watching her expectantly as she said, "It's time for your contribution."

"I'm sorry?" She looked past Dechtire. The sun had set, the gray day they'd spent in isolation having fallen into a darker night. Rain had left the surrounding tree limbs heavy and dripping, but now the clouds thinned overhead. She blinked, replaying the words. "My contribution?"

"Yes, to your sister's cure."

Behind the queen, Alanna slept next to Rigo, who sat cross-legged and listened intently to a rather animated story Aurelia was telling. The king, no doubt at his wife's request, stoked the fire beneath the cauldron.

Still confused, Jastyn asked, "What do you mean? I gave you all the ingredients. Yesterday you said you were certain the cure was coming along fine." Panic spiked in her chest. Jastyn hadn't noticed the narrow strip of parchment in the queen's hand, which she raised and read from.

"'Combine ingredients with one cauldron of water on the first new moon of the autumnal equinox.'" She glanced up. "That's tonight. 'Add blood, mixed.'" She lowered the parchment, meeting Jastyn's gaze pointedly.

Finally, Jastyn understood. "It calls for blood that is both human and fae. Mixed blood. Blood from someone like me." The queen stood unmoving, watching her. Jastyn felt suddenly small, like a child being asked to do a task they'd never imagined having to complete. Jastyn shifted in a vain attempt to bring herself closer to Dechtire's height. "Grannus told you who my father is."

The queen's eyes roved her face like she was counting the dirt-smudged freckles or perhaps simply searching for traces of Jastyn's selkie father in her features. "Did you know?"

The queen's question caught her off guard. "Did I know who my father was, or did I know he was a fae?" Crossing her arms, Jastyn's gaze fell to her boots. "My mother told me he was fae right before I joined the search party for Aurelia. It wasn't until we made it to the western shore that I had any idea about the selkies." She swiped a hand down her braid, cutting her gaze at the queen. Surprised at how easy it was to tell Dechtire all of this, she added, "Tove, my father, knew about me. But I had no idea until a few weeks ago."

Dechtire's eyes crinkled at their edges. What was that in them... sympathy? Jastyn wasn't sure.

After a moment, the queen merely nodded, gesturing to the fire. "Shall we?"

Silently, Jastyn followed her. For a time, Dechtire stood with her hands on her hips, scrutinizing their surroundings.

"What are you looking for, darling?" asked Grannus.

"We need something sharp."

Aurelia and Rigo, who had halted their conversation to watch, frowned. At their inquisitive looks, Jastyn said, "I need to add my blood to the cure."

"What?" Aurelia scurried to her feet, then bent apologetically as Jastyn held a finger to her lips, pointing at Alanna sleeping. Aurelia lowered her voice, but it remained tight with worry. "Mother," she said, mirroring the queen's stance, "what is she talking about?"

Dechtire looked tired but patiently reread the recipe. Aurelia's brow creased, then her eyes lit with recognition. "Oh."

"It's okay," Jastyn assured her. "It's the least I can do to help Alanna."

Aurelia caught one of her hands, squeezing it. "You've already done so much."

Jastyn smiled but remembered Aurelia's parents and was grateful when Rigo stepped forward.

"Here." He unsheathed an arrow from the quiver propped against a log. "You may use this."

Both Dechtire and Grannus froze. A flash of something lit the queen's gaze, her face falling. Even Aurelia's breath caught, and for a moment, Jastyn struggled to follow. She had almost forgotten it was an elf's arrow that had caused the prince's death. All three pairs of Diarmaid eyes fixed on the arrowhead. Jastyn looked at Rigo, who also seemed to realize what was happening.

"Thank you," Jastyn told him, taking the arrow carefully, pulling it close and away from the frightened looks across from her.

Wordlessly, she stepped to the cauldron, one hand out over the simmering liquid. The golden yellow surface popped sporadically, the bursting of each bubble emitting the scent of fresh flowers. Jastyn placed the tip of the arrowhead against the pad of her left thumb. Taking a deep breath, she dug the sharp point in deeper.

A small gasp drew Jastyn's gaze to Aurelia. Her eyes were on Jastyn's thumb where a small pool of blood appeared. Aurelia seemed lost in a memory as Jastyn turned her hand over. They all watched as blood trickled into the liquid, small hisses of steam unfurling with each droplet.

After the fifth drop, Jastyn looked up. Dechtire nodded, and Jastyn retracted her hand. Aurelia, seemingly recovered from whatever had occupied her mind, already had a strip of cloth ready and began bandaging Jastyn's thumb.

Rigo took back his arrow and asked, "What's next?"

The queen stirred the cauldron's contents. "It settles for a day. Then the cure will be ready."

On her pallet of leaves, Alanna stirred. Jastyn was elated at the queen's words, but her bliss was cut short when footsteps stormed through the brush outside the meadow. In one motion, Rigo stood between Alanna and the meadow's border, the arrow now nocked in his bow. Jastyn moved past him, as did Aurelia. When Roisin stumbled from between two trees, Aurelia rushed through the protection spell and dragged her maiden within its confines.

"Roisin, it's nightfall, what are you doing out of the castle?"

Her face was red as the apple Jastyn had eaten for dinner. She stood with one hand clutching her midsection, her robust chest heaving. "Had to come, m'lady." She took two deep breaths. "Announcement made…baroness told the court…"

The king and queen joined them. Despite struggling to breathe, Roisin gave them each a bow. Jastyn's patience waned with each huff. She was glad Aurelia seemed to sense this when she asked, "Roisin, what did you hear, what news?"

After another gulp of air, Roisin's gaze found Jastyn, who went cold at the horror she saw staring back at her. "The baroness tried and found your parents guilty of conspiring against the royal family. Branna and Elisedd are to be executed at dawn in three days' time."

CHAPTER TWENTY

A urelia reached for Jastyn's hand. She didn't need to ask if Jastyn wanted to leave, run to the castle to help her mother and Elisedd. So Aurelia clutched tightly to her as they stood in the dimly lit meadow and listened to Roisin.

"It was terrible, Your Majesties. They were brought to the main hall and had to stand before Baroness Enya. Gods, if you could've seen it." She trembled, shaking her head. "She didn't even give 'em a chance to speak, just named their crimes and sentenced them right there." Her voice quivered as she glanced fearfully around.

"Surely the court tried to do something, tried to intervene?" Her father's question was met with a sad snivel.

"'Fraid not, Your Highness. I could tell they wanted to say somethin', the court I mean. Some of 'em looked angry."

Her mother asked quietly, "But no one did?"

Aurelia gave her mother a look to reinforce her words. "They're scared. Too scared to stand up to her."

Roisin continued, "When the baroness reminded the court of your mother's past," she said, turning to Jastyn, "there wasn't anything anyone could say."

Jastyn's face was contorted with rage, her lips set in a thin line, and her jaw tense. She threw a look at Aurelia's mother, who, to her credit, seemed appalled at Roisin's news.

"I'm sorry." Roisin held Jastyn's gaze, wiping frightened tears from her cheeks.

"How did you leave the castle?" Aurelia asked, stepping closer to Jastyn and wrapping one arm around her waist, added security to keep her in place.

"Coran, m'lady. He's been watching the guards, learning when they alternate posts. He snuck into the stables and met me there."

Jastyn spoke, her voice unnervingly calm. "If you snuck out, that means you can sneak back in. You can help me sneak in to see them."

Roisin stammered as Aurelia replied, "No. Absolutely not."

"Aurelia, they need my help."

"It's too dangerous."

Jastyn held her gaze, then pulled her hand away. "I can't stay here and do nothing."

Aurelia didn't know what to say. She agreed with Jastyn and knew she didn't like to wait. But things were happening too fast. She still couldn't fathom the baroness making such a proclamation. Were Jastyn's parents really such a threat? Or was she simply trying to prove a point, that a new time was dawning over their kingdom? And no one would stand in her way on her quest to true power.

They all stood in silence. Roisin took a drink Rigo offered. Aurelia was still trying to think about what to say when a small voice said, "Jastyn?" Alanna stood near the fire. Aurelia tried not to stare at her sunken eyes, her brittle figure like a spirit clinging to this world, holding tight to life in the fabric of her sister's cloak around her shoulders. "What's going on?"

Aurelia and the others exchanged looks. Jastyn's eyes glistened before she took a slow, deep breath. The look on her face made Aurelia's chest feel like it was being constricted.

"Alanna." Jastyn stepped toward her but faltered as she glanced back, her gaze pleading. "Mother and Elisedd…"

Before Jastyn could say anything else, Aurelia's mother pushed past her, moving swiftly to Jastyn's sister. After a moment's hesitation, she wrapped a careful arm around Alanna. "Your parents are still in the dungeons, sweetheart. But they are alive. They're okay."

Alanna's brow crinkled. "But—"

Aurelia's father joined them, hurrying to pour a fresh cup of tea. "Roisin came to tell us they're still safe," he said, receiving a nod from Dechtire. Alanna seemed as startled by this sudden display of concern as Aurelia. At first, she didn't understand and even felt angry at the sight of her parents cajoling Jastyn's sister, lying to her about what they'd just learned. But as her mother led Alanna to a seat near the fire and her father handed her a cup of warm chamomile, she began to understand what Jastyn had been talking about before.

Aurelia's parents' instinct to protect their children, or any children, from the harsh realities of the world were something she couldn't fully comprehend. But those instincts were something that existed in order to keep a sense of safety. A sense of order. Alanna might have wanted to know the truth, and she might know it eventually. But adding another burden to her already difficult life wouldn't have been helpful. Not now.

Jastyn, meanwhile, looked blankly upon Aurelia's parents with her sister.

"Jastyn?" Aurelia placed a hand on her arm.

For several moments, Jastyn continued to watch them. Aurelia scrutinized her face, watching it shift from great sadness to hardened determination. Afraid at what Jastyn was planning to do, she reached out. No words came to her, though. She felt overwhelmed with love and fear, both sticking like tree sap in her mouth, running her throat and words dry.

"I need to go." Jastyn started to take a step, but Aurelia shot out her hands, grabbing Jastyn's arms.

"Jastyn, wait." She swallowed, trying to find the right thing to say. "I know this is terrible, but…" She glanced at her parents. "The cure is nearly ready. Your sister's health is on the brink of revitalization. That's what you've always wanted." Pleadingly, Aurelia slid her hands to Jastyn's, searching her eyes for a sign that she wouldn't be rash, that she wouldn't run.

Jastyn's gaze fell, and she ran her thumbs gently over Aurelia's knuckles. "I need to walk, Aurelia. Just for a little while. I need to think." When she looked up, Aurelia saw the truth shining among her tears. "I promise I won't do anything without telling you first."

Aurelia tugged her into a hug. "I love you so much. We'll get through this, I promise."

Both of them sniffling, Jastyn gave Aurelia's hand a quick kiss before she said, "I'll be back soon," and stepped through their protection spell and disappeared into the Wood.

Taking a moment to collect herself, Aurelia joined Roisin and Rigo near the fire where Alanna was finishing the last of her tea and already looked half-asleep again. Aurelia was surprised to see her mother remove her cloak, then lay it atop the pile of leaves Jastyn's sister had slept on. Catching her mother's eye, Aurelia raised her brow in acknowledgment but said nothing.

"I'm not sure how much more of this I can take, m'lady," Roisin whispered when Aurelia sat next to her. "My head aches each moment of the day, and my heart feels too big with fright each time the baroness so much as looks at me."

"Does she suspect anything?" Aurelia asked.

Roisin shrugged. "Hard to say, m'lady. She and Drest keep behind closed doors mostly, only comin' out for meals or proclamations, like the one I told you about," she added, lowering her voice even more with a subtle nod to Alanna, who was being tucked in by Aurelia's father. "Everything's a rotten mess."

Once it appeared Alanna was asleep, Aurelia's parents joined them, her mother giving another stir to the cure before sitting down.

"Something I've been wondering," her mother said, adjusting her tunic at the wrists, "Enya told the court I died, correct?"

Nodding, Roisin replied, "Yes. And…" She hesitated, fidgeting with the end of her belt. "She's also claimed a new tragedy about you." She turned to Aurelia.

"Me? What has she said?"

Roisin had a guilty look on her face. "The baroness said the queen died on the journey to find you. But you…" Her voice trailed off.

"What, Roisin? What did she say happened to me?"

"She said you were killed…by Jastyn."

Aurelia felt as if she'd been kicked by a horse. She clutched her stomach.

"It's horrible, I know, m'lady."

Aurelia's fists balled atop her thighs. She'd felt a lot of things toward the baroness over the years, but thinking about her now made Aurelia want to do things she wasn't sure she was actually capable of. She shook with fury and tried to calm herself. Mostly, she was grateful Jastyn wasn't present to hear this.

Her father pulled Aurelia's focus back. "What news of me?"

Frowning, Roisin said, "I don't think she's mentioned you, Your Majesty. So I presume you're still alive in their eyes." She shook her head. "Gods, this makes me dizzy."

Aurelia stared across the fire at her mother. She seemed to be contemplating something, her face turned down in thought. Aurelia could see the reflection of the fire dancing against her blue eyes.

"There's a part of all this I don't understand." Her mother's gaze lifted, finding Aurelia's. "If Drest is the one who took you after Brennus's Remembrance, why did he leave you unharmed? Why did he spare you for so long?"

Holding her arms across her chest, Aurelia shook her head. "I remember him saying to the elves the first night that I was 'of no use dead.'" She glanced at Rigo.

"That is true. His only direction was to keep guard over you while we traveled. To make sure you were not harmed."

"Where was he taking me?" Aurelia asked. She'd worked so hard to escape, she never considered what his end goal was in kidnapping her.

"We were to meet my queen. She would handle things once you were in her custody. I imagined she would do the dirty work that would aid in their twisted tales regarding your family's demise."

Aurelia swallowed, feeling faint at the thought of being handed over to the elf queen, whose stories were filled with terrifying feats of powerful magic.

"Well, I'm certainly glad it didn't come to that," she said, tossing a tight smile to Rigo. Then, feeling her parents' attention on her, Aurelia fidgeted. Her knee throbbed as if her body, like her mind, was reliving the awful memories of her kidnapping. "Each time he caught up to us, he always had an offer for me." She licked her lips, recalling Drest's frantic, delusional rants.

"Like he wished to make a deal, m'lady?"

"He asked me to join him." She forced herself to look up and wasn't surprised to find wide-eyed expressions from her parents.

Her father leaned forward. "He *what*?"

"He was mad, completely unhinged but"—she took a breath—"I think perhaps, in his own demented manner, he thought he was showing me kindness."

Her parents' immediate objections barraged her ears. Roisin placed a hand on her back, and Aurelia defensively threw up her hands. "I know he's mad," she said. "He and Enya are some of the worst things to ever happen to Venostes." She inhaled slowly. "But I think he wanted to see if I would side with him because to him, that was merciful."

Aurelia knew the thoughts that filled her parents' minds. She had them, too. How could it be possible for Drest to care about anything, let alone her? It couldn't be, not after what he'd done to Brennus. Mercy wasn't the right word. No, like his mother, Drest only wanted to own the kingdom and everyone in it, including her. He wanted to conquer her, have her be the one to bend the kingdom to his will and shape it in his terrible image.

"Perhaps we could use this." Her mother's voice lifted, pulling Aurelia from her thoughts. "Maybe we can convince him that you are on his side just long enough to distract him and get to Enya."

Aurelia blinked. Her father sat up straighter. "Dechtire, what are you saying? You want to throw Aurelia at that madman?" She could hear the disbelief in his voice, and she had to agree that this was a complete uprooting of everything her mother had said thus far.

Seeming to realize this, her mother sighed, her head dropping into her palm. "I don't know, Grannus. I'm only thinking aloud."

Her mind racing, Aurelia said timidly, "Why don't we simply walk up to the castle? Request an audience?" She laughed. "Not that we should need permission to enter our own home."

"Darling," her mother said, "we're dead, remember? What do you think will happen if we suddenly appear in the village?"

"Then everyone will know we're alive," Aurelia replied. "Everyone will know the baroness is lying."

"Or they'll think we're spirits from the Otherworld."

"Mother, you don't think—"

"M'lady." Roisin said, wincing at interrupting. "If I may, the kingdom is in an unstable place. Nobody knows what to think. If you show up out of nowhere…" Her face pinched in concern. "It'd be even more chaotic than things already are. People would be scared. I fear they'd act out."

Frustrated, Aurelia propped her chin in her hand. "Then what do we do? How do we stop Enya from taking over completely?"

"If we can get close and there's enough of us, there are spells to bind her wind powers." Her mother spoke to the fire, lost in thought.

"There are?" Aurelia thought back to that day on the beach. The baroness had shocked them with her magical strength. If her own mother, the strongest woman Aurelia knew aside from Jastyn, couldn't handle Enya, Aurelia wasn't sure who could.

"Yes." Her mother and father exchanged glances. "They're difficult to conjure and maintain, as are any binding spells, but it is possible. She'd need to be isolated. Combined with Drest, I fear they are too powerful."

"How do Your Majesties propose we deal with the Dark Fae?" Rigo's question drew their collective gaze.

"Last time I saw Drest, he said the Dark Fae is under his and Enya's control." Aurelia pulled her cloak tight against the wind. "Perhaps if we defeat them, we can neutralize the Dark Fae, banish him, even send him to the Otherworld for good."

When she glanced up, her mother was watching her, a small smile in her lips.

"What?"

"That was spoken like a true queen."

Aurelia bit her cheek to hide her surprise. Quickly though, the pleasant feeling her mother's comment gave her brought another wave of emotion: regret. Regret that Brennus wasn't a part of this. She smiled sadly. Her brother would have been eager to take action, to go and face the baroness head on. He was like Jastyn that way.

For a moment, Aurelia stared at the conjured image of Brennus standing beside their fire. His color was bright, like the hazel in his eyes. He had one hand on the hilt of his sword, the other rubbing his chin thoughtfully.

Just like that, the image vanished. A sharp crackle from the fire brought Aurelia back to the present. A present vacant of her brother's life. Like it had many times since his death, a deep, agonizing sense of anger filled her chest.

But now was not the time to give in to that anger, nor was it time to cry. She didn't have time to mourn Brennus. There was too much at stake.

"Once the cure is ready, we can set our sights on getting to Enya."

Glancing toward the dark line of trees outside Eegit's meadow, Aurelia frowned. "What about Jastyn's parents?"

"I can help her." Roisin's voice wavered, but Aurelia saw a new determination in her gaze. "Jastyn was right before. I can sneak her in to the castle. At least to see her parents before…"

Simultaneously, their gazes fell to Alanna, fast asleep on her bed of leaves atop the queen's cloak.

"Her cure will be finished in another day's time." Her mother's voice was even, calm, and Aurelia clung to it as if to a boulder along a raging river's edge as her thoughts left her floundering. "Then we'll take back our kingdom."

CHAPTER TWENTY-ONE

Jastyn ran her fingers along the damp tree bark. She closed her eyes and breathed deep, relishing the smell of saturated moss and boysenberries heavy with moisture. The scent of upturned earth beneath her feet made her think of Aurelia, the faint fragrance of tulips on her skin a memory so prominent she could conjure it at a moment's notice.

Her saol bobbed one step ahead, waiting patiently as she leaned against a tall birch tree. Outside of Eegit's meadow, the realm seemed too dark, a new moon shrouding Venostes in a black veil that made it impossible to see more than ten paces ahead. This darkness left her feeling like it was impossible to know what the coming day might bring.

But she always felt ready for the unknown. She was built for difficult times. They seemed inescapable. Now, a new obstacle stood before her. How was she going to keep her mother and Elisedd from execution?

Undoing the bandage around her thumb, she found the wound already closed. She smiled at the spell Aurelia must have used when dressing the wound. A red patch of new skin had grown. Tucking the cloth into her tunic pocket, she glanced at the branches dripping with the day's rain. It was ironic that now she had sided with the Diarmaids, something like this was happening to her family. She could beg the queen and king to pardon her parents, and they might. Except they weren't the ones in charge anymore.

The kingdom had been overrun by evil. Enya, Drest, and their grandfather. He would always be the Dark Fae to Jastyn, but knowing what she did now gave her hope that he could be defeated.

A wolf's howl pierced the sky to the north. Peering through the trees, she half expected to see Eegit standing nearby, bartering with a gnome over a handful of quartz. Jastyn wondered where she was now. She had mentioned needing to see someone about…what was it…some minerals? Jastyn could only guess where she was and wasn't entirely surprised by Eegit's lack of interest in the kingdom's upheaval. Eegit was a master of survival, something she'd achieved by keeping to herself. Still, Jastyn wouldn't mind if she popped up now to share in the tired state.

"Chin up, child," Jastyn could hear Eegit say. "Did you not get what you wanted? The cure is nearly ready."

And she would be right, Jastyn mused, pushing herself off the tree. Her sister's cure was almost done. Soon, Alanna would be healthy and able to lead the life she deserved. Then Jastyn could focus on helping her mother and Elisedd.

Upon returning to the meadow, Jastyn found her sister asleep. She glanced twice at the fine, deep blue material Alanna slept on, the queen's cloak. Dechtire, now only in her tunic and riding pants, seemed to have fallen asleep sitting up, leaning against a dozing Grannus before the simmering cauldron.

Nodding to Rigo, who stood watch on the opposite side, Jastyn vanquished her saol as she rounded the logs where Aurelia and Roisin sat deep in conversation.

"What did I miss?" she asked.

"You're back." Aurelia smiled up at her, the glint from the firelight reflecting in her clear gaze.

"Don't sound so surprised, Princess." Jastyn smirked and sat, thrilled as Aurelia placed a hand on her thigh when she spoke.

"We were discussing the plan to infiltrate the castle."

Roisin's wavy locks seemed as frazzled as her expression when she said, "Yes. We've determined that after I speak with Coran, you'll meet us in the stables. From there, I'll help you to the dungeons to see your family."

Jastyn stared, processing the words. Then she turned to Aurelia. "You're letting me go?"

"Never." She smiled, squeezing Jastyn's leg. "But you should be able to see your mother again." Jastyn was grateful she didn't add, "before her execution," to that sentence. Though the look in her eye told Jastyn she understood Jastyn wasn't going to give up without a fight.

"Are you coming with us?" Jastyn asked after a moment.

Aurelia shook her head. "I'm afraid not. Though I'd love nothing more, but as much as I hate to admit it, my parents are right that it's too dangerous if one of us simply appears in the castle. It would be chaos if the princess who's presumed dead walked up to the guards and asked to be escorted inside." She gestured to the brewing cure. "Besides, I can watch Alanna." She smiled, brushing a few stands of hair from her forehead. Jastyn caught the look in her eyes and knew what she was thinking. Aurelia was aware of Jastyn's continued distrust toward her parents. Yes, the queen was helping. Yes, the king spoke to her like a person now. Still, Dechtire was distant, and something in her curt replies and unreadable gaze made Jastyn wary.

Smiling back, Jastyn was grateful for Aurelia's willingness to keep an eye on her sister. She was the singular Diarmaid Jastyn could depend on.

Roisin seemed to sense the unspoken words between them and pushed back in her seat as if to give them space. Jastyn stared into Aurelia's eyes. She was certain they were both picturing the day they'd met: standing opposite each other in the stables, uncertainty and intrigue swirling around them in the air.

"Go help your family," Aurelia said, her voice thick with emotion. "Then come back to me."

"I won't let anything happen to her, m'lady," Roisin said, prompting laughter from them both. "I'm tougher than I look, thank you," she added behind a fake pout.

"I believe that," Jastyn said. "Coran wouldn't like you so much if you weren't." At this, Roisin blushed. "When do we go?"

Aurelia scooted closer, one arm resting protectively behind her. "Tomorrow night," she explained. "That should give you and Coran time to prepare, right?"

Roisin nodded. "I still need to tend to the other ladies of the court during the day. Plus, I should make sure the baroness doesn't suspect anything. Once the sun starts to set, I'll be able to leave." She yawned, covering her mouth to stifle it. "Apologies, m'lady."

"You've a right to be tired," Jastyn told her. "It's the middle of the night."

"Maybe I'll lie down, just for a minute." Roisin was already on the ground, leaning against the log, her head lolling atop her chest.

"Of course, Roisin," Aurelia said. "Rest until dawn. It will be safer to travel then."

Roisin muttered a response. Jastyn smiled. She hadn't slept well in the last week; too many thoughts occupied her mind despite how fatigue plagued her. However, catching the look in Aurelia's eye now made Jastyn feel wide awake and suddenly nervous. Aurelia's fingers danced along the small of her back, around her waist.

Her throat dry, Jastyn said, "So…"

Aurelia gave half a smile. "Everyone seems to be asleep."

"Save for Rigo."

"He never sleeps."

"No. He doesn't."

They held one another's gaze. Aurelia bit her lip, then said, "I noticed a lovely spot near the brook the other day." Her pulse quickening, Jastyn could only nod. "I also noticed our flasks need refilling."

Now Jastyn's body raced with heat that poured over her as if she'd stepped out from a shadow into the sun. With another look around, Jastyn stood, trying to keep her voice even. She picked up a flask and didn't care that it was nearly full. She hesitated. "The guards…"

"Are focusing their efforts to the north, according to Roisin."

Jastyn held out her hand. "Are you sure?"

Aurelia smiled. "I've never been more certain." She took Jastyn's hand, and they slipped into the night.

Heading to the brook, Jastyn could almost feel Aurelia's saol trilling against her own fingertips, aching to be closer. The sensation left her hyperaware of not only Aurelia but the vibration of life that filled the surrounding Wood. Jastyn could hear the buzz of fairy nests; she could smell the berries, ripe and ready on their limbs; she could feel the cool night air beckoning them to a modest, smooth patch of grass partially hidden by the fallen trunk of a wide ash tree.

When Aurelia gently pulled Jastyn to kneel the same way she had on the selkie ship, Jastyn had to remind herself to breathe. She wanted nothing more than to lose herself forever in Aurelia, to clear her mind of everything except for this.

She swallowed her nerves as she ran a hand down Aurelia's arm. They'd done this before, so why did she feel like this was the first time?

Seeming to sense her trepidation, Aurelia caught her hand. She held Jastyn's fingers, placing two of them at the pulse point on her neck. Slowly, Aurelia pulled them down, leading Jastyn's fingers along her collarbone.

The feel of Aurelia's skin awoke all of Jastyn's senses as her eyes drifted lower.

Even in the dark, nearly pitch in the night's darkest hour, Jastyn could see Aurelia clearly. Touching her, being with her, helped everything make sense. Jastyn didn't want to break the silence she felt building as the space between them closed.

When Aurelia kissed her, Jastyn pulled her close. She ran her hands down Aurelia's back. When her fingers danced up and over Aurelia's shoulders, they faltered on the torn material of her tunic.

Jastyn pulled back, her gaze falling to the scarred skin beneath. Ever so gently, she pushed aside the material to find skin. Meeting Aurelia's gaze, she grazed the newer, raised flesh below her shoulder, careful not to press too hard.

Aurelia's breath caught. Jastyn gripped her waist and tugged it to press against her own. It was like a roar of spell-fire burst between them, heat boiling over until Jastyn could hardly stand it. They leaned in, foreheads pressed together.

"Jastyn." Aurelia's voice was barely a whisper. "Please."

They would have to go back. They would have to face everything about their terrifying reality. But here in this moment, in the in-between time, Jastyn let herself fall uninhibited into Aurelia.

CHAPTER TWENTY-TWO

The next day passed painfully slowly. Jastyn took solace in the memories of the night before, but she still fell prey to fits of agitation. It was like she could feel every miniscule movement of the sun across the sky. It teased her, making her conscious of the ceaseless simmer of her sister's cure on its way to completion, as well as the hours before she would leave to meet Roisin in the stables.

Jastyn knew she was trying the queen's patience, but she didn't care. She spent most of the day either staring at the cauldron or shooting Dechtire looks while trying to get Alanna to drink water between coughing fits. At one point, the queen, staring diligently into the cauldron, said, "Everything in due time," to no one in particular, though everyone knew it was Jastyn she spoke to.

"Be patient, Jastyn," her sister said meekly, her voice as broken as the skin on her chapped lips.

"You know that's not my strong suit."

Alanna held her gaze. "I'll be well in no time. Just wait."

Grimacing, Jastyn crouched, wiping sweat from her sister's pale forehead with a strip of cloth. Bouts of chills came and went, but they were taking a toll on Alanna. She hardly ate, and the shadows beneath her eyes were frighteningly prominent.

"Soon, Alanna. Soon this will all be over."

The Diarmaids kept a steady hum of conversation over the cauldron. Jastyn couldn't bring herself to join what she could tell was a planning session. She could hardly listen to a word, her mind was so preoccupied. She wanted to get to her mother. She wanted to free her, to tell her about Tove and the caves and have her near when Alanna's cure was complete.

When the moment came and the queen announced, "It's ready," Jastyn's head jerked up so fast from her overcooked tree-dweller that something in her neck cracked. Her gaze flew from Dechtire to Aurelia to her sister sitting beside her. Alanna's tired eyes lit up, a faint smile gracing her lips.

Tossing the rest of her dinner into the fire, Jastyn walked carefully to join the queen where she hovered over the cauldron she hadn't left for days. Peering over the top, Jastyn saw deep gold liquid shimmering under fading afternoon light. She could hardly believe it was there, her sister's cure, the one she'd crossed the realm for. The one she, Aurelia, and Coran had nearly died for was finally ready.

"It needs to cool and settle overnight. Then I'll prepare it for her to drink at dawn." Even Dechtire sounded excited, though Jastyn could see her working to keep an air of sensibility as she used one of Eegit's ladles to stir. The king stood.

"Wonderful," he said, hands triumphantly on his hips. "Truly wonderful."

Jastyn rolled her eyes but bit her lip to keep from grinning when she saw the sheer happiness on Aurelia's face. Then, not caring that the king and queen stood near, Jastyn pulled Aurelia into a fierce hug as tears blurred her vision. She caught sight of her sister, seated opposite them with Rigo. She looked content in a way Jastyn had never seen before.

"Dechtire." Jastyn stepped back, releasing Aurelia and meeting the queen's gaze. "Thank you, for helping Alanna."

A smile crinkled at the corner of Dechtire's eyes, which stayed focused on Alanna. It bothered Jastyn that the queen still struggled to even look her in the eye. After everything, she thought they'd attained some sort of respect for one another. Though Jastyn had to admit, she couldn't fully trust the queen. She figured it was because she was the one responsible for locking up her mother. Old disdain was hard to let go of. The queen's attitude toward her didn't help matters.

"We'll see how tomorrow goes." The queen swiped the hair from her face that had fallen loose from her braid. As the royal family fell into conversation, Jastyn crouched in front of Alanna.

"Try to eat something while I'm at the castle, okay? And don't forget to drink water." Jastyn rested her hands on her sister's knees.

Alanna sighed. "I know, Jastyn." She glanced past her, then asked, "Are you going to try to get them out?"

Smiling, Jastyn replied, "I really can't get anything past you, can I?"

"It's amusing you still try." Alanna giggled, but a disturbing rasping erupted from her chest, and she doubled over. The rag she grabbed to cover her mouth was splotched with blood when she pulled it away. Both stared at the glaring red in silence.

Eventually, Alanna took a shaky breath. "If you can't get them out," she said, her hands trembling as she wrung the rag, "tell Mother and Father that I love them."

"You tell them yourself." Her sister smiled, but it was grim. "I broke you all out before," Jastyn said, trying to keep her voice light. "I can do it again."

"Jastyn—"

"I know. Be careful."

Alanna faced her. "I was going to say, thank you. You've been the best sister I could have ever hoped for." Jastyn clenched her jaw to keep from crying. Alanna grabbed her hand. "I love you, Jastyn."

"I love you, too, Alanna."

They hugged tight until a gentle voice said, "Are you ready to go?"

Sitting back, Jastyn wiped her face and looked up at Rigo. "To go to the stables?" She blinked, confused. "Yes, but…are you coming with me?"

He nodded.

Jastyn glanced between him and Alanna. Rigo said, "Your sister will be safe here. The royal family will watch over her. Your excursion holds greater risk."

Raising one eyebrow, Jastyn said, "Aurelia asked you to go with me, didn't she?"

The skin around his gray eyes crinkled.

Jastyn shook her head. Alanna chuckled, leaning into her. "I'll stay close to the princess. Besides, we both know all I'm going to do is sleep." She yawned for effect.

Finally, Jastyn clutched her sister's hands. "I'll go get our parents. Then we'll be together when the cure is ready."

"Go safely, Jastyn."

After saying good-bye to Aurelia—who snuck a quick kiss on the cheek—Jastyn and Rigo headed out into the Wood toward the royal stables.

❖

With the sun beginning its descent at their backs, Aurelia and her parents sat around their small fire, lit with bright orange edges from her father's saol. Smoke unfurled lazily skyward. Roisin had mentioned that the guard parties were focusing on the northern portion of the Wood, seeming to think a fugitive Jastyn would keep close to fae territory. There hadn't been any guard activity close by in nearly three days.

Alanna had managed to eat a handful of gooseberries but nothing else. They'd made her a cup of chamomile, which Aurelia thought might have had an added herbal sedative due to how quickly Jastyn's sister fell into a deep slumber after finishing it.

Leaning forward, Aurelia listened to her family's plan. Rather, she watched her parents discuss the dangers of the only plan they'd been able to come up with.

"Grannus, you're certain you feel confident about this?"

"Yes, darling." He munched on a raspberry. "Enya probably still thinks I'm under her influence, at least to some extent."

"She'll know you broke free from it as soon as you were out of the castle."

"Regardless, Dechtire, I can do it. It won't be difficult to play the lowly brokenhearted monarch, desperate to return home." He paused. "For a while, I really did think I'd lost you." He faced Aurelia. "Both of you."

"Even if she thinks I'm dead, she'll know Aurelia is alive," her mother countered.

Her father nodded. "But I'm the one who carries Diarmaid blood in my veins. She'll want to use me. If she thinks she can manipulate me again, she won't be able to resist," he added with a glance toward Aurelia's mother.

Aurelia sighed, looking between them. It wasn't much, but her father requesting a meeting with the baroness to tell her he would take her side—accompanied by the single request that he be able to return to the castle—was incredibly risky. But if he could get close, her mother knew a spell to bring her to the Wood, where together, they would bind her powers and take her into custody.

"Remind me how this spell works," Aurelia said, wringing her hands. "Are you certain we need to split up?"

"I'm afraid so, sweetheart." Her mother shivered slightly as the sun dipped below the tree line, and her eyes cut to her cloak still draped over Alanna's sleeping figure. "The spell's original intention was to swiftly dismiss unwelcome individuals from the castle during a time when the guards were extremely vigilant."

"Prior to the Fae-Diarmaid Treaty," Aurelia added, her tone flat.

"Yes. Several Diarmaid monarchs ago. The guards could use the spell like a sort of entrapment mirror." She held her hands shoulder-width apart, palms facing one another. "One guard who had captured the suspected party within the castle"—she made a fist with her left hand—"could use this spell to send the individual through to the other side, where the second guard waited outside royal grounds." Her fist smacked into her open right palm, which closed around her left as if taking hold of the captive party. With her right hand now in a fist, she said, "From there, the guilty party was out of the castle and no longer a threat."

Aurelia snorted. "The *suspected* party, I think you mean." Her parents fidgeted, saying nothing. "What happened to them? What happened once the fae or the unwed women carrying children were sent to their fate?"

Aurelia could see her mother's mind racing, considering how much to share. Then with surprising remorse, she said, "Oftentimes, they were executed there and disposed of in the Wood."

Swallowing, Aurelia could only stare.

Her father cleared his throat. "Obviously, times have changed."

A stray tear fell, and Aurelia swiped it away. She was struck with the memory of Vreis's story: his father petrified for eternity in his elemental form, never able to embrace his son. "Well, if this spell is the best we've got, then we better not muddle it up."

"Muddle what up, exactly?"

They all turned. Ten paces away, Drest stood directly behind Jastyn's sister. "Oh dear," he said, his sickening smile widening. "Did I interrupt a family meeting?" His eyes were wide, an alarming glint reflecting from the flames. "There was once a time when I would have been welcome in a setting like this." He twirled his pointer finger, making a circle around their group. Then he placed a hand over his chest, pouting. "I'm rather offended."

Aurelia was on her feet, fingers itching with spell-fire. Her mother and father stepped in front of her as her gaze flickered from Drest to Alanna still asleep at his feet. Aurelia's chest tightened as Drest's eyes began to go clear.

"How did you get through the protection spell?" her father asked, one hand going for a sword that wasn't there.

"Two ways," Drest said. "That dim-witted hedgewitch left several holes. Additionally, Mother has taught me a lot in the last week. We actually sniffed you out days ago but thought we'd let you feel safe for a time. More fun that way."

Drest had his saol conjured over one open palm. He turned to glance around the meadow. "Aren't we missing a few?"

None of them answered. Aurelia felt frozen. She wasn't sure if she could get to Alanna quickly enough to shield her, move her, do anything to help. She had promised Jastyn she would watch her sister. Now Alanna was inches away from a madman.

"No matter. Who would like to go first?" His spell-fire grew, and he toyed with it between his hands.

Before she could blink, a bright orange saol shot from her father's hand. It flew at Drest, who deflected it, sending smoke and sparks sailing. Aurelia winced as the debris settled over Alanna. How was she still asleep?

A giant yellow orb erupted from Drest's hands. Dechtire threw up a protective shield, narrowly encasing the three of them to avoid being hit.

"That won't last forever, Dechtire." Drest stretched out his arms, new saols forming at each of his fingertips. "Perhaps I should start with the weakest one."

When he looked at Alanna, Aurelia shot forward. "No! Don't you touch her."

But Drest pulled back his arms, lifting them higher, building his spell-fire. Aurelia screamed when he let the flames go right at Alanna.

CHAPTER TWENTY-THREE

Night had completely fallen when Jastyn and Rigo arrived outside the royal stables. They'd had to wait for a company of guards to leave the castle first. After an agonizingly long time watching them complete a sweep of the surrounding pasture, Jastyn waited for the final guard to disappear into the opposite stretch of trees before venturing out, Rigo at her heels.

There was a rustling noise behind a stack of hay along the fence near the horse pens. Rigo nocked an arrow, but it was only Coran who leapt out, hands up protectively.

"Gods, Coran." Jastyn eyed the bits of straw in his hair and across his tunic. "How long have you been back there?"

He brushed himself off. "Since midday. Wasn't so bad," he added at their incredulous looks. "Roisin visited when she could. And my mum packed me some bread for dinner."

"Where is Roisin?" Jastyn asked, taking in the outdoor pens. A couple of pigs grunted on the far end of the low fence, and several chickens clucked nearby.

"She's on the other side of the door inside, waitin' for ya. How's the preparation for Alanna's cure?"

"It's done."

His eyes widened. "It is? Has she had it?"

Jastyn shook her head, keeping her eyes roving across the grounds for signs of any unwelcome guardsmen. "Not yet. It'll be ready to drink by dawn."

He inhaled deeply, as if he was letting the information sink into his chest. "You've done it, Jas. You've got your sister's cure."

She scooted dirt around with the toe of her boot. "Well, I can't take all the credit. Rigo helped, too."

When she looked up, Coran was grinning. He punched her arm playfully. Rigo shook his head in the way she'd come to know as his resigned inability to understand their sense of humor.

"Ya better get goin', Jas. The guards that left will be back in an hour to rotate out. Best not be here when they get back."

She nodded.

"I'll find higher ground to help Coran keep watch until then," Rigo said, his bow resting in one hand.

Coran walked Jastyn to the stable doors. They stood side by side for a moment, neither saying anything. When Jastyn reached to open the door, Coran said, "Be careful, Jas. I…" He faltered, one hand fidgeting with the hem of his tunic. "I don't know what I'd do without ya."

She opened her mouth to reply, but her usual snarky retorts fell short. She didn't know what to say. She didn't know how to tell Coran what he meant to her, how *she* was the one who would be lost without his friendship. Or at least the one who would have been thrown into the dungeons a dozen times without him. He gave her life consistency which she sometimes took for granted. How many friends would travel across the realm on an extremely dangerous journey, after all?

He smiled, and Jastyn wondered if he had heard all those thoughts. "Go on, then," he said, shoving her forward. "See ya on the other side."

"This way."

Jastyn followed Roisin into another stone corridor until they reached a passageway she remembered as the one leading to the dungeon. Peering around the wall, they found two guards posted before the door just like last time. In the stables, Roisin had explained that the baroness required members of the court to be present at all meals, which was why they'd had no trouble keeping hidden on their way here.

Roisin held up a hand, instructing Jastyn to wait. Then she fixed her dress, smoothed her hair, and ventured down the hall.

Jastyn strained to hear her. "Her Greatness the Baroness Enya requests the presence of all guards in the main hall immediately."

Within seconds, Jastyn heard the hurried tread of the guards' boots as they ran toward where she stood, then shot down the opposite corridor toward the heart of the castle.

When they were gone, Jastyn joined Roisin, who was already shoving open the door after utilizing the same spell Aurelia used previously. "That was easier than I thought it'd be."

Roisin smirked. "I've become a well-respected maiden now that I see to the daughters of the women who serve Enya. Besides," she added, "all of the guards are terrified of her."

"Wait," Jastyn said as they climbed down a set of stone steps. "No keys?"

Roisin faltered. "Oh. They'd have suspected something if I'd asked for them, wouldn't they?"

Grimacing, Jastyn said, "Probably." She shook her head. "It's fine. We'll think of something." The rotten stench of filth overwhelmed her, and she fought the urge to gag as Roisin led her past the first row of cells. When she spotted the familiar lone torch in its sconce, she ran to the cell opposite, relieved to see her mother and Elisedd inside.

"I'll wait here," Roisin called, but Jastyn focused on the cell door as she gripped the vertical bars. Elisedd slept in one corner atop a pile of straw. Her mother flew to meet her.

"Jastyn." Her hands were nearly frozen. She was pale, and dirt smudged her face and arms. Her voice, though, remained strong.

"I've come to get you out." Jastyn felt like water pressed against a dam, brimming with everything she wanted to tell her mother. Searching her eyes, she said, "The cure is ready. The queen was true to her word. At dawn she'll prepare it for Alanna." Tears ran down her cheeks. "Alanna will be well."

"Oh, my girl." Her mother's hands gripped hers. "Gods know how long we've dreamt of this time." She smiled, her own tears falling. Then she stepped back. "Elisedd will want to know."

"Wait." Jastyn reached out. "Before you tell him, there's something else I need to say."

Her mother's brows knit, and she moved closer. "What is it, love?"

"It's about my father."

The smallest flash of surprise lit her mother's gaze. Uncertainty seeped into her lungs, but Jastyn forced herself to continue. "He's here."

She blinked. "Here?"

"Just offshore. He brought Coran and me back to Venostes. He's making me a new dagger. I know about the dagger now. And he helped me get to the cave." Her mother's mouth had fallen open, one hand holding her tunic below her collar. "I met him," Jastyn said when the silence continued. "I met Tove."

Like the snap of a tree branch, her father's name broke her mother from the shocked state she'd seemingly fallen into. "Tove." She said his name slowly, as if testing it out, as if her tongue had forgotten how. Jastyn wanted to share so much about Tove and the selkies and the cave. Gods, the cave. She wanted to know what had happened; she wanted to ask her mother everything. Most importantly, she wanted to tell her mother she forgave her. She was sure, on some level, her mother knew. But it was another thing entirely to say the words out loud. She was about to tell her when Roisin called, "The guards are coming."

Jastyn spun around. The rush of footsteps sounded overhead, then there was the clank of a key hurrying to unlock the dungeon door.

"Jastyn," her mother said, "you need to go."

"Branna? What's going on?" Elisedd was awake. Upon seeing Jastyn, he shot to his feet. "Jastyn, what are you—"

"What are we going to do?" Roisin asked, swaying frantically.

"I'm not leaving them," Jastyn replied, scanning the dungeon for something to help them. Maybe there was something that could pick the lock. She cursed herself for not thinking this through.

"You have to go," her mother said again.

But Jastyn couldn't run and leave her mother again. Not now. Not when they were so close to having the life they'd always wanted, a life where Alanna was healthy, and there were no more secrets between them.

"Roisin." Jastyn spun around. The dungeon door scraped open. "How's your attack magic?"

Roisin paled. "Decent, but—"

"Good. You're going to need it."

Her mother grabbed her hand once more. Jastyn ignored the pleading look. She spoke quickly. "One of them will have keys. When I get him against the cell, grab them. Coran and Rigo are in the stables. If anything happens, meet them there."

Both Branna and Elisedd stepped away from the cell door at the same time Jastyn grabbed Roisin, pulling her into the shadows against the far wall.

"Where are they?" one of the three guards barked, spittle flying from his mouth as he leered toward her parent's cell. The other two split up, searching the rows.

"Where's who?"

"Don't play dumb, you wretch."

Elisedd had conjured yellow spell-fire. It burned menacingly at his fingertips as he glared at the large guardsman who was even taller than him.

The guard sneered. "You're just as bad. Marrying a whore who bore an Odium."

Before the guard could finish laughing at his own remark, Elisedd and Jastyn fired their saols. Their spell-fire hit him simultaneously. He groaned and fell to his knees, lamely reaching for his sword. The other guardsmen came running.

With a shriek, Roisin fired purple spell-fire at one of the men. It hit him in the neck, bowling him over.

The third rounded on Jastyn, sword drawn. She ducked as he swung at her head, then pushed her saol at his stomach. He blocked it with his own, then lunged for her. His sword scraped her pant leg. When he lunged again, she brought up her knee, ferociously connecting with his nose. A red saol zoomed close and hit him, knocking him out completely. Jastyn gave her mother a grateful nod, but the other two guards were back on their feet. Roisin scurried to stand beside her.

"One down," Jastyn said between breaths.

Roisin replied, "I hope you know how much I hate this." Her voice pitched to a yell as they both dodged the swords that swung at them.

Jastyn and Roisin shot their saols. One of the guards stumbled when the flames hit his hip with a hiss of smoke.

The largest, with the ring of keys on his waist, stalked closer. Jastyn conjured her saol again. Roisin, looking petrified, did the same. The guard grinned, looking between them.

"Do I get two for the price of one?"

Jastyn hurled her saol at his chest. To her dismay, he deflected it with the hilt of his sword and she watched in horror as it ricocheted, hitting Roisin. She clutched her arm, stumbling to the ground.

"Roisin!" Jastyn leapt to help her.

"Look out," she cried, pointing past Jastyn. The guard raised his sword when two saols hit him in the back. He dropped his sword, grunting and staggering. Mustering her strength, Jastyn rammed into him, pushing him until she felt him hit the cell door. Elisedd shot a hand out of the cell, wrapping one arm tightly against the guard's throat.

"Grab the keys," he said, and Jastyn fumbled with the ring when a sickening scream sounded behind her. Roisin doubled over, unmoving on the floor. One of the other guardsmen had a new saol burning over his open palm as he stepped around her limp figure.

The ring of keys came loose, and Jastyn's fingers trembled. "Which one is it?"

The eyes of the guard Elisedd held rolled back and he slumped, unconscious. The other one moved closer at her back. Her mother fired a saol, but the guard's footsteps only faltered.

"Jastyn, hurry."

"I don't remember which one it is."

She was shaking too much. She couldn't think. The image of Roisin unmoving blazed in her mind. The awful weight of the guard pressed close was suffocating.

The keys fell from her hand.

"Jastyn!"

She met her mother's frightened gaze when something hit her hard in the back of the head, and the world went dark.

CHAPTER TWENTY-FOUR

E verything happened at once.
Aurelia and her parents fired their saols at the same time
as Drest, their spell-fire erupting in a showering spray of sparks over
Alanna. With a noise like a snarl, low and animal, Drest conjured
another saol. Aurelia ran at him. He grinned before sending an orb into
her shoulder. She fell back, the pain hot and sharp.

Her parents charged. This time, he spun the air around them until
two funnels formed at his side. Before her parents could retreat, they
were swept up, blown halfway across the meadow.

"This is more fun than I anticipated," Drest said, unsheathing the
short sword from a scabbard at his waist.

Alanna stirred. Aurelia threw two saols at Drest. He deflected one,
but the second hit his left arm. He shouted, then lifted his sword above
Jastyn's sister.

"No!" Petrified, Aurelia was certain of the terrible inevitability
when a small figure appeared with a *pop*, hunched over Alanna.

"Eegit?" Aurelia said in disbelief.

She snatched a large ladle that lay nearby on the grass, then
slammed it into Drest's groin. He groaned, doubling over.

"Thank the gods," Aurelia said, hurrying over while he tried to
stand. "Please help us, Eegit."

The look in her eyes, however, was not one of benevolence when
she put her hands on Alanna's shoulders. Alanna was awake now but
struggled to keep her eyes open. "I'm not here to help," Eegit finally
said.

Aurelia shot a saol at Drest, knocking him back. "I don't understand. I thought—"

"You thought wrong. My allegiance is to Jastyn, not the Diarmaids." She snapped her fingers and disappeared, taking Alanna with her.

Still wincing, Drest stood. "Well, that was unexpected." He wiped soot from his cheek with the back of his hand, smearing ash along his jaw. Bits of scorched grass and splinters drifted into his blond hair.

Aurelia stared at where Alanna had been. She was gone. Gods, what were they going to do?

"Aurelia, darling." Her mother's voice made her turn. It sounded distant, as if she was hearing it from underwater. Her mother stumbled toward her, still looking dazed from Drest's spell. Her father was several steps behind, looking haggard and holding his left arm.

It wasn't until she heard a splash that Aurelia whirled back to face Drest. He had picked up the ladle Eegit had hit him with and plunged it into the cauldron holding Alanna's cure.

"This looks important."

Flinching, Aurelia tried to keep her face even. Her parents stood on either side of her, all of them breathless.

"What do you want, Drest?" her mother asked, and Aurelia knew she was trying to distract him.

"Are we really still asking those questions?" He peered into the cauldron, leaning close. Aurelia took a step forward when he sniffed it.

Her father tried next. "Aren't you tired of doing your mother's dirty work?"

Drest spoke matter-of-factly. "I'm helping clear the path to my mother's ascension." He straightened, the ladle twirling in his hand, sending flecks of the cure flying.

"Then why isn't she here?"

"She's on her way."

Her mother scoffed. "Coming to help?"

"I don't need her help."

Quickly, her parents fired their saols. Aurelia knew they were hoping to catch Drest off guard. Part of their spell-fire hit his hip before he rolled nimbly to the side.

"Be careful," Aurelia said under her breath. The cauldron had wobbled atop its tower of logs.

Her parents sidestepped, moving opposite one another, rounding on Drest, who hurried to his feet. Though his eyes had regained their color, some of his power drained from their attack, his gaze was glassy. His tunic was singed. A line of blood ran from a cut on his arm. A large gash oozed where Rigo's arrow had been extracted from his thigh. His shoulders hunched as if tired.

Her parents stood ten paces from him on either side. Still holding the ladle, Drest paused and raised it to his nose. Aurelia took another step.

"This smells like old magic." He waved it mildly. "Whatever were you doing?"

Her mother said, "That is none of your concern."

They'd all taken a few steps in so they formed three points of a triangle surrounding him. Aurelia caught her parents' gazes. Her mother lifted her chin in recognition. When Drest began to tip the cauldron with the toe of his boot, Aurelia vanquished her saol.

"Wait." She raised her hands, palms facing him.

Looking unimpressed, he tossed the ladle aside. "Really, Aurelia, more questions?"

"No," she said, moving to stand on the other side of the cauldron. She glanced down, relieved at the sight of the cure still intact. "No more questions."

Drest, short sword still in his right hand, gestured skyward. "On with it, then. I was supposed to have things ready by sundown." She was silent, but he seemed to read the question in her eyes. "I'm supposed to have your mother's corpse in my possession, to be specific."

She hoped he didn't catch her frightened glance sideways. She took a deep breath. "Take me with you."

An immediate grin spread across his face. He swiped his free hand down his chin in an effort to hide it. Her father's voice was pitched high when he said, "Aurelia, what are you doing?"

"Take me with you, Drest," she said again, ignoring her father but knowing her mother sensed what she was trying to do. "Your offer before…it still stands?" She walked slowly around the cauldron as she spoke.

Her mother's saol burned brighter in her hand. "Aurelia, what are you saying?"

"Hush," Aurelia spat, receiving an impressed look from Drest. She forced herself to meet his gaze. "I want to know she'll be safe. I want to know that the Dark Fae won't harm Jastyn."

Drest's shoulders relaxed. Aurelia knew she had his attention. Gods, she hoped this worked.

"What made you change your mind?" he asked.

"We both know how my parents feel about Odiums." She saw his upper lip rise at that last word. "They would never let me be with her." She glanced over her shoulder at her mother, adding a sneer for effect. "But you, you have power over the Dark Fae. With my face at the forefront of the change you'll bring, I know Jastyn and I can be together."

"Aurelia," her mother said, stepping closer as Aurelia placed herself between Drest and the cauldron.

"Promise me Jastyn will be safe, and I'll go with you."

Drest's gaze roved over her. She could see his mind turning, weighing her words. From the corner of her eye, she saw her mother quietly close in.

When Drest lifted his sword, the sharp end hovering inches from her cheek, Aurelia forced herself not to blink. He drew the blade close, carefully lifting strands of hair that had fallen over her face.

"You remind me so much of Brennus." He spoke softly. Aurelia could feel his breath on her face. "But there's one thing that sets you apart."

"What is that?" she asked, her saol sparking to life at her fingertips, ready.

His lips lifted in a grin as he leaned in and whispered, "Brennus was a better liar."

She didn't have time to strike before he grabbed her, spinning her until her back was forced against his chest. She cried out as his sword flew to her neck, the edge digging into her skin below her jaw.

"I wouldn't do that if I were you," he said when her parents aimed their saols.

"Let her go." Her mother looked as menacing as that day at the beach. Aurelia tried to wriggle free, but Drest was too strong.

"I'm afraid there's only one way that's going to happen."

To their right, her father shouted. "Drest, you fiend."

"Grannus, no."

But her father charged, his saol ready. Pressed against Drest, Aurelia could feel a surge of power course through him. The hand holding her waist shot out, and a burst of wind hurled her father skyward across the meadow. He slammed into the trunk of an elm tree, then crumpled to the ground.

"Father!" She scratched and kicked Drest's shin, but he only laughed, holding her tighter.

"He *was* warned."

She met her mother's gaze. Dechtire's eyes brimmed with tears. She shook when she said, "What do you want?"

"You always were the more sensible one," Drest said, lightly dragging the edge of the sword along Aurelia's throat. "As I was saying, there's one way I will let her go." She tried to calm her breathing, still fighting against his grip. "Take your own life, Dechtire. Take your life in exchange for your daughter's."

"You're mad," Aurelia managed to say, receiving a small cut in her neck in return.

"That is a matter of opinion." He snarled. "What do you say, Dechtire?"

Her face was tight, her brows knit in the way Aurelia knew from years of scolding. When she remained silent, Drest continued, "It seems an easy decision to me. Lose both your children or give up your own life to save one."

Aurelia grabbed Drest's arm to try to pry the sword away. He only gripped her tighter, pressing the blade against her pulse point. She felt sharp pain and something warm run down her neck.

"You murdered Brennus," her mother said.

"Well, I can't take all the credit."

Aurelia felt sick at the joy dripping from his voice. She tried conjuring her saol, but as soon as her fingers grew hot, Drest squeezed her waist so tight she couldn't breathe.

"Mother, it's all right," she gasped. If she could convince him to take her to the castle, they had a chance.

"No." Her mother stood back. "Aurelia, if we give madmen like him what they want, the kingdom will fall."

Drest laughed, the sword shaking at her throat. "So no deal?" He moved them forward, closer to Alanna's cure. Aurelia tried to break free, tried to loosen his grip, but nothing worked. She tried to summon more strength. She pictured Jastyn. Was this what it was like facing endless days of fear and unrest? Of torment and struggle?

Her mother's eyes widened but only for a moment. She heard something familiar, but she was dizzy, too faint to concentrate on anything but the lack of air in her lungs and the blade at her throat.

"Mother," she gasped, her throat dry. "Please."

"Have it your way then."

Aurelia prepared for the sickening swipe cutting across her throat. Instead, a piercing sound cut through the air behind them, and Drest groaned and fell forward into her.

His grip loosened, and she sprang out of it. Running to her mother, she looked back. Drest stood, howling, an arrow embedded near the center of his back. She scanned the trees, looking for Rigo.

"You fools," Drest shouted. Then he lunged, one of his legs rearing.

It took a moment to realize what he was doing. Her mother ran forward, arms desperately outstretched.

They both screamed when Drest kicked over the cauldron and watched helplessly as Alanna's cure spilled out, evaporating in a scorching sizzle of smoke in the fire.

CHAPTER TWENTY-FIVE

"No!" Aurelia collapsed, falling forward and driving her hands into the hot, charred logs. The golden liquid of Alanna's cure hissed against the embers, dissipating into choking smoke. She hardly registered the pain as she snatched the nearby ladle, scooping frantically through the fire for a drop of the cure. But there was nothing left.

"Oh my," Drest said. He stood awkwardly, one arm behind him to cast a wind spell that tugged the arrow from his back with sickening ease. "Was that the cure for the horse master's daughter?" He grimaced, though there was no sincerity behind his eyes.

On her knees, Aurelia felt ill. She dropped the ladle and pulled back her hands to stare at the gray ash, the skin blistering on her palms. The cure Jastyn had searched for was gone. Everything they'd worked for…her heart ached. Gods, this couldn't be happening.

"Aurelia, look at you. It's hardly worth sniveling over." His voice grated on her ears. She clenched her jaw. In one motion, she stood and aimed two saols at his chest. One hit him, knocking him back, but he blocked the second. Fury surged through her hands as she conjured more spell-fire.

"Aurelia." Her mother hurried forward, her magenta flame brewing at her side.

"Truly, Dechtire, you make this harder than it needs to be." Drest shot out an arm, his hand making as if to catch her mother by the throat. She halted mid-step. Yellow spell-fire wrapped around her neck.

"Let her go." Aurelia wondered if this feeling was like Jastyn's dark place. She'd felt anger and distrust toward Drest since her kidnapping. She'd grown to despise him upon learning his role in her brother's death. Now...this was different. This feeling was black and loud and made her want to send him to the darkest reaches of the Otherworld where he belonged.

"I'm afraid I can't." He glanced down, seeming to take in his haggard state. His face was pale, yet he seemed to remain upright out of sheer mad determination. He snapped his fingers, and six guards appeared in the meadow. At first, they looked confused, but after a wave of Drest's hand, their eyes glazed over, and they all stood at attention before dispersing, heading toward her parents.

Aurelia's breath staggered as the darkness worked through her mind. Her thoughts were on fire, each flicker a glaring scream for her to act. She needed to do something, but the cacophony of hatred toward Drest blinded her and froze her in place. Her gaze fell to the firepit. The empty cauldron lay on its side, a brutal reminder of what had just transpired.

"Aurelia, listen to me—" Her mother's voice cut off. She was being held between two guards, one with a hand over her mouth. The yellow saol around her neck was gone. Behind them, her father lay unconscious on his back as two other guards grabbed his wrists and began pulling him toward the trees. Her mother was shoved brusquely, forced to follow.

"There will be time for good-byes soon enough." Drest seemed tired, but his smile was sick when he looked at her.

A wave of despondency washed over her. She felt adrift. She hadn't been fast enough to stop Drest. She hadn't been good enough to keep the cure safe.

Drest took one of her arms, forcing her to follow the guards out of the meadow. "Come now. Mother is waiting."

Jastyn was on her back and could feel the grubby hands of someone pulling her by the wrists. The hard ground scraped by beneath her, rocks and fallen tree bark prodding her legs and hips. Her eyes fluttered open. It was dark. The crunch of leaves sounded beneath boots, multiple pairs. How many were with her? She couldn't see. Her head pounded.

Another rock jammed into her back, but she worked to keep her face slack. Closing her eyes again, she inhaled through her nose. The smallest sense of hope kindled; she was in the Wood.

Her captors dragged her deeper through the trees as she tried to recall what had happened. Where had she been?

Aurelia.

No. That was too long ago. Aurelia was with Alanna. Jastyn left the meadow with…Roisin. A pang of dread hit her like the gnome hill beneath her head. Roisin had been on the dungeon floor, unmoving. Why?

The guards. They'd been attacked when she'd tried to rescue her parents. What had happened to them? She remembered the guard against the cell, pinned between her and Elisedd. His keys had been in her hand, but then…she searched her mind. There was only pain and dark and a frightened look in her mother's eyes.

When she heard the familiar trickle of the brook near Eegit's meadow, Jastyn kept her eyes shut. One of her wrists was released.

"Which way, Baroness?" a deep voice asked from somewhere above her. She heard a lighter tread as somebody strode past. She also smelled something. It was too sweet, like over-ripe plums. Her stomach turned.

"Patience. We must wait." Jastyn didn't recognize the voice but presumed it belonged to the baroness. Hadn't Aurelia said something about her before?

She was scooped up into a wide, burly pair of arms. Peeking through her nearly closed eyelids as her head flopped against the guard's right shoulder, she saw another guardsman and a tall woman with features that reminded Jastyn of a crane she'd once seen near the river. Her long neck held a pointed face in every sense, from nose to chin. Her red tunic and navy cloak looked new, and Jastyn caught the glimmer of jewels on her fingers and a dragonfly pin pulling back her blond hair.

Closing her eyes, Jastyn kept her breathing calm and sporadic in hopes of not drawing attention.

"He's here." The baroness's voice was gleeful as footsteps drew near. A loud, shallow breath crackled on the night wind and flew toward her along with the smell of rotten flesh. The guardsman holding her stumbled back while the other let out a startled cry.

"Oh, do pull yourselves together," the baroness said. It took all of Jastyn's willpower not to cover her face at the stench. What could possibly smell like that and be well enough to walk? "Don't just stand there," the baroness said. "Bow before the great king who will bring forth the old glory of this land." She giggled and inhaled sharply before announcing, "My grandfather."

Jastyn had to see. She cracked her eyes open. Her breath caught. He was no longer a phantom, no longer a figure in her nightmares. The hooded rider from her past had found her.

The Dark Fae stood next to the baroness only five paces away. His hood sat back atop his head, exposing a garish mix of mottled skin and tangled muscle lifted in what could only be a grin.

"Odium Child." His mouth maintained its skewed, serrated look from the mountains, but flesh had grown in distorted patches along his face, neck, and arms. The glaring white of bone stuck out between visible ligaments near his jaw and at his wrists below the sleeves of his black tunic. He was alarmingly incomplete yet the most whole Jastyn had ever seen.

"The more power his descendants gain, the more alive he grows," the baroness said, answering Jastyn's silent question.

Fear overwhelmed her as he seemed to smile wider, his gnarled lips turning up and revealing decayed gums. His eyes matched the baroness's. He lowered his hood to look from Jastyn to the guardsmen.

"Set her down," he said.

The guardsman dropped her, and she landed hard. Her head still ached, but she tried to focus on her surroundings. She scooted backward.

"Once the Odium is gone, the princess will be easier to eliminate. My son's foolish notions that he can sway Aurelia are mistaken. There's no place for Odiums in this world." The baroness crossed her thin arms. The Dark Fae moved closer, and Jastyn turned to crawl before pushing herself to stand. She hadn't noticed the two additional guards, who moved to block her way. She tried to conjure her saol, but she was too weak. Spinning back around, she looked past the Dark Fae to the baroness.

"Where are my parents?" she asked.

"Right where you left them."

Dismay crept down Jastyn's neck. She'd failed. She hadn't been able to save her mother and Elisedd.

"In two days, their execution will be carried out."

"Why didn't you leave me there?" Jastyn asked, keeping the Dark Fae in view. He'd slowed his steps even more, seeming to relish her fear.

The baroness uncrossed her arms and took a defiant stance. "Odiums don't deserve the dignity of a public execution."

This woman was as terrible as her demented son. Jastyn felt the faintest flicker between her fingers. The Dark Fae began to laugh, low and deep. The baroness joined in.

"So like an Odium," she said once her laughter subsided. "Always quick to anger." She started forward, her cloak billowing as she passed the Dark Fae. "Prone to fits of rage, not caring about anyone but themselves." She lifted a brow. "That is your downfall." She loomed over Jastyn. "Odiums are worse than fae, though it's a close call between them." Her eyes shifted, growing dark. "You're a biproduct of what loose laws can create. It's only when the land is cleansed of you and the fae filth that Gultero can rise again to prosperity."

Jastyn swallowed, forcing herself to hold that gaze.

"We were once the supreme example of power and success in the realm. But then the fae brought their wretched famine to our shores. Gultero never recovered."

"The famine was a tragedy," she replied, "but it wasn't the fae's fault."

"Liar!" The baroness raised one arm, her saol burning next to Jastyn's face. She could feel the heat against her cheek, but she didn't move. The baroness closed her eyes and took a breath. "You're trying to trick me." She vanquished her saol and lowered her arm. "Very clever. But I won't deny my grandfather the satisfaction of finally collecting you."

Jastyn tried to think beyond the pounding ache and the debilitating fear rushing through her veins. When the baroness stepped aside, the Dark Fae stood an arm's length away.

She took in his cloak's colors, still faded, but now she recognized the kingdom's markings in the belt. His dark pants and boots looked outdated. It was all too much. He couldn't be here, be real. It couldn't end like this.

She stepped back, but the guards drew their swords in warning. She scanned the trees for something, anything, that could help her. But there was only darkness. At least Alanna was safe. At least she had the cure. Even if her mother and Elisedd couldn't escape, even if Jastyn was facing her final moments, as long as Alanna was safe, it would be okay.

After a rush of footsteps, a guard appeared from behind the trees. "Your Greatness, the Diarmaids…we have them."

Jastyn's stomach dropped.

The baroness smirked. "Excellent."

"No." Jastyn went cold. She tried to move, to rush the baroness, but the Dark Fae shot out an arm, catching her throat in his grip. She pulled at his hand. Her mind raced as familiar pain squeezed around her neck. What had happened to the Diarmaids? Was Aurelia okay? They had been fine when she'd left them. The cure was nearly ready. Where was Alanna?

Slowly, the Dark Fae lifted her off the ground. Jastyn tried to gasp, searching for air, willing it into her lungs. But with each attempt, his grip tightened. Searing pain tore through her head. She heard the baroness say something, but like her vision, her hearing was unclear as she grew dizzy. She kicked at the Dark Fae but missed. The longer he held her, the weaker she became and the more hopeless she felt.

When he opened his mouth, she closed her eyes. She hated herself for being afraid, but fear was all she could feel. What was left to hold on to? Soon, her mother was going to be executed. Aurelia was captured, which meant Alanna was in danger of not getting her cure. Everything she'd fought for, everything she'd worked for was slipping away.

Everything she had done had been for nothing.

A muffled cry sounded, and for a moment, Jastyn thought it was her making another strangled effort to breathe. But the ghastly intake of breath from the Dark Fae halted.

"Idiots! Stop him."

Opening her eyes, Jastyn saw three guards sprinting toward the back line of trees where one of their fellows lay motionless. A dark figure was yanking a blade from the guard's gut before running toward her.

The Dark Fae turned to look. Jastyn peered past him, but her vision was too blurry. She could see the guardsmen shouting at the dark figure. He moved swiftly, expertly dodging the guardsmen's swords. The baroness conjured her saol and stalked toward him.

As if amused, the Dark Fae chuckled and turned back to Jastyn. She choked out a noise to protest, but he opened his mouth again. This time, before he could begin to drain her life, another figure leapt onto his back, driving a bone-handled dagger into the exposed muscle of his neck.

"Get your hands off my daughter."

Tove drove the blade in deeper. The Dark Fae howled and released her. She fell to the ground, the impact shooting pain through her feet. Stumbling, she blinked, clearing her vision and regaining her senses. She swiped at her neck to be rid of the lingering feeling of the Dark Fae's fingers. She gulped at the air, filling her lungs and regaining her strength.

Her father was still on the Dark Fae's back. He pulled the dagger out, leaping nimbly to the ground before running to her.

"Jastyn, are you all right?"

She nodded, her throat burning.

"Here." He pulled a dagger from a loop on his boot.

"My dagger." Her voice was hoarse. She took a blade just like the one he held. At its touch, a surge ran through her fingers. The Dark Fae roared.

Her father moved to stand beside her. Behind them, Fortan had taken out two of the guards and was currently trying to shake off the remaining one. At the Dark Fae's howl, the baroness turned back. Even from where they stood, Jastyn could see her eyes blaze.

More footsteps sounded from beyond the tree line.

"Alanna, do you know where she is?" asked Jastyn.

"She's with Eegit."

Relief washed over her. "You're sure?"

"Yes. She brought us the serpentine stone to finish your dagger. Alanna was with her. They're on the ship."

Feeling reinvigorated, Jastyn straightened. There was still hope. Her sister was safe. They just had to get through this, and come sunrise, Alanna would finally be healthy.

"At least the pooka's not here," her father said, and they exchanged grins as the Dark Fae moved in. The baroness stood beyond, watching them.

Jastyn and her father lunged. They jabbed at the Dark Fae, who moved quickly to dodge their blades. Beyond, Fortan kicked the fourth guard, then stabbed his shoulder. He rushed to join them, but the baroness squared off with him. She fired a golden saol, but he rolled and dodged. He ended up right behind the Dark Fae, and Jastyn caught a flicker of joy in his eyes as he jammed his dagger into the Dark Fae's lower back.

Screaming, the Dark Fae reared backward. Her father leapt, taking his own shot at the torso. His dagger went easily through the Dark Fae's tunic below his ribs.

"No!" The baroness ran at them, two saols burning over her hands. One hit Fortan in the back. He fell forward, stumbling away. The other narrowly missed Jastyn's right shoulder. The Dark Fae, bleeding but recovered, flung out his left arm, sending Fortan flying. Her father lunged, but the Dark Fae dodged the dagger and shoved Tove with such force, he was thrown twenty yards back, falling awkwardly into a tree.

Jastyn looked from her father to the Dark Fae. The baroness stood next to him. Strands of hair had fallen loose from her pin and covered her pale, rageful face. When Jastyn conjured her saol, the baroness's eyes flickered to something behind her. Jastyn didn't care if there were more guards coming. She wanted to fight this evil once and for all. She wanted to shove her saol into the baroness. She wanted to fight until the Dark Fae was gone. She was tired of this. It had to end.

Her dagger in her right hand, she raised her left arm, a fiery saol ready. The baroness smiled. "I wouldn't do that if I were you." Then she pointed behind Jastyn.

"Your guards don't scare me."

She was about to fire when a voice shouted, "Jastyn!"

She turned. Aurelia.

CHAPTER TWENTY-SIX

Aurelia." Jastyn took a step toward where Drest held her, but the baroness threw a golden wall of spell-fire.

"Not so fast, Odium." The baroness didn't need to keep her hand up to hold the wall in place, unlike the way Dechtire had earlier. Jastyn felt no heat from the flames, only a claustrophobic closeness. Through the saol, Jastyn looked from Aurelia to the guardsmen flanking Drest. The king lay on the ground nearby, unmoving. Jastyn couldn't tell if he was alive. The queen seemed to be trying to wriggle free from the guards keeping her arms pinned at her sides. Aurelia, to Jastyn's surprise, didn't struggle against Drest as he held her hands behind her. She'd been crying. What had happened in Eegit's meadow? Was King Grannus dead?

A vicious snarl drew her attention. Fortan dove for the baroness. She conjured a wind funnel that easily upended him. But he stood quickly, motioning to Tove. They attacked. This time, the Dark Fae flew to stand between them and the baroness. He grabbed both by the throats, and while he couldn't seem to lift them, his mouth stood open, ready.

"Tove!" She tried to run to him, but the baroness's saol encased her. Horrified, she could only watch as the Dark Fae drained Fortan and her father. After unceremoniously dumping them on the ground, the Dark Fae turned. More skin had grown where before had been only muscle and bone. Thin blond hair fell to his shoulders. A few patches of flesh remained decayed near his scalp, but now the old king was nearly whole.

On the ground, her father groaned. Relieved he was still alive, Jastyn faced the baroness. "It's me you want." She glanced at Aurelia, who stared, seemingly lost. "You're a smart woman. I have a deal to offer you." It was a longshot, but Jastyn had to try something. They were outnumbered and outpowered, but knowing Aurelia was alive gave Jastyn the spark she needed to fight.

"I don't make deals with Odiums." The baroness sneered, and the Dark Fae cackled. He ran a fully fleshed hand through his hair and down his arms, seeming to admire his newly acquired skin.

"Take me and let the Diarmaids go." If they're free, she thought, they can help Alanna. They can get the cure to her.

The baroness looked incredulous. "Did I just hear an Odium offer her life for the Diarmaids? Anything really is possible, isn't it?" She looked to Drest. He laughed, but it was tired. Blood ran down his tunic and pant leg. Why was Aurelia making it so easy for him?

"Take me in exchange for the Diarmaids and pardon my family."

"Now that's simply being selfish." The baroness walked toward Drest and the royal family. "You ask too much." She ran her fingers down Aurelia's hair, who seemed to barely register the action as tears streamed down her cheeks. "Besides, I can't cancel my very first execution as queen. That would look absolutely awful in the eyes of the court."

"The court you've bewitched." Dechtire spoke through gritted teeth.

The baroness rounded on her. "I've only opened their minds to the truth."

Dechtire continued to try to free herself from the guards' grasp. To Jastyn's left, her father and Fortan moaned as if in great pain.

"Jastyn," her father said. "Your dagger."

Still encased in the baroness's spell-fire, Jastyn glanced at her dagger gripped tightly in her right hand. Did it really work? Would the luck inside stave off the Dark Fae? He hadn't touched her since it came to be in her possession. Could it work against the baroness, too? She had to get out of this saol first. If she could free Aurelia and the queen, they could fight back. Again, she looked at Aurelia, but she only stared into the trees beyond.

Jastyn didn't like the dejected look in her eyes. What had happened?

"You never answered me." Jastyn pulled the baroness's attention back to her. "Do we have a deal?"

The baroness seemed to scrutinize her from across the stretch of wood between them. Her gaze roved over the bodies of her fallen guardsmen. Then she motioned to the guards on either side of Grannus's body. They marched to where her father and Fortan lay. After forcing them to stand, the baroness slowly walked toward them, hands clasped behind her back.

The look in her eyes was chilling. Jastyn placed her open hand against the saol holding her. She could feel its strength. Trying to punch through it with her own spell-fire proved useless. Everyone in the clearing seemed to watch as the baroness looked back at the Dark Fae.

"What do you propose we do with these?" she asked.

The Dark Fae ran one hand down the tail of his belt, then rubbed his fingertips together as if warming them for a spell. He walked to join the baroness and faced Tove. The baroness eyed Fortan.

The Dark Fae's voice was hollow as he said, "Break them."

A demented smile lit the baroness's face as she waved her arms in a flourish. There was a flash of wind followed by a sickening crack. Both Fortan and her father screamed, their teeth bared in agony. Their elbows bent out of place, and their shoulders drooped awkwardly. Fortan fell to his knees, still screaming. Her father's face contorted, but he set his lips in a thin, hard line.

"Father!" Jastyn pounded against the spell-fire.

The baroness turned to Jastyn. Her eyes had gone clear like Drest's did. She sent a small funnel of air at Tove's chest. More bubbling cracks and he gasped, doubling over.

"I always wondered if selkies have the same number of ribs as we do."

"Stop it." Jastyn shoved the end of her dagger against the saol, trying to puncture it. She couldn't stand watching another member of her family suffer on her behalf.

"I'm merely demonstrating my point," the baroness said, her face pulling in a pout. She gestured to the Diarmaids. "You see, they don't care whether these fae live or die. It's pointless to offer your life for theirs because deep down, we all know the truth." She approached Jastyn, and Jastyn could see the terrifying white of her eyes. "A Diarmaid could never care about the fae. Nor could a princess ever love an Odium. It's all a wishful fantasy that I am more than happy to help you end."

"Enya!" The queen had one arm loose.

Seeing this, the baroness only seemed amused. "I'm only telling the truth, Dechtire. I'm the only one brave enough to say what everyone thinks. I'm the one willing to bring about the pure kingdom Venostes has failed to become but secretly wants to be."

The queen conjured a small saol, firing it at the guard to her right. He fell. Dechtire ran forward, shoving a magenta flame at the baroness.

Deflecting it, Enya shot out her arm.

"Mother!" Aurelia's first words pulled Jastyn's attention but only for a moment before Dechtire was lifted from the ground. The baroness held one palm facing the queen, then moved as if to shove the air between them. Dechtire gasped and flew backward across the Wood, inches above the ground. A loud smack reverberated when she hit a towering ash tree. Golden spell-fire wrapped around her arms like rope, tying her to the tree trunk only a few yards away from where Jastyn stood trapped.

"You just gave me a wonderful idea, Dechtire." The baroness lowered her arm.

Jastyn felt like the world was at a tilt. Too much was happening. Her father and Fortan winced and their arms dangled limply. The night sky between the trees began to lighten. Time was running out. Alanna needed to drink the cure at dawn. Jastyn felt dizzy. If she had the ability to move freely, her legs would give out, and she'd fall, slipping from the earth into nothingness.

"Let me go," she begged, pounding harder against the saol. "Please."

In a flash the baroness was before her, staring through the spell-fire. The golden hue made her skin look sickly when she clucked. "You fight so hard, Odium. For what?"

"Her sister." Drest's voice pulled their attention.

Jastyn felt panic rise within her chest. Beside her, the Dark Fae grinned.

"The poor horse master's daughter." It wasn't a question, and Jastyn hated to think how much the baroness knew about her family. "That's right. Your epic journey." Her voice rose in mocking. "What was it you were searching for again?"

Jastyn's jaw clenched.

"A cure, wasn't it?"

She gripped her dagger so tightly, her hand hurt. The baroness's taunting was driving her mad. She wanted to dive through the saol and fight her way to Alanna. Surely, Aurelia knew, too, that time was running out. Why wasn't she fighting?

Drest's low laugh made her stomach turn. "She doesn't know yet."

"Oh? How awful." The baroness smirked. "The truth is always best, no matter the pain."

Aurelia was crying now. Jastyn struggled to understand. "What do you mean?" Drest and his mother looked overjoyed, eerie grins plastered to their faces. Jastyn couldn't take this anymore. "Aurelia, please look at me," she shouted. "What are they talking about?"

"Tell her, Aurelia. Tell your lover the truth."

Jastyn willed her knees to keep her upright. She was sinking, falling away with each second that passed.

"Tell her," the baroness screamed, spittle flying.

Aurelia's cheeks were wet with tears.

Jastyn's voice was small. "Aurelia?"

"Jastyn, I'm so sorry." Her words were barely audible between choked sobs. "The cure. Jastyn…the cure is gone."

"What?"

Aurelia's shoulders shook as she cried. "I'm so sorry, Jastyn."

"It's gone? The cure is gone?"

Aurelia dropped her head against her chest. It bobbed in sad acknowledgment. Jastyn was sure she was falling now. The ground had to have dropped out beneath her feet. She was in a freefall, staring at the end of her efforts. She looked up as if from the bottom of a well at the lightening sky. The stars were dimming, their glow disappearing.

"You see? You see how foolish it was to trust a Diarmaid? Now you understand. Now you know why they are not fit to rule."

How could the cure be gone? What had happened? Jastyn blinked, clearing her blurred vision as she stared through the tree tops. Wind rattled the leaves, their rush typically a soothing balm that now seemed empty, useless. They were out of time. She shivered. The baroness's words echoed in her mind. What if she was right? What if she'd been wrong to trust the queen?

The Dark Fae broke the silence. "Release her."

The baroness waved her hand, and the spell-fire disappeared. Jastyn stumbled forward. Her mind felt numb, but a faint, nearly forgotten rage buzzed behind her eyes.

"You must be collected, but perhaps you can be of use before you die."

Jastyn hardly heard the baroness. She stared at her hands, one clenching the dagger. The cure was gone. Alanna's one chance at a better life…no more. The past six months, the danger she'd put Coran and Aurelia in. Every narrow escape had been for what, to have the cure in her hands only to have it snatched away? But it hadn't been in her hands. She'd given it up. She'd trusted somebody she swore she never would.

A drop of moisture fell onto her wrist. Glancing up, she expected to find rain, but it was her own tears. Slowly, her gaze slid to the queen.

"Yes," the baroness cooed, stepping behind her. A strong wind pushed her toward Dechtire, still strapped to the tree. "Harness your anger, your rage, your hate, and take the revenge you seek. The vengeance you've always wanted." Jastyn's grip tightened on her dagger as she stared at the queen. The buzzing in her mind began to roar when the baroness leaned in. Next to her ear, she said, "Kill Dechtire. She's the one who lost your cure. She never wanted to see your sister well. She's a Diarmaid."

The queen's cloak looked ragged as Jastyn walked slowly toward her. Dirt was smudged beneath her jaw, and a thin trickle of blood ran from her hairline. Still, her blue eyes stared stoically back.

The baroness walked in step with Jastyn. The same saccharine smell wafted around them. It made Jastyn nauseous, but that only made her focus more on the fury in her mind. When the baroness spoke, it was like Jastyn's thoughts followed easily, tethered to a tight, unrelenting leash. "You left the cure to Dechtire. A great healer but a Diarmaid. A part of you knew she couldn't be trusted. After all, she's responsible for the life you've lived."

The baroness's hand reached up to her temple. Her vision narrowed until she could only see the queen splayed helplessly before her.

Aurelia called, "Jastyn, please. Don't listen to her."

"Dechtire and Grannus made sure your mother was imprisoned. They made sure you were born in the dungeons. Dechtire never wanted to know you. She doesn't care about you or your sister."

A horrible thought filled Jastyn's mind, overruling everything else. "That's why you kept such a close eye over the cure." She was only ten paces from Dechtire now. "You were the only one who could touch it."

"Jastyn—" Aurelia's voice was cut off.

"She knew the best way to hurt someone is to crush their hopes, their dreams." The baroness's voice was like a constant wind berating her mind, kicking her thoughts into a frenzy. "Dechtire must be punished for what she did to you."

Jastyn nodded. Her life had been bent to the will of the Diarmaids. Dechtire had only been using her since their meeting, toying with her emotions. She enjoyed watching Jastyn suffer. A lifetime of horrible thoughts, nights of sinister unspoken words swam around her. Black spirits rose from the back of her mind, screeching unforgiving curses Jastyn had wished upon the Diarmaids in her darkest, weakest moments. A small voice in her mind told her to fight, told her to keep these voices at bay, but they were too loud, too tall from a lifetime's worth of hate.

The queen's entire body strained against the spell-fire holding her to the tree. But when Jastyn was an arm's length away, Dechtire stopped fighting. Jastyn's fingertips glowed hot with her spell-fire. She gave the dagger in her right hand a turn. She no longer sensed the baroness behind her, but her voice sounded clear.

"She doesn't want you in her life. She doesn't want you near her daughter. Her heart is full of hate."

Jastyn stepped forward but faltered at the sound of her father's voice. She couldn't hear what he said, but for a moment, the darkness parted in her mind. She shook her head as conflicting emotions battled. Old resentment bellowed, angry and clawing through her chest to be heard. It willed her to raise the dagger to the queen. She glanced sideways as a separate voice shouted. Aurelia was fighting Drest, her eyes on Jastyn, pleading.

A burst of wind forced her forward again as the baroness spoke. "The Diarmaids are to blame for everything. You hate them. You hate Dechtire for what she did to your mother."

Jastyn closed her eyes. Memories flooded her mind. Freezing nights spent on the brink of starvation. Mornings running from the guards after stealing in the market. A life of hiding, all thanks to the woman before her now.

Yes, Jastyn thought, I've always wanted this. She'd always wanted justice for her lot in life. Now was her chance to take it.

Her body went numb. Rage had taken hold of her limbs. This desire had always been there, buried deep in her darkest dreams.

SAM LEDEL

Leaping forward, Jastyn pressed her left hand against the tree above Dechtire's right shoulder. The other held the dagger to the queen's throat. Dechtire flinched.

"Kill her!" The baroness's voice boomed over the Wood.

Jastyn leaned in, raising the blade at the angle that would tear open the queen's throat. All it would take was a single, swift swipe. Then it would be done. She would have her revenge. She could avenge her mother, absolving them both from the life they'd been forced to live.

"Kill her now."

Jastyn drew her other hand downward. Her saol hovered in her palm. The baroness screamed in her mind as she moved the flame over Dechtire's collar. The blue spell-fire popped, the edges singing the queen's tunic.

Dechtire's eyes gleamed. Did she feel sympathy now, tied here, her wrongdoings lying bare?

"Why?" Jastyn didn't recognize her own voice. It was small, a pleading whimper like a child's. Her saol shook in her hand.

Dechtire's gaze had been on the dagger, but it lifted to meet Jastyn's. "I thought we were doing the right thing."

"You forced my family apart. You forced me to live half a life." Her saol burned brighter. Dechtire winced at the heat against her skin. "Why?"

The baroness screamed again. "Do it now."

There was a muffled cry, then Aurelia shouted. "Jastyn, please don't!"

Jastyn slammed her eyes shut. Everything was jumbled. She didn't want to hurt Aurelia, but the queen had to pay, didn't she? She'd offered to help Jastyn only out of some twisted sense of manipulation. Opening her eyes, she pressed the point of the dagger to the queen's neck. A line of blood ran from the blade's tip. She had to fight to keep her hand from shaking. She had to be strong.

"Jastyn."

A tremor seemed to run beneath her feet at the sound of her name on Dechtire's lips. Flustered and shaking, she swallowed hard. Behind her, footsteps sounded fifty yards off. The queen took a breath, then said, "Inside my cloak." Confused, Jastyn followed her gaze.

"Enough. Kill her now or you die with her."

Jastyn could feel her closing in, but her eyes were fixed on a pocket she hadn't noticed inside the queen's cloak. It was small, hardly noticeable, but large enough to hold a vial. And while it seemed hard to believe, Jastyn knew it was true because looking at Dechtire, the darkness cleared, scampering from her mind like fearful rabbits. Like her daughter, the queen continued to surprise Jastyn, continued to inspire hope that their fight didn't end here.

Whirling around, Jastyn found the baroness with her arm raised, a single golden orb poised. Jastyn wasn't sure if the scream she heard was her own or the final, grasping tumult in her mind. Either way, it fueled her, driving her forward, blade first.

CHAPTER TWENTY-SEVEN

Aurelia kept screaming Jastyn's name. She had to. It was the only thing she could think to do while Jastyn stood with a dagger and spell-fire at her mother's throat. Drest kept stifling her cries while holding her hands behind her back. She bit his hand in order to yell again. She had to reach Jastyn before Enya's spell took her mind and made her do something she'd never be able to take back.

When Enya closed in, Jastyn spun away from Aurelia's mother and drove her dagger into the baroness. The look Jastyn wore was a mix of rage and disconnection. She seemed to look through the baroness as she pierced her chest, as if she only saw the Dark Fae beyond as he howled as if feeling the blade himself.

The attack seemed to halt Enya's magic. Whatever held her mother to the tree vanished, and she fell to the ground, catching herself on one knee.

Drest cried, "Mother!" He tossed Aurelia toward one of the guards. For a moment, she watched him rush to Enya, but only for a moment.

"Drest!" When he didn't stop, she threw her saol at his back, a scorching explosion of red spell-fire that knocked him face-first to the ground. More spell-fire ready, she stalked forward. Everything was boiling to the surface inside her. She could feel it shoving against her skin, pricking at her fingertips and beneath her palms as red flames licked hungrily. It all swam to the forefront of her mind: years of friendship thrown from the window by Drest's actions, Brennus lying motionless in the dining hall, her kidnapping, Drest's maniacal misconceptions of what was right. No, she thought as she pressed forward, he doesn't get to run to his mother. Not when Aurelia never got a chance to say good-bye to her brother.

Her hands blazing, she raised them high. The spell-fire agitated her blistered palms, but she didn't care. The guards near her father shouted and ran for her, but she fired on them in a single turn, knocking them out. Conjuring more, she hit Drest again as he struggled to stand.

Beyond, her mother stood beside Jastyn, who had recovered her dagger, now bloodstained to the hilt. Enya bent at the waist until Aurelia's mother waved, casting magic that forced Enya to the ground with her limbs splayed. The wound had to be deep; blood ran from below Enya's ribs, seeping from the tear in her tunic. Two dozen more guards appeared after a feeble snap of Enya's fingers. The Dark Fae snatched one up, quickly draining his life before seeming to search for more. While Aurelia's mother held the baroness in place, Jastyn ran to her father, and Aurelia returned her attention to Drest.

The back of his tunic was shredded, an arrow hole visible through torn fabric and burned skin exposed. Somehow, he stood. Unsteady, he faced her. His eyes were clear, and a single funnel twisted beneath his downturned palm. Aurelia let her ire fill her up, and when he shot the funnel at her, she fired back with her saol. The two elements met in midair, rebounding off one another and knocking them onto their backs.

Aurelia gasped, trying to recover her breath and pushing up on her elbows. Drest groaned where he lay. She stood when a series of sharp barks broke through the Wood, the sound bounding between the trees. Aurelia swung her gaze to Jastyn, and they both smiled briefly in recognition of the selkie cries. Then a high whistling followed, and between where she and Jastyn stood streamed a long slender arrow. The guard it hit fell dead.

"Rigo!"

He leapt from the treetops, and Aurelia had never been so happy to see him.

"Your Highness, I'm sorry it took us so long." He nocked another arrow, aiming and firing at a guard.

"So long? I didn't know you were coming," she replied, firing a saol to finish the guard. She was breathless, trying to figure out how he had known to be here.

As usual, he seemed to follow her thoughts. "Revna told me where to find you. Some of my clan are coming, too."

"Revna is here?" She glanced at Drest, who was still on the ground with one arm over his face. His legs shook as if in great pain.

"Somewhere, yes."

Tove and Fortan lay at the base of a tree, both looking on helplessly, their arms listless at their sides. "Please, can you help them?" she said, pointing to the selkies.

Rigo promised her he would before disappearing into the branches overhead.

Aurelia ran to Jastyn as she took out a guard with spell-fire. She grabbed Jastyn's sleeve and pulled her aside, careful to avoid the clashing selkies and guardsmen. Ducking behind a tree, Aurelia said, "Gods, Jastyn, I'm so sorry." She hugged her fiercely. "The cure—"

But Jastyn cut her off, holding up a small blue vial. "Your mother had this." Inside the glass, golden liquid shimmered.

Aurelia gawked. "But how? When did she—"

"It doesn't matter."

"That must've been what she was trying to tell me before." Aurelia glanced at her mother, who seemed to be contemplating what to do with Enya. Facing Jastyn again and finding her face fallen, she asked, "What is it?"

Jastyn fingered the vial's edge. "Aurelia, I almost did it. I could feel myself ready to…to hurt your mother."

Aurelia cupped her cheek. "But you didn't do it. I knew you were stronger than Enya. I had faith in you, Jastyn. I always will." Adrenaline had been coursing through her for the last hour, and she could hear the cries from the selkies, the guardsmen shouting, and the steadily growing number of elven battle cries. She needed to get out there. She needed to help her mother. Looking to make sure Drest was still incapacitated, she noticed that the air had begun to brighten. "Go." She pushed the vial back at Jastyn. "Get that to your sister."

Jastyn kissed her hard, one hand pulling her close. Before Aurelia could catch her breath, Jastyn had gone, disappearing between the trees.

"Look alive, Princess."

Turning, Aurelia's mouth fell open. She lunged forward, throwing herself onto Sif. "You're alive."

Sif laughed, then carefully pushed Aurelia off. Aurelia scanned her strong figure, amazed at the clean tunic, her lively dark eyes, and the familiar old scar running down her neck. There was no evidence that she'd been nearly dead, shot with an enemy arrow.

Sif pushed back her dark hair and smiled. "Nice to know you were worried about me." Aurelia felt light when she added, "We came as soon as word reached us that the royal family was in danger."

Aurelia frowned, about to ask why the selkies, especially Sif, cared enough to help. She was stopped before she could start.

"Diarmaid or not," Sif said, "we can't have the princess dethroned before she has a chance to make things right."

Her breath caught, and gratitude filled her chest. Not sure how to say how happy she was about seeing Sif, about her willingness to help, Aurelia could only shake her head.

Sif squeezed her arm gently. "Come on," she said, tugging Aurelia to follow. "We've got a fight to win."

Aurelia took in the crude battleground. Her mother continued to hold Enya, whose head lolled back and forth where she was trapped in magenta flames. Sif ran to assist Rigo, easily disposing of two guards along the way. She spotted the Dark Fae moments before he retreated into the clouds. Drest, meanwhile, struggled to crawl toward his mother.

She took a deep breath, the air now mingling with upturned earth and the faintest scent of iron. Taking it in, she also opened her mind to the awful memories she had spent months trying to repress. Walking toward Drest, whose bleeding, battered limbs dragged him toward his mother, horrible visions barraged her senses. She heard the sick gurgle of blood in her brother's throat. She felt his cold skin. She saw Drest's gleeful face as he retold Brennus's final moments.

From the ground, Drest began to conjure a funnel, but Aurelia fired her saol. It hit the back of his hand, knocking away his magic. He screamed, the high sound mixing with the clash of metal on shields as the fae battled the remaining guards. His now charred hand stretched toward Enya, still encased in the snare.

"Take my offer, Enya," her mother was saying over the battle's clamor. Her mother's disheveled appearance did little to dull the majesty in her stance. Aurelia squinted and realized her mother was actually sending a healing spell to Enya's wound.

The baroness didn't seem to care. "Your reign will end, Dechtire." Her hands balled into fists, looking ready to punch through the saol. Aurelia's mother kept her other arm steady, holding the spell-fire snare in place.

"Maybe it will," her mother said, "but not by your hand and not today."

Enya sneered, and Aurelia's mother withdrew the healing spell. Blood flowed again from the baroness's wound. Aurelia's mother's jaw was firm as wind whipped her hair across her face. "Enya, chains are better than the Otherworld. Live to stand trial before the court. Face your crimes and you may live a long life yet."

The baroness looked to Drest. Aurelia expected to see affection, worry, something sympathetic toward her dying son. In her eyes, there was only disappointment.

Enya lifted her chin. "I accept." She nodded to Drest. "Let me help him." Her voice took on a pleading, broken tone. "Please, Dechtire. He has only minutes left."

Her mother hesitated, then the magenta flames vanished. The baroness had barely landed when she leapt for Aurelia, unhinged evil in her eyes. The wind picked up, and Aurelia didn't even have time to scream.

A sharp crack made the moment freeze. Aurelia had one arm up to shield herself, but the baroness didn't move. Aurelia's mother's eyes blazed, and her arm was outstretched, hand level with the baroness's neck. With a turn of her wrist, Enya's neck twisted, breaking. Hazel returned to her eyes before she fell.

Aurelia stared at the baroness's body: one arm crushed beneath her torso, blood pooling in the grass near her face, her cheek smashed where she'd landed, her empty gaze seeming to stare at her son.

"No." Drest clamored to his knees.

Aurelia's mother was breathing hard, looking ready to move when Drest managed a small wind-spell. It wasn't much; his power was nearly gone, but it was enough to buffet her.

Aurelia threw a saol that knocked him forward. He caught himself, then turned over, crawling backward until he lay protectively over his mother. Burned skin showed between tears in his tunic. Bruises and cuts littered his face, neck, and arms. His breathing was ragged, his pallor like that of a spirit. He moved as if to say something but coughed, blood spewing into his hand. He stared at it as if surprised.

Aurelia stood over him. He grimaced and unsheathed his sword.

"Give up, Drest," she said.

Another awful gurgle came from his throat. His eyes rolled back. His chest heaved, and his shoulders shook when his lips curled up. Was he laughing? His grasp on this world was slipping away, and Aurelia couldn't believe his sardonic display. Her saol tingled at her fingertips.

"I don't know what happened to you or if this is always who you were." She felt compelled to speak, to explain her thoughts as her saol flickered. "Maybe your mother poisoned your mind. Maybe she only helped groom what was inside you. Whatever the truth is, I can't care about it anymore." She was struck by the realization that she didn't know what to do. Her mother shoved against the barricade he'd conjured. Was she saying something? Aurelia couldn't hear. The pounding of her heart was like a thousand drums. This was her chance to…what? Kill Drest? Get her revenge? She couldn't bring Brennus back. Nothing could. Drest might not have fired the arrow that killed her brother, but he'd orchestrated the opportunity.

Every part of her felt stripped raw. Like her saol had encompassed her entire body, leaving her exposed and aware of every single thing surrounding them. She smelled the stale scent of iron. She saw the vacant, desperate look in Drest's eyes, then heard him scream before more blood ran down his chin. He staggered to his feet, lunging with his sword. She sidestepped easily and kicked the blade from his hand.

Her mother's voice broke through the wind barrier. "Aurelia!"

The sword hit the grass. Aurelia dove, reaching it moments before Drest did. She scooped it up and swiftly pressed the tip below his ribs, the same place Jastyn had stabbed Enya.

She held it there, blinking and realizing the harried breaths were her own. Hunched, Drest swayed, his own breath weak. Looking into his eyes, she could see it.

Drest was gone. Her childhood best friend, her brother's confidante, their companion in castle mischief. Maybe he was never really any of those things.

"Aurelia." His voice crackled like the dying embers of a fire. Blood sat between his teeth and had pooled onto his collar. Glancing down, she kept the sword to his torso, waiting. The blade shook, and she looked from her trembling hand to his vacant gaze. "Please."

Through her tears, she willed her hand to move, to do something, but she couldn't.

Drest wrapped his hands around hers on the sword grip. By the time she realized his intention, she couldn't pull her hand back. She cried out as he pulled her toward him, sinking his sword into his chest. He gasped, a sickening sound like cutting meat as he drove the blade farther in, his hands tight around hers.

His knees buckled, and Aurelia fell with him. He collapsed on his back, bringing her to her knees. He smiled before his face went slack with a final heave from his torso. She slowly pulled her hands from the blood-covered hilt and rocked back. Her stomach turned, and she watched his chest, waiting for the sword to push itself out. She waited for his hand to lift and flick her away like a pesky fly.

Her stomach heaved, and she retched onto the grass. A deep, agonized wail broke through her chest and poured out into the early morning air. She doubled over, weeping into her fists. Tears mingled with blood and dirt. A door had opened inside her, one she'd locked and had never been willing to look at since Brennus's passing. But now the door sprang open wide, and her grief came flooding out.

The wind stopped, and Aurelia lifted her head. Her mother was at her side, her voice soft. "Oh, my darling."

A wave of sorrow washed over her, and Aurelia threw herself into her mother's arms. She let herself be held and burrowed into her mother's tunic, clinging to her as if to the edge of a cliff that she'd been unwilling to look over for the last six months. She'd seen the other side now, and she knew. It was time to feel again, time to release the anguish she'd shoved down in order to continue forward. But she hadn't moved forward. She'd been stuck, ignoring the pain she was too afraid to feel.

More sobs racked her body. "He's gone," she said, her voice muffled between cries. "He's gone."

CHAPTER TWENTY-EIGHT

A s she tore through the Wood, Jastyn kept her grip tight around the vial. She leapt a fallen log, relishing the feel of the soft, moss-covered ground that seemed to lift her feet faster with each step. Even the low-lying branches appeared to part as she sped past, as if the Wood sensed her urgency as sunlight crept over the realm.

It felt like she was flying as she descended toward the shore. Sweat trickled down her spine. The selkie ship floated two lengths from the beach. Frantically, she searched for the rowboat. Not finding it, Jastyn felt panic rise in her throat. When the first sliver of sunlight broke over the dunes at her back, she shouted, "Alanna!"

A familiar *pop* and Eegit stood ankle-deep in the water before her. "Stop screaming, child, and come on."

Jastyn ran to her. Eegit grabbed her hand. A feeling like the ground had fallen out from under them made her stomach drop, but then wooden floorboards creaked in greeting beneath her boots, and she looked around the cabin of her father's ship.

"Jastyn."

Alanna sat, hunched and pale, against the opposite wall.

"Alanna, I'm here. I have it." Shaking, Jastyn worked to uncork the vial. Alanna shivered, coughing so much, it shook her entire body.

"Child." Eegit's voice came from behind her. "Where's the rest of it?"

"This is all that's left." Finally, she yanked the stopper free. Glancing over her shoulder, she asked, "Will it be enough?"

Eegit's wide eyes held uncertainty. "It'll have to be."

Jastyn helped Alanna lift the vial to her dry lips. She took a shaky breath as if to will her lungs to quell their struggle long enough to drink. Jastyn nodded, trying to encourage her. "That's good." Together, they tipped the vial upward. Jastyn cupped her sister's trembling hands to steady them.

Even the creaky boat seemed to pause its sway as Jastyn pocketed the empty vial and waited. She and Alanna stared at one another, Jastyn searching her for a change, any kind of sign that the cure was working. Eegit stepped into her line of sight, watching.

Alanna frowned, one hand moving to her chest. She took a deep, clear breath before smiling. Jastyn returned it, reaching out. "Alanna?"

Alanna's smile fell. Her eyes rolled back. Her neck lolled to one side, her chin limp against her shoulder.

Dread rushed through Jastyn. "No." She shook Alanna. Her hands scrambled to her neck, searching for a pulse. "Alanna, wake up."

"Child." Eegit's scratchy voice seemed to reach out, coaxing Jastyn away.

"No." She turned, glaring. "The cure will work. It has to."

Eegit opened her mouth. With tears burning her eyes, Jastyn faced her, ready to fire back a retort when Eegit's face scrunched. She tilted her head to one side as if listening. After a look back at Alanna, Jastyn asked, "What is it?"

With a roar like a giant beast, the right wall tore open, sending broken planks and splintered wood flying through the cabin. Eegit fell backward. Jastyn covered her ears as she ducked to shield Alanna from the debris.

The Dark Fae stood framed in a jagged opening, the wall blown apart, now only smoking fragments that revealed the shoreline and the slowly brightening light reflecting off the ocean.

"Enough now, Odium Child." He looked just as he had in the Wood, a resurrected tyrant here to fulfill his demented mission.

"She's had enough of you." Stepping out from behind an overturned barrel spilling wine, Eegit raised both arms, palms directed at the Dark Fae. He bellowed but staggered backward by a wall of green spell-fire. Jastyn gaped. The fiery saol was three times the size of Eegit as it blazed from her hands. The Dark Fae seemed taken aback by her strength, his eyes wide as he was nearly forced from the haphazard entrance he'd just made. His arms shot to his sides, his fingertips catching the edges of the broken boards to keep from falling into the sea. Eegit walked closer, muttering a new spell.

The Dark Fae regained his balance and met her magic with his own. The wind he conjured picked Eegit up like a doll and threw her against the far wall.

"Eegit!" Jastyn stood, her stance wide to obstruct his path to Alanna, though she knew it was only her he wanted. Her saol burned to life in both hands. She shoved it forward. He waved it aside. She glanced at Alanna still limp against the wall. Jastyn conjured more, clinging to the hope that everything hadn't been in vain.

Firing, she managed a snare of blue flames that wrapped around the Dark Fae's arms and chest. Eegit emerged from a pile of detritus. She wore the same look of determination as when working on a difficult spell. Her hands shot out, adding green flames to Jastyn's blue that twisted around his waist. He screamed, and the noise was so similar to the pooka's, Jastyn was afraid it might appear to join their fight. There was a splash from outside. Holding her spell-fire in place, she braced herself for the creature to break through the ceiling.

Her blue flames faltered at her fear, and the Dark Fae broke one arm free. Eegit stepped closer, fighting to keep him locked in spell-fire. Jastyn glanced again at Alanna. What if the cure hadn't worked? What if it hadn't been enough? Jastyn winced at the energy she forced into her hands to maintain her magic. She was so tired. Tired to her core. Tired of running. Tired of fighting. If Alanna was gone, and if the Dark Fae being here meant the worst for Aurelia in the Wood, what was the point? She shuddered, thinking how easy it would be to pull back, to extinguish her fire and let things end. The cabin swayed under the tumult of their fight. She considered hurling herself at the Dark Fae, throwing them both into the rocky sea. Then it would be done. She imagined what it might be like, the stark, peaceful quiet of the ocean floor.

The Dark Fae screamed. His eyes met hers.

No. She couldn't let him win. She couldn't give in to the years of torment, of hiding, of living in fear. So many had left their marks on her, creating indelible scars and forcing her to believe she wasn't worth it. It had taken a long time to learn, and Jastyn knew she was still learning, but she knew...she deserved a whole life. A life full of love and family, a life lived without fear. That was what she deserved. That was what she would have.

"Eegit." Jastyn wasn't sure how long they could hold him. Even if they could, what were they going to do? She could draw her dagger, but doing so would break her concentration. It wouldn't take long, but she couldn't risk it.

"We need more power," Eegit shouted. Her thin arms shook. As powerful as she was, even she had limits.

Jastyn's flames thinned, dimming around the Dark Fae. He sneered, pulling his shoulders up to free his arms. He had nearly twisted out of their waning spell-fire when a second splash sounded from below, followed by a thud and footsteps running overhead.

Jastyn tried to prepare herself for who it probably was: an enchanted guardsman, Drest, or his mad mother. When the cabin door fell in, Jastyn couldn't believe who stood in the doorway.

Revna took in the cabin with a quick sweep of her dark gaze. Stepping forward, she spoke an incantation Jastyn didn't recognize. A rush like at a waterfall's edge swept up from under the ship, rocking it. Through the broken wall, a line of water rose up like a snake. Revna lifted one hand, still speaking in a quiet rhythm until the water shot into the cabin and coiled around the Dark Fae's neck.

Eegit cackled, a wide grin lifting her sallow cheeks. "Selkies. Now I have seen everything."

Revna shot her a look but held her charm steady. Bolstered by her presence, Jastyn burned her saol hotter. Eegit followed suit. The Dark Fae screeched as the three of them closed in. Maybe now Jastyn could get to her dagger.

As she leaned down, Revna said, "Wait." Jastyn followed to where Revna's other hand pointed. "Look."

A wound appeared in the Dark Fae's chest. It grew larger, a coin-sized tear that expanded to the size of an apple. Blood seeped down his tunic.

"That's where I stabbed the baroness," Jastyn said over the roar of their spells.

"His descendants," Eegit said, "they control him. They must be connected."

The Dark Fae looked down. His face fell in disbelief, then slowly began to change. He screamed again, this one tight with rage. When he lifted his head, sending them all a disdainful scowl, the recently acquired flesh on his face began to mold, crumbling off his bones in chunks.

Ignoring the bile in her throat, Jastyn shouted, "What's happening?"

"Keep your spell going," Revna said.

When a second, deeper gash cut into his chest, a mirror image of the first, his scream made even Revna step back. Blood ran from both wounds as more of his body withered into decay.

Their streams of magic flowed steadily, encircling him tighter as the Dark Fae weakened. He threw back his head in an anguished howl. Jastyn couldn't take her eyes off him, afraid the scales of power would shift, and he'd be whole again.

"Keep going," Revna roared over his shrieks. Now their magic engulfed him completely. Fire and water met in clouds of steam, scolding bright bursts of energy that stoked the Dark Fae's decay. Smoke rose in colorful columns in a circle around him. His shouts devolved to that of a ghoul or some other garish spirit. The blood from his wounds had curdled and slowed. For a moment, he met Jastyn's gaze.

Years of hauntings, sleepless nights, and fretful dreams were ending. Jastyn could feel it. She could see it in his eyes moments before those too shriveled and shrank. She felt sick but couldn't look away. His clothes also fell apart, stitches unraveling into fragments that turned to dust as they hit the floor.

The Dark Fae twisted as if to fight against his final moments. Now only pieces of ligaments clung to a black-boned skeleton overcome by their magic. From between rotted gums, he directed a last screech at the sky. Jastyn cried out with Eegit and Revna as they let their final ounces of strength and magic fly from their hands. What seemed like a storm cloud exploded from where the Dark Fae had stood, rolling over them until the entire cabin was shrouded in mist.

The screeching stopped.

Jastyn coughed as they waved at the smoke as it dimmed and dissipated out the broken wall. Jastyn felt weak, maybe the weakest she'd felt since she'd had to fight off starvation as a child. Her knees buckled, but she caught herself, stumbling and staring at the pile of ashes, all that was left of the Dark Fae.

Revna stepped closer, peering at the sizzling fragments. Eegit hobbled over to join them, hacking and spitting between agitated breaths.

Jastyn leaned carefully over the gray ashes. Had they really, finally defeated him? It seemed surreal. Part of her wanted to reach out and touch it, make sure it was true. Instead, she looked at Eegit.

She pushed back her mane of white hair with a wrinkled arm.

"Thank you," Jastyn said, her voice breaking. "Thank you," she said again, this time to Revna, who adjusted the sealskin atop her black hair. She bowed her head in response.

"Jastyn?" Alanna sat upright. Her complexion was fair, but pale pink filled her cheeks, and her eyes were bright, despite the confused look in them. "What happened?"

"Alanna." Jastyn ran over and fell to her knees beside her sister. She scanned her, clutching her hand before tracing her fingers down her hair. "How do you feel?"

She frowned, thinking. She took a wonderfully deep breath. They both grinned when not a single cough followed.

"You better make more of that, child," Eegit said, but Jastyn hardly heard her as she tackled Alanna in a hug. She let herself feel how much she'd missed her sister. She'd missed Alanna on every step of the journey across the realm. Only now did she realize she'd missed her sister like this, able to live more than a life resigned to poor health, the results of a curse that never should have been.

"What is—" Alanna pointed, and Jastyn turned as Revna and Eegit kicked the last bits of ashes out the wall. Some drifted upward for a moment before falling to the water below.

"Just in case," Eegit huffed.

Jastyn wasn't sure whether to laugh or cry. She smiled, shaking her head. Looking back, she said, "We did it, Alanna. It's over."

CHAPTER TWENTY-NINE

A urelia wasn't sure how long she sat curled in her mother's arms. Eventually, her cries came only in waves, without tears but still wrenching her with pent-up grief. However, with each exhausting exhale, she felt part of her heart mending. The blackness marring her brother's memory brightened as she let her guilt for not being willing to mourn him go. The sun was nearly above the trees when she finally collected herself.

Dazed, she leaned against a tree as her mother did what she did best: commanding order. She disenchanted the guards that had been under Enya's spell, though a handful remained loyal to the baroness's cause despite her rigid body being carried toward castle grounds. Those committed to the baroness's ideals would be imprisoned until they could stand trial before the court.

"Grannus," Aurelia's mother called between releasing more guardsmen from the spell. He turned, hunched and battered, between Rigo and another elf. "Order the immediate release of Branna Rhinehart and Elisedd Eidhin."

Her father looked from her to Aurelia. His bushy eyebrows rose. Aurelia gave a tired smile before he left. Her mother quickly returned to her counter-spells, mending wounds where she could.

For a time, Aurelia watched, glancing occasionally at Drest's body before it, too, was carried away. What had happened to the Dark Fae? She could only hope their assumptions had been true, that with Drest and the baroness gone, so was he. Her mother seemed to float around the stretch of Wood, assessing the damage done to the land. Several fairy leaders had emerged from their nests, along with a handful of gnomes from the hills at the base of nearby trees. Her mother conversed with each, and Aurelia couldn't help but admire how eloquently she seemed to navigate their grievances regarding the damage done to their homes in the battle. Had her mother always been such a good overseer?

Aurelia had never paid much attention to her parents' responsibilities when she'd been living in the castle. She'd been so caught up in her own dreams and begrudging her lack of freedom. Perhaps she'd been so fixated on her family's horrible past that she'd forgotten her parents were capable of good. She'd thrown herself into hating them and lost sight of the fact that they could be benevolent monarchs, even if they had a lot to learn.

"I suppose I do, too," she said to herself, scanning the Wood.

When her gaze fell on the stained patch of grass where Drest had lain, she swallowed and closed her eyes. Her body had been a mix of emotions in the aftermath. Despite feeling like she'd been hollowed out with a carving knife, the new lack of tightness in her chest was liberating. Still, an odd sensation kicked up in her stomach, and she turned away, forcing her gaze back toward the brightening sky.

"Jastyn." She hoped she'd found her sister. Gods, she hoped the cure had worked. She'd tried to say something to her mother about it once the baroness had been taken away. She had tried to thank her, but her mother had only pulled her into a tight hug before getting to work setting this part of the Wood right again. Aurelia hoped the cure had been strong enough.

Tears reemerged, and she leaned her head back, trying to keep them at bay. Why was she still crying? She felt raw. Hadn't she wept all her tears by now? She'd grieved, finally, for her brother's passing. Why did she still feel like this? She looked at her bloodstained hands. She caught her breath, remembering Drest's hands around hers, driving his own sword into his chest. She saw his eyes dim before what little life left in him was gone.

She jumped when Sif took her by the elbow. "Come on, Princess. Let's get you cleaned up." Taken aback, she walked silently beside Sif, who led her to a creek. She tried to clear her mind until Sif helped her kneel at the creek's edge.

"Here." Sif took her hands and dipped them into the water. The cold startled Aurelia, and she gasped, pulling back. "It's okay." Sif met her gaze. "Let me help you," she said, and Aurelia could only nod as Sif began to scrub the blood off.

The shock of the cold water seemed to part the mist shrouding her mind. The agonizing screams of Drest began to fade, though not completely. Slowly, she was able to clean the final caking blood off her wrist.

"Are you okay?" Sif asked.

A quick reply came to Aurelia, but upon opening her mouth, nothing came out. She scanned Sif's face, tracing the furrowed brows beneath her sealskin, the mouth tight with concern. Then she looked around at the tightly packed birch trees, their knots like curious eyes waiting to see what she would do. The early morning air was crisp. She shivered.

Finally, she said, "I don't know."

Sif nodded, and Aurelia saw understanding in the crease of her smile. At the sound of a morning jay, Aurelia asked, "Will you help me find Jastyn?"

Sif pulled her up and helped adjust her mother's cloak on her shoulders. "Of course." Gesturing for her to follow, she added, "Let's go get your Odium."

Eegit took Alanna home to the village while Revna healed Tove and Fortan, who'd showed up at the ship not long after Alanna woke up. Njal and Gorm had helped them swim to the ship. Jastyn had panicked at the sight of their clearly broken arms, but Revna's healing powers reset them, and after a few piercing barks of protest, their arms were realigned and forced into slings.

"Remind me to never get mixed up with humans again," Fortan said, though a slight grin lifted his bruised face. "Could be worse," he said before stooping awkwardly over a goblet to lap up the wine.

Tove laughed, and Jastyn adjusted his sling carefully. He winced. "Revna says it's done."

Jastyn wiped her hands on her pants, avoiding his gaze and glancing at the spot where the Dark Fae's ashes used to be.

"She says he's gone."

"I'm afraid..." she started, then cleared her throat to begin again. "I'm afraid to leave."

Her father frowned. "Why?"

"I'm afraid to leave because what if...what if this isn't real? What if he's still out there? What if as soon as I leave this ship, everything goes back to how it's always been, with Alanna sick and the Dark Fae waiting in the shadows to collect me?" Her voice had risen, and she took a breath.

Her father glanced at Fortan, who used his teeth to grip the edge of the goblet and wander out of the cabin. "Jastyn," he said, leaning closer. "I know it can seem impossible. But it's real." His emphatic tone made her look up. "You did it, Jastyn. You found the cure. You healed Alanna, and the Dark Fae is gone."

"But—"

"He's gone, Jastyn."

She swiped at her tears. Sniffling, she searched the cabin. "I don't know what to do now," she finally said, her voice a whisper.

He stood. "Revna said the king was on his way to the castle with a pardon for your mother and Elisedd. I think meeting him halfway would be a good start."

She nodded. "Will you come with me?"

Her father's eyes widened. "To the dungeons?"

"To see Mother."

"I'm not sure that's a good idea."

"Why? Because of Elisedd?"

"Branna and I..." He trailed off, looking at his hands. "I don't know what I'd say."

"Neither do I. But maybe we can figure it out together."

He looked up, his dark eyes shimmering. "Okay," he said. "Together."

With all the chaos following the battle in the Wood, it was easy for them to slip into the stables and through the castle. Guards and court members ran in every direction, some screaming for their family members, some barking orders, a few crying at the news of what had befallen the baroness and her son.

Catching part of a conversation, Jastyn and Tove exchanged glances: "Still alive," and "Her Majesty disposed of the baroness single-handed." In too much of a hurry to sort out the truth, Jastyn and Tove followed the passageway she'd walked with Roisin to the dungeon door. Jastyn skidded to a halt, Tove barking in pain when he collided with her, making Grannus turn as he finished unlocking the door twenty paces ahead.

It took Jastyn a moment to realize Rigo was one of the elves on either side of the king.

"His Majesty is weak," Rigo said, following her silent question. "We're here on orders from Queen Dechtire."

"And I agreed..." the king started to say, then waved a hand. "Oh, never mind." He pulled open the door with help from the elves as Jastyn and Tove joined them. Hurrying inside and running past the first hall of cells, Jastyn was relieved to not see Roisin still lying there, then feared the worst.

"Coran came and got her after several ladies of the court sent out a search party." Her mother's voice pulled Jastyn's attention to the cell. "She was weak but alive."

Jastyn gripped the bars. Her mother and Elisedd stood, expectant looks on their faces. She knew they'd been aware of the days passing and that this morning had been their final opportunity to get the cure to Alanna. She also realized how much had happened since their imprisonment and decided the entire tale was a story for another time. What mattered most was Alanna. "She's better," Jastyn said as Grannus arrived to unlock the cell door. "We did it."

Inside the cell, her stepfather moved to her mother, wrapping one arm around her. They both stared. The king, mistaking their stunned silence for their sudden freedom, cleared his throat.

"By order of the queen and king, you are hereby pardoned of all alleged crimes against the kingdom. You are free to go."

But her mother and stepfather didn't move. Jastyn stepped inside the cell. "She's well. Alanna is well and finally home."

Her mother was crying, and Elisedd looked up as if to keep his own tears from falling, though it proved futile. They hugged, and her mother stepped back before pulling Jastyn into their embrace. She let herself join in their happy cries, relief mingling with years of worry.

Again, the king cleared his throat. Jastyn led them out of the cell.

"Where is she?" her mother asked.

"Eegit's with her at the house."

Elisedd made a snorting noise, but Jastyn laughed. "Don't worry, she's too tired to try to brew anything before we get home."

"Thank you," Elisedd said to Grannus before he turned to leave. The king chewed his lips, seemingly at a loss for words. Then he reached out, and after a moment, Elisedd took his arm. They nodded, and the king led his guards from the dungeon.

A light footfall behind Jastyn made her turn. Tove emerged from the back wall where he'd been standing beneath the torchlight. Her mother looked from her to him, and her mouth fell open.

Stepping aside so Tove could stand opposite her mother, Jastyn watched them, surprised when Elisedd didn't try to pull her mother closer. Instead, he straightened his shoulders, which gave him even more height on them all. Jastyn caught Rigo's curious gaze before she nodded reassuringly, and he followed the king out.

"Hello, Branna."

Her mother seemed lost in her father's gaze, then finally looked him over. "You look well," she finally said, a soft smile at the corner of her eyes.

"As do you." He paused, giving a quick glance to Elisedd. "It is good to see you."

Jastyn wasn't sure how to feel. On top of everything that had happened in the last day, a reunion between her mother and father was another bewildering occurrence. Though somehow not as surprising as it once would have been. Her parents gazed at one another, a silent conversation taking place in the space between them.

"Mother," Jastyn said after a long silence. "Alanna..."

She nodded. "We should go to her."

Elisedd stepped closer, and her mother wrapped one arm around his waist. "I imagine there is much to talk about," he said, looking between the three of them. "Tove?" Jastyn's father finally tore his gaze from her mother. "Would you care to join us?"

His surprised look vanished quickly, and he smiled. "Very much."

Elisedd nodded. Arm in arm, he and Branna started for the doorway. Tove watched them go.

"Ready?" Jastyn asked.

"I'm not sure." He faced her. "Are you?"

She watched her mother and stepfather as they left the dreary, suffocating confines of the royal dungeons, headed for home. "I don't know. But I know someone who is excellent at making you feel ready for anything."

He returned her smile. "Well, then," he said, "let's go find your princess."

CHAPTER THIRTY

By late afternoon, Jastyn's home was buzzing with activity. Alanna had greeted them all enthusiastically, tackling Elisedd and their mother in hugs which were returned with equal ferocity. She had been set up by the hearth by Eegit, who had arranged an old blanket and sacks of cornmeal stacked as a makeshift seat. As her mother and Elisedd fussed over her, still seemingly in shock at her healthy state, Jastyn had pulled Eegit aside while Tove stood respectfully near the front door pretending to look interested in Elisedd's tools.

"Do you think it will last?" Jastyn asked.

Eegit seemed to have recovered some since the showdown against the Dark Fae on the boat, but she still wheezed occasionally and leaned when she walked. "The cure was still the cure. The ingredients were the combination needed to heal."

"To counter the selkie curse," Jastyn said, her words sharp.

She grunted. "So it was. You still have the vials?"

Jastyn reached for the satchel that wasn't draped over her. "I'm not sure. I think…they were in the Wood." She met Eegit's gaze. "Do you think we should make more?"

"Couldn't hurt. Maybe I can help Dechtire with it now that I've finished bottling luck." She guffawed at her own idea as she started to go, but Jastyn ran after her.

"Wait." She grabbed Eegit by the elbow, turning her. "What do you mean?" She searched Eegit's knowing eyes as realization dawned. "All this time…you've been working on my new dagger? But how… the old one wasn't even lost yet."

Eegit wagged a finger, grinning as she started off again. "Come by my meadow later, child, and I'll tell you all about it. Though I've had to relocate after all the chaos you caused."

Shaking her head at Eegit's abilities, Jastyn tried not to grin. "I'll find it, don't worry."

Eegit waved as she passed Tove, then gave a solid thwack to his back. He shouted in surprise, and Eegit cackled as she wandered out the door.

Tove walked over to Jastyn who said, "She likes you."

He grimaced, slowly moving his shoulders as if to soothe the area she'd hit. "That's good. I think."

When her mother motioned for Tove to join her, Elisedd, and Alanna by the hearth, he didn't move.

"Go on," Jastyn said. "My sister wants to meet you."

His eyes twinkling, he took a deep breath, then joined them. Jastyn watched for a moment, smiling at Alanna's enthusiasm until she remembered what her mother had said about Roisin. "I'll be right back," she called to her family, gesturing in the direction of Coran's house.

She hurried down the hill until she saw the familiar off-kilter door, the savory-smelling smoke curling out of the small chimney. She knocked and was immediately greeted by Kyra.

"Jastyn!" Kyra pulled her into a hug, dragging her inside. "Gods, Coran has told me all about it. Come in. He's in his room tending to Roisin. Poor girl got hit with a nasty batch of spell-fire." Jastyn grimaced, knowing it was her own saol that had knocked Roisin out. "Come, sit. I've just made a stew. Let me make you a bowl."

Jastyn noticed the limp in Kyra's step, and how her left hand didn't open completely, the lingering effects of the arrow she'd taken in the back during the elf invasion. She started to scoop out a ladle of stew when Jastyn said, "Stew smells great, Kyra. Save me some for later? I'd like to go see them first, if that's okay."

Kyra kept spooning chunks of meat and carrots into a bowl but looked up between long red-orange curls that fell over her forehead. "O'course. Go on." She nodded, and Jastyn smiled, slipping into Coran's room.

He sat near the head of his bed where Roisin lay on her side. Her eyelids looked heavy. Coran stroked her arm as they carried on what seemed like an intimate conversation. Jastyn had to contain her joy at seeing her best friend safe in his home again. She stood quietly, her gaze on her boots for a time before she cleared her throat.

Coran whipped around and stood. "Jas!"

They met each other halfway in a hug. "Gods, it's good to see ya. I'm sorry I didn't stay to help, but..." He stepped back, motioning to Roisin.

"Roisin," she said, "I'm so sorry."

Roisin shook her head and pushed up, leaning against the wall behind the bed. "Nonsense." She winced, and Coran helped situate a blanket behind her head.

"But," Jastyn said, "my spell-fire..."

"It was an accident," Roisin said, holding her gaze steady.

"She told me what happened, Jas." Coran sat back in a chair pulled close to the bed. "Really, it was the guards who should be blamed."

Jastyn reached out, resting a hand on Roisin's. "Still, I'm sorry."

"I may have gotten accustomed to castle life, but I'm still tougher than I look."

Jastyn and Coran exchanged looks. "Well, I'm glad you're okay."

"I saw Alanna made it home with Eegit," Coran said. "She looked well." The look he gave her said how happy he was for her, how glad he was to know Alanna was finally on the path to a healthier life.

"She is," Jastyn said. "We did it," she added, punching his arm.

He rubbed it dramatically, then lowered his voice. "When I went over to see Alanna, Eegit said something about the selkie ship. Something about Revna and...ashes?"

No matter how many times she replayed the memories, she still found it difficult to believe her own words. "He's gone," she told him and was met with awe. "We defeated him, Coran. The Dark Fae is done."

He looked at Roisin, who seemed equally rapt. Jastyn could see his hesitancy before he asked, "And...you're sure, Jas? He's really gone?"

She pictured the Dark Fae's remains, nothing but a pile of ashes kicked out to sea by Eegit and Revna. She smiled, and finally believed it herself. "He's really gone."

Coran reached out, and Jastyn grabbed his hand, squeezing it. He, better than almost anyone, knew how tormented she'd been. She'd laid bare to Coran over the years the terrible visions she didn't want to tell her mother about. She'd trusted him with her fears. Now, she saw his happiness for her and felt his shared relief at her no longer having to bear the weight of the Dark Fae's looming presence.

A sudden shriek from the main room made them turn. Kyra sprinted through the doorway, holding a ladle that dripped bits of potato. She used it to point over her shoulder as she stammered, "Coran, there's a…a tall…he's a…there's an elf…in the house."

"Oh, mum, it's only Rigo," he explained as Rigo silently stood behind his mother, who ducked away back toward the main room.

Rigo, looking confused, turned to Coran. "Your mother looks like you," he said as Coran tugged him into the room.

"Not usually how that sentence goes, but thanks," he replied. Roisin nudged herself back but didn't look as startled by Rigo's presence as she had in the Wood.

"I've come to offer my assistance, if I may," Rigo said, looking at Roisin.

"That's awful nice of you," Coran said. He looked to Roisin. "If it's okay with you."

She glanced between them. "If m'lady Aurelia trusts you, I trust you."

Coran smiled as Rigo turned back to Jastyn. "Speaking of Her Highness, I saw her coming up the far hillside."

"She's okay?" Jastyn asked, trying to swallow the thudding heartbeat that seemed to rise in her chest.

"I can't answer that," Rigo replied. "But she was walking unassisted."

Jastyn had so much to tell Aurelia and so many questions for her in equal measure. She wanted to know what had happened in the Wood and wanted to tell her the good news about Alanna. She wanted to hold Aurelia close, not just this day, but every day from here onward. She wanted what she could finally see now that the Dark Fae was gone: a future of her own.

"Go on, Jas," Coran said. "We'll be here. I'll introduce Rigo to mum's stew."

Smiling, Jastyn said good-bye and tore from the room, waving to a frazzled Kyra before she ran back up the hillside. She spotted Aurelia and Sif clearing the final line of trees on the other side of the low wall outside her house.

Jastyn nearly flew up the hill as Aurelia clambered over the wall, stumbling a bit but pulling herself up in time for Jastyn to pull her into a hug.

They held one another tightly. Jastyn cherished the feeling of Aurelia pressed against her. She inhaled the scent of earth and tulips that always seemed to cling to her. She closed her eyes to fall farther into Aurelia's arms. Eventually, she leaned back, searching Aurelia's eyes which stared lovingly back at her.

"You're okay," Aurelia said, pushing back Jastyn's hair.

"Actually, I'm exhausted."

Aurelia laughed, tears sitting in the corner of her eyes. "Gods, me, too."

Jastyn leaned in, kissing her.

After a few moments, Sif cleared her throat. "Save it for later, Princess."

Another quick kiss and Aurelia leaned back, giving a dramatic groan. "Very well."

Jastyn's head felt light, dizzy with Aurelia being here, outside her home, kissing her, wanting her. "Aurelia," she said, pressing their foreheads together, "he's gone."

Aurelia didn't seem surprised as she gave a small nod. "So are his descendants." They stood like that for several seconds, letting their latest deeds sink into one another. Aurelia's presence was like a gentle balm, and Jastyn let the nearness soothe her mind.

"Come on." Jastyn took her hand. "You have a big admirer who would love to see you again."

Aurelia grinned and followed her inside.

Sif and Tove eventually left to assemble the other selkies. They were going to determine their immediate next steps as well as the future of their alliance with the Diarmaids. Tove and Branna had gone outside to talk before he left. From a seat near the fire in the common room, Aurelia could see Jastyn straining to listen, only replying in short sentences as Alanna told Elisedd what she remembered from the selkie ship.

Aurelia was so weary, she feared she might never get up. Her body felt heavy, her muscles tingled with fatigue.

Branna returned from outside. "Tove says they're going to have a meeting with the king in the coming days," she said, taking a seat next to Elisedd behind Alanna.

"They're staying?" Jastyn asked. She probably wasn't ready to let Tove go.

Aurelia wasn't sure if Jastyn wanted to go back with him. Maybe not now but perhaps someday. For now, Alanna's good health should keep her here for a time.

"They'll stay for a week." Branna accepted a cup of tea and took a drink. She'd just set the cup down when there was a knock on the door.

They all stood, save for Alanna. Jastyn placed one arm protectively over Aurelia. Gently, she laid a hand on Jastyn's back. "It's okay."

Jastyn blinked, seeming to collect herself as Elisedd strode to the door.

"Mother?" Aurelia rushed forward. Her mother had re-pinned her hair, though strands still strayed across her face in the evening breeze. Her face had been scrubbed clean, but a few cuts lined her forehead. Her cloak billowed behind her until Elisedd ushered her inside.

Aurelia asked, "Mother, what is it?"

Her mother, who had been doing a sweep of the room with her wide gaze, turned to her. She pulled Aurelia into a hug, then swept off her cloak, placing it over one arm. "I've come to see how Alanna is doing."

The entire room seemed to inhale; even the fire flickered in astonishment. Aurelia glanced back to Jastyn, whose jaw clenched, but her typically hard stare had softened. Behind her, Branna and Elisedd exchanged glances, then nodded. Aurelia returned to Jastyn's side, leaving her mother near the doorway.

Eventually, Elisedd reached for her cloak. "May I take that for you, Your Majesty?"

"Yes, thank you, Elisedd. Please," she added, adjusting her collar, "use my first name." She moved toward the hearth, closer to Alanna. They all situated themselves around the small space, forming a half circle opposite the warm orange fire. Elisedd joined them and passed Aurelia's mother a cup of tea.

Nobody seemed to know what to say. Aurelia even felt at a loss for words, bewildered by her mother sitting in Jastyn's home, with Jastyn's parents sitting like proud recipients of the realm's greatest prize in

Alanna, their youngest daughter leaning easily against their legs from her seat on the floor. Branna ran a hand through her daughter's hair, constantly reaching out as if to make sure Alanna was real.

"When did you do it?" Jastyn asked, breaking the silence.

Aurelia's mother took a sip of tea, cupping it gently between her slender hands. "When did I capture the extra vial of your sister's cure? The night it was done. I'd seen several spare vials among your friend's assortment of items."

Aurelia tried not to smile at her mother's careful choice of words regarding Eegit's eclectic belongings.

"I always like to err on the side of caution."

"We're so grateful," Elisedd said, giving Alanna's shoulder a squeeze.

"Well, I'm happy to have helped." She shifted in her seat, and Aurelia was surprised at her sudden uncertainty.

Alanna asked what they were all wondering. "Will it last?"

Her mother flattened her lips, her eyes pinching at their corners in thought. "I think so." This time, a collective exhale filled the room.

"But if it doesn't…" Jastyn trailed off, and Aurelia squeezed her hand. It was naive to think her realistic outlook would shift to optimism after such a dramatic day. Still, the validity of the question pained Aurelia.

"I'm afraid the vials were lost, but I remember each of the ingredients vividly and recall the recipe word for word. I can reach out to our contacts in the East and see if they might be able to procure the ingredients. That way, we can have a constant supply just in case."

Jastyn and her family exchanged looks before nodding vigorously. Branna said, "That would be wonderful."

Aurelia's mother said, "Consider it done."

Jastyn seemed at a loss for words, a continuing theme of the evening since Aurelia's mother arrived.

"I also wanted to apologize for your unauthorized capture at the baroness's request."

Elisedd nodded as if this was already forgotten. Branna, however, held her gaze as if waiting.

"We…Grannus and I…the court as a whole have many things to consider."

Aurelia nudged her mother's knee with her own, prompting her to continue.

"To reconsider, I suppose. There are many things to discuss and a lot my husband and I are going to try to understand. Things our kingdom has been neglecting."

Aurelia smiled.

"I can't take back what was done. None of us can." She glanced at Aurelia. "But we are going to try to fix what's broken in our kingdom. We want Venostes to be a place that's warm and receptive. I thought we were…" Aurelia's mother trailed off, then, seeming to remember who she was with, lifted her chin. "Clearly, we have a lot to learn. Our meeting with the selkies will be a start."

Overcome, Aurelia took her mother's hand. She saw tears in her mother's eyes when she set her cup down and stood. To Alanna, she said, "I am glad you are well. Perhaps I can come check in some time." Alanna nodded eagerly before Branna placed a hand on her shoulder.

"That would be very kind," Branna said.

"Wonderful. Well, I have many matters that need sorting before sundown." Then she was at the door, donning her cloak. "Aurelia," she called over her shoulder, "don't be too late, darling. It's been a trying day, and your father and I…we would like to see you home soon."

"I'll be home by nightfall," Aurelia replied. Her mother's gaze gave one more sweep of the room before she smiled and was gone.

Alanna's stomach growled, and she gripped it in surprise. "Gods, I'm starved. I could eat a whole plate of lamb." Branna smiled, and Elisedd leaned down, placing a kiss on Alanna's forehead.

Jastyn stood. "Kyra's made three cauldron's worth of her stew. I bet she's got extra."

"Sounds delicious," Alanna said, turning to warm her hands.

"We'll fetch some," Jastyn said, reaching for Aurelia's hand. "When we get back, I think it's time we told you all the whole story." Jastyn squeezed her hand. Aurelia's heart fluttered as their fingers intertwined. Happiness filled her chest. Everything seemed brighter as a clear vision of possibility flew before her eyes. Jastyn turned as they stepped outside. "From the beginning."

EPILOGUE

S ee you in the spring," Coran shouted, waving alongside Jastyn and Aurelia where they stood upon the southern shore. They shielded their eyes from the sunlight reflecting off the water. Wind whipped their hair across their faces, but Jastyn didn't let that diminish the joy she felt as she waved good-bye to her father and the other selkies.

"Is it strange I miss them already?" Rigo stood a few paces behind them, easily watching over their collective heads as the ship sailed toward the horizon.

"Not at all," Aurelia said, leaning into Jastyn. In her clean tunic and bright navy cloak, Aurelia looked stunning. She'd donned the newly polished starfish pin in her hair. It tried unsuccessfully to keep some of her braided strands in place in the strong wind.

"Their Majesties said the meeting went so well, they may consider gatherings between the kingdom and the selkies," Roisin chimed in from Coran's other side.

Jastyn's chest swelled with pride at what had—according to Aurelia in her recount of the meetings she'd attended with her parents over the last week—been an extremely successful reworking of some of the Fae-Diarmaid Treaty guidelines. She had nearly burst into Jastyn's home a couple nights ago, brimming with excitement at the willingness of her family to concede some of the water back to the selkies, even opening Venostes' shores to a bi-annual gathering. Jastyn knew it was a big leap for the Diarmaids to sit down with fae, let alone begin the changes Dechtire had promised and Aurelia was helping to push along.

When the ship was out of sight, they started back for the mainland, ascending toward the trees.

"Anyone up for some of mum's fish stew?" Coran asked as he helped Roisin up the sandy embankment.

"I'd love some," she replied, and he grinned, giving her a quick kiss.

Jastyn kept her hand in Aurelia's, who gave her a look that said she had other ideas. "Maybe later. Tell Kyra to save us some."

He nodded. "Rigo?"

Rigo stood beneath an elm tree, looking alarmingly tall compared to the four of them. "Is this one of those things humans do when they don't want someone to leave? Offer them tasty sustenance?"

They all laughed. Yesterday, Rigo had shared his plan to return to his homeland to find his mate. Jastyn had been surprised with how sad she'd felt at the news, and Coran had openly wept at the prospect of him leaving.

"You know you want some, Rigo," Coran called, now several steps ahead with Roisin.

Rigo smiled and looked to Jastyn and Aurelia.

"He's not going to let you say no," Jastyn said.

He chuckled. "I suppose one more bowl of stew could only do me good."

"Say good-bye before you leave?" Aurelia asked.

"Of course, Your Majesty."

He caught up to Coran and Roisin, then disappeared below the hillside.

Jastyn turned to Aurelia. "I see that look in your eye. You're up to something." She grinned as Aurelia's face tightened in mock anger before lifting in a knowing smile.

"Can we stop by the market? There's something my mother wanted me to pick up." She tugged Jastyn to follow. Eventually, they made it to the market streets, which weren't as busy as they once were since the commotion of the last few weeks. Most villagers rejoiced at learning the Diarmaids were well, evident in the many bows and exclaimed greetings Aurelia received as they strolled between carts, something Jastyn still wasn't used to experiencing. A few people inside the court had evidently been aware of the baroness's scheme. Some had gone into hiding, but Dechtire and Grannus held most in the dungeons until they could be questioned thoroughly. There was an undercurrent of change vibrating throughout the kingdom, and for once, Jastyn had a feeling it was something good. A walk like this, for one, would have been unbearable a year ago. Now, hardly anyone reacted to her the way they once had. Children weren't hurried away. Old men didn't grumble disparaging remarks as she passed. A couple villagers seemed to eye them with curiosity but nothing more.

When Aurelia strode up to a wooden cart covered in woven tapestries and silk hangings, Jastyn asked, "What are we doing here?"

"I told you," Aurelia said, handing the woman a trio of gold coins, "I'm picking something up." The redheaded, matronly woman handed Aurelia something wrapped in parchment and tied with twine. "Come on, then," she said, package in hand as she retraced their steps toward the village.

Jastyn followed. "What is that?"

Aurelia tossed her a grin, her braid swaying happily at her back. "You'll see."

Content, Jastyn walked alongside Aurelia, losing herself in the memories from the last few days. She recalled sitting at home, laughing at stories Tove and her mother told over a shared loaf of bread and a bowl of stew. She'd walked with Alanna up to the well to fetch water, something Jastyn had never done with her sister. Sliding her gaze sideways, she recalled one night she and Aurelia had joined the selkies for dinner on their ship and had slipped out to their favorite spot in the Wood and spent a night under the stars next to a warm fire.

Lost in thought, Jastyn was surprised when Aurelia asked, "Should I knock?" Looking up, Jastyn found they were standing in front of her home.

Shaking her head at Aurelia's question, she opened the door as she tried to figure out what Aurelia was up to. Inside, they found her mother by the fire, mending a pair of socks. Elisedd was no doubt at the stables. Alanna sat at the table, leaning over a book Aurelia had gifted her two days before.

"Jastyn," her mother said, looking up and smiling. "Your Highness." At Aurelia's frown, she corrected herself. "Aurelia." She shook her head. "That is going to take some getting used to." She set her handiwork aside and stood. Jastyn began to shed her cloak when her mother gestured to Aurelia. "May I take yours?"

"Oh, no, thank you. We're not staying long."

Jastyn paused. "We're not?"

Her mother smiled, placing one hand on her hip. "Is it time already?"

Aurelia nodded, but Jastyn glanced between them, confused. "Aurelia, what's going on?"

Ignoring her, Aurelia stepped forward. "First things first." She held the wrapped item out. "I come with a special delivery." Jastyn didn't miss the pitch in her voice, which drew Alanna's attention from her book. "The queen has a gift for Alanna."

Within moments, Alanna was at her mother's side. She looked stronger already, her face rounder and full of healthy color. "A gift?" Her excited gaze flew between them, then to the parcel. She reached out but paused.

"Oh, go on," their mother said, smiling.

Alanna squealed, then carefully took the gift. She scurried to the hearth to sit on the rug in front before tearing into the parchment. "By the gods," she said, one hand over her mouth.

Aurelia seemed to be working hard to look like she had no idea what was going on. When her mother joined Alanna, she too gasped, then turned back to face them with tears in her eyes.

Overcome with curiosity, Jastyn crouched next to Alanna, pulling back some of the parchment to see. In her sister's lap was a beautiful, folded, patchwork quilt made of material that seemed to shimmer even in the dim firelight. Jastyn, Alanna, and their mother all fell quiet.

"I told my mother about what happened," Aurelia said. Her gaze was on Alanna. "Regarding your quilt when the guards…well, you remember." A flash of anger flew over her face, but it vanished quickly. "She had this made for you as a replacement."

"Some replacement," Alanna said, sounding awestruck, and Jastyn snorted. Simultaneously, they reached out, caressing the soft material. It felt like the downy feathers of a chick but softer.

"Thank you," Alanna finally said. "It's wonderful." Then she stood, handing the blanket to Jastyn before running to Aurelia. "I'll sleep with it every night," she exclaimed before attacking Aurelia in a hug.

"I'm glad," she replied, and Jastyn caught her pleased look.

Jastyn felt a swelling of emotion at the look in her mother's eyes. She saw in them the same contentment that had settled in her chest the last few days. Slowly, their lives were beginning again.

"Tell the queen we're very grateful," her mother said finally, busying herself with the charred pots over the hearth.

Aurelia nodded. "I will."

Clearing her throat, Jastyn stood. "So is anyone going to tell me what you were talking about earlier? What is it time for, exactly?"

Her mother laughed, wiping her face and turning to grab a rag she used to clean off the table. "I didn't want to spoil it. Besides, Aurelia told me not to tell."

Raising her brows, Jastyn glanced between them. Normally, she'd be annoyed and uneasy at not knowing what was going on, but the fact that Aurelia had confided in her mother was too astounding to be angry about.

Turning with a flourish of her cloak, Aurelia said, "I'll have her home before the moon is high." Then she motioned for Jastyn to follow, her arm outstretched. Jastyn took her hand but not before tossing her mother a look.

Alanna called, "Have fun."

"What is going on?" Jastyn asked when Aurelia led her outside.

"Now, don't be mad," she started, the first sign of nerves evident in her tight lips.

"Aurelia…"

"I only wanted to surprise you."

"I think we need to have a talk about surprises, considering, you know, everything."

Aurelia frowned. "I didn't think about that. But I see your point."

Jastyn smiled despite having no idea what was going on. But with Aurelia by her side, she felt ready to take on anything. These confident thoughts faltered, though, when she found herself standing outside the palace gates.

Aurelia said, "My mother and father said you could visit but only until nightfall."

Jastyn stared at the towering castle, the piles of gray stone looming over this part of the hillside. She traced the turrets, then down to the main doors she'd never stood this close to before.

"Aurelia, wouldn't it be safer to…sneak in?" she asked, swallowing at the guardsmen framing the doors.

"Nonsense."

"Are you sure it's okay?"

"Jastyn—"

"Aurelia." She sighed. "Your parents don't exactly…care for me."

Aurelia faced her, looking offended. "That's not true." At Jastyn's pointed look, she scrunched up her face. "Well, they don't *not* care for you. But they're ready to start listening and are open to getting to know you. They're the ones who said I should bring you around today."

Jastyn squinted. "They did?"

Aurelia crossed her heart. "Princess promise." Seeming to sense Jastyn's uncertainty, Aurelia moved to stand shoulder to shoulder with her. "No more sneaking through the stables. No evil baroness." She took a deep breath. "No more Dark Fae."

Shaking her head, Jastyn knew she was right, but it was still so new. Like discovering a new way of life, a completely different way of doing things, a reality that had been hidden just beneath the one they'd always known. Now that it was uncovered, the realm upended by the last six months, it all seemed too good to be true.

Aurelia placed a kiss on her cheek. "Jastyn, your sister is healthy. You don't have to worry about her anymore."

"She's my sister. I'll always worry."

Rolling her eyes, Aurelia smiled. "You know perfectly well what I mean."

Jastyn grinned. "I know. I've just…never felt like this."

"Like what?"

"Free."

Aurelia squeezed her hand, and they both stared at the bright clear sky. "Well, what would you like to do with this new freedom?"

Jastyn turned, scanning the royal grounds, the village over the hills, and the Wood beyond. "There's still so much to do."

Aurelia nodded. "There is."

Jastyn faced her. "I think I'd like to do it all with you."

The smile on Aurelia's face widened, and Jastyn could see her trying to contain her excitement, bouncing on her toes. "That sounds wonderful."

The castle gates opened, and they walked inside.

About the Author

Originally from Dallas-Ft. Worth, Sam Ledel currently resides in Southern California with her girlfriend and their Jack Russell terrier. Her debut novel, *Rocks and Stars*, was a 2019 Goldie finalist. She is currently working on her next book.

Books Available from Bold Strokes Books

A Fae Tale by Genevieve McCluer. Dovana comes to terms with her changing feelings for her lifelong best friend and fae, Roze. (978-1-63555-918-7)

Accidental Desperados by Lee Lynch. Life is clobbering Berry, Jaudon, and their long romance. The arrival of directionless baby dyke MJ doesn't help. Can they find their passion again—and keep it? (978-1-63555-482-3)

Always Believe by Aimée. Greyson Waldsen is pursuing ordination as an Anglican priest. Angela Arlingham doesn't believe in God. Do they follow their vocation or their hearts? (978-1-63555-912-5)

Best of the Wrong Reasons by Sander Santiago. For Fin Ness and Orion Starr, it takes a funeral to remind them that love is worth living for. (978-1-63555-867-8)

Courage by Jesse J. Thoma. No matter how often Natasha Parsons and Tommy Finch clash on the job, an undeniable attraction simmers just beneath the surface. Can they find the courage to change so love has room to grow? (978-1-63555-802-9)

I Am Chris by R Kent. There's one saving grace to losing everything and moving away. Nobody knows her as Chrissy Taylor. Now Chris can live who he truly is. (978-1-63555-904-0)

The Princess and the Odium by Sam Ledel. Jastyn and Princess Aurelia return to Venostes and join their families in a battle against the dark force to take back their homeland for a chance at a better tomorrow. (978-1-63555-894-4)

The Queen Has a Cold by Jane Kolven. What happens when the heir to the throne isn't a prince or a princess? (978-1-63555-878-4)

The Secret Poet by Georgia Beers. Agreeing to help her brother woo Zoe Blake seemed like a good idea to Morgan Thompson at first...until she realizes she's actually wooing Zoe for herself... (978-1-63555-858-6)

You Again by Aurora Rey. For high school sweethearts Kate Cormier and Sutton Guidry, the second chance might be the only one that matters. (978-1-63555-791-6)

Coming to Life on South High by Lee Patton. Twenty-one-year-old gay virgin Gabe Rafferty's first adult decade unfolds as an unpredictable journey into sex, love, and livelihood. (978-1-63555-906-4)

Fleur d'Lies by MJ Williamz. For rookie cop DJ Sander, being true to what you believe is the only way to live...and one way to die. (978-1-63555-854-8)

Love's Falling Star by B.D. Grayson. For country music megastar Lochlan Paige, can love conquer her fear of losing the one thing she's worked so hard to protect? (978-1-63555-873-9)

Love's Truth by C.A. Popovich. Can Lynette and Barb make love work when unhealed wounds of betrayed trust and a secret could change everything? (978-1-63555-755-8)

Next Exit Home by Dena Blake. Home may be where the heart is, but for Harper Sims and Addison Foster, is the journey back worth the pain? (978-1-63555-727-5)

Not Broken by Lyn Hemphill. Falling in love is hard enough—even more so for Rose who's carrying her ex's baby. (978-1-63555-869-2)

The Noble and the Nightingale by Barbara Ann Wright. Two women on opposite sides of empires at war risk all for a chance at love. (978-1-63555-812-8)

What a Tangled Web by Melissa Brayden. Clementine Monroe has the chance to buy the café she's managed for years, but Madison LeGrange swoops in and buys it first. Now Clementine is forced to work for the enemy and ignore her former crush. (978-1-63555-749-7)

A Far Better Thing by JD Wilburn. When needs of her family and wants of her heart clash, Cass Halliburton is faced with the ultimate sacrifice. (978-1-63555-834-0)

Body Language by Renee Roman. When Mika offers to provide Jen erotic tutoring, will sex drive them into a deeper relationship or tear them apart? (978-1-63555-800-5)

Carrie and Hope by Joy Argento. For Carrie and Hope loss brings them together but secrets and fear may tear them apart. (978-1-63555-827-2)

Death's Prelude by David S. Pederson. In this prequel to the Detective Heath Barrington Mystery series, Heath discovers that first love changes you forever and drives you to become the person you're destined to be. (978-1-63555-786-2)

Ice Queen by Gun Brooke. School counselor Aislin Kennedy wants to help standoffish CEO Susanna Durr and her troubled teenage daughter become closer—even if it means risking her own heart in the process. (978-1-63555-721-3)

Masquerade by Anne Shade. In 1925 Harlem, New York, a notorious gangster sets her sights on seducing Celine, and new lovers Dinah and Celine are forced to risk their hearts, and lives, for love. (978-1-63555-831-9)

Royal Family by Jenny Frame. Loss has defined both Clay's and Katya's lives, but guarding their hearts may prove to be the biggest heartbreak of all. (978-1-63555-745-9)

Share the Moon by Toni Logan. Three best friends, an inherited vineyard and a resident ghost come together for fun, romance and a touch of magic. (978-1-63555-844-9)

Spirit of the Law by Carsen Taite. Attorney Owen Lassiter will do almost anything to put a murderer behind bars, but can she get past her reluctance to rely on unconventional help from the alluring Summer Byrne and keep from falling in love in the process? (978-1-63555-766-4)

The Devil Incarnate by Ali Vali. Cain Casey has so much to live for, but enemies who lurk in the shadows threaten to unravel it all. (978-1-63555-534-9)

His Brother's Viscount by Stephanie Lake. Hector Somerville wants to rekindle his illicit love affair with Viscount Wentworth, but he must overcome one problem: Wentworth still loves Hector's brother. (978-1-63555-805-0)

Journey to Cash by Ashley Bartlett. Cash Braddock thought everything was great, but it looks like her history is about to become her right now. Which is a real bummer. (978-1-63555-464-9)

Liberty Bay by Karis Walsh. Wren Lindley's life is mired in tradition and untouched by trends until social media star Gina Strickland introduces an irresistible electricity into her off-the-grid world. (978-1-63555-816-6)

Scent by Kris Bryant. Nico Marshall has been burned by women in the past wanting her for her money. This time, she's determined to win Sophia Sweet over with her charm. (978-1-63555-780-0)

Shadows of Steel by Suzie Clarke. As their worlds collide and their choices come back to haunt them, Rachel and Claire must figure out how to stay together and most of all, stay alive. (978-1-63555-810-4)

The Clinch by Nicole Disney. Eden Bauer overcame a difficult past to become a world champion mixed martial artist, but now rising star and dreamy bad girl Brooklyn Shaw is a threat both to Eden's title and her heart. (978-1-63555-820-3)

The Last First Kiss by Julie Cannon. Kelly Newsome is so ready for a tropical island vacation, but she never expects to meet the woman who could give her her last first kiss. (978-1-63555-768-8)

The Mandolin Lunch by Missouri Vaun. Despite their immediate attraction, everything about Garet Allen says short-term, and Tess Hill refuses to consider anything less than forever. (978-1-63555-566-0)

Thor: Daughter of Asgard by Genevieve McCluer. When Hannah Olsen finds out she's the reincarnation of Thor, she's thrown into a world of magic and intrigue, unexpected attraction, and a mystery she's got to unravel. (978-1-63555-814-2)

Veterinary Technician by Nancy Wheelton. When a stable of horses is threatened Val and Ronnie must work together against the odds to save them, and maybe even themselves along the way. (978-1-63555-839-5)

16 Steps to Forever by Georgia Beers. Can Brooke Sullivan and Macy Carr find themselves by finding each other? (978-1-63555-762-6)

All I Want for Christmas by Georgia Beers, Maggie Cummings, Fiona Riley. The Christmas season sparks passion and love in these stories by award winning authors Georgia Beers, Maggie Cummings, and Fiona Riley. (978-1-63555-764-0)

From the Woods by Charlotte Greene. When Fiona goes backpacking in a protected wilderness, the last thing she expects is to be fighting for her life. (978-1-63555-793-0)

Heart of the Storm by Nicole Stiling. For Juliet Mitchell and Sienna Bennett a forbidden attraction definitely isn't worth upending the life they've worked so hard for. Is it? (978-1-63555-789-3)

If You Dare by Sandy Lowe. For Lauren West and Emma Prescott, following their passions is easy. Following their hearts, though? That's almost impossible. (978-1-63555-654-4)

Love Changes Everything by Jaime Maddox. For Samantha Brooks and Kirby Fielding, no matter how careful their plans, love will change everything. (978-1-63555-835-7)

Not This Time by MA Binfield. Flung back into each other's lives, can former bandmates Sophia and Madison have a second chance at romance? (978-1-63555-798-5)

The Dubious Gift of Dragon Blood by J. Marshall Freeman. One day Crispin is a lonely high school student—the next he is fighting a war in a land ruled by dragons, his otherworldly boyfriend at his side. (978-1-63555-725-1)

The Found Jar by Jaycie Morrison. Fear keeps Emily Harris trapped in her emotionally vacant life; can she find the courage to let Beck Reynolds guide her toward love? (978-1-63555-825-8)